Urban Myth

By the same author

Rollover

Urban Myth

James Raven

ROBERT HALE · LONDON

ISBN 978-0-7198-0543-1

Robert Hale Limited
Clerkenwell House
Clerkenwell Green
London EC1R 0HT

www.halebooks.com

2 4 6 8 10 9 7 5 3 1

Typeset in 10/14pt Palatino
Printed in Great Britain by the MPG Books Group,
Bodmin and King's Lynn

This one is for Catherine – with love.

prologue

Genna Boyd thought she was alone in the house. That's why she believed it was safe to make the call. But she was fearful nonetheless.

Her heart pounded as her thumb hovered over the keys on her mobile phone. For a long, agonizing moment she hesitated, knowing that she was about to take a monumental risk.

But she felt she had no choice. It was the right thing to do. If she did not make an effort to warn him then the guilt would be an unbearable burden for the rest of her life. She'd done some horrible and despicable things during her twenty-six years on the planet; things that would shame and disgust most decent people.

But she couldn't bring herself to do this. Not now that she had thought it through.

She should have rung him sooner. She knew that now. But at least it wasn't too late. There were still a few days to go. She swallowed hard and depressed the zero key on her phone. But then she froze, convinced that she'd heard something downstairs.

She held her breath as her heart thumped against her ribcage. The house remained silent. After fifteen seconds she stepped up to the open door and looked out onto the landing. It was clear and no sounds reached her. She let the air out of her lungs and stepped back into the bedroom with its pink walls and cheap pine furniture. It was not to her taste; too quaint by far. But she had to admit they had done a pretty good job of making it bright and homely.

Through the window she could see the flat, gorse-covered landscape of the New Forest. In the distance, dark hills loomed against the horizon. Dusk was slowly descending on a cool, autumnal day, washing the view with a strident orange glow. But for her its beauty was marred by the knowledge of what was going to happen here if she didn't do something about it.

She could feel an icy chill in her gut as she punched the number into her phone, beginning with the 001 dialling code for the United States. There were several seconds of silence before the unfamiliar ringing tone kicked in. She prayed that he would be in and, more importantly, that he would take her seriously.

After what seemed an eternity the phone was answered. But the crackling on the line distorted the American's voice.

'Hello,' he said. 'Jack Keaton here.'

'Can you hear me, Mr Keaton?' Genna asked.

As she spoke his name she tried to picture him. She had no idea what he looked like. All she knew was that he had a wife and two children and lived near Houston in Texas. She conjured up an image of a middle-aged man with brown, wavy hair and a warm, genuine smile.

'I can just about hear you,' Keaton said. 'But this line is not good.'

'I'm calling from England, Mr Keaton. I'm on my mobile phone and the signal is poor.'

'You're not kidding. So who are you and what can I do for you?'

He had a deep, crusty voice and if it hadn't been for the accent he would have sounded much like her late, repulsive father.

'It doesn't matter who I am, Mr Keaton,' she said. 'My name won't mean anything to you.'

'Oh really? Then what do you want?'

After a pause, she said, 'To warn you not to come to the house in England, Mr Keaton. You have to stay away from this place.'

'I don't understand.'

'There's no time to explain. But you have to believe me when I tell you that your family will not be safe here. You must—'

'What the hell are you on about?' Keaton interrupted. 'The house is all booked, along with the flights.'

'I know that, Mr Keaton, but you shouldn't come here. Cancel your plans and go on holiday somewhere else.'

'I have no idea what you're talking about.'

'I'm trying to stop you from making a terrible mistake,' she said. 'For the sake of your family just forget about the house.'

'Do I know you? Is this some sick practical joke?' Keaton said.

'It's no joke. I'm telling you the truth. You have to believe me. If you don't you'll regret it.'

He said something in response but his words were drowned out by a blizzard of static.

'I can barely hear you, Mr Keaton,' she yelled into the phone. 'I'm losing the signal. I'll hang up and call you straight back. Please answer the phone. You have to listen to me.'

She severed the connection with her thumb. Then she took a long, deep breath to calm her nerves, blowing the air out through pursed lips. Her whole body was trembling now and her throat felt dry. She realized it wasn't going to be easy to convince him, not unless she told him everything, and she couldn't do that. She went to hit the call key again, but at that moment something else seized her attention. It wasn't a noise this time. It was the sudden, overwhelming sense that she was no longer alone. She stood rooted to the spot, afraid to turn towards the open bedroom door.

A chill of fear rushed through her body. Then the familiar smell reached her, that heady cocktail of cheap aftershave and pungent tobacco; a smell that she had come to associate with pure evil.

Her body immediately succumbed to a fear-induced paralysis that was almost painful in its intensity. She couldn't move, not even to breathe.

'You stupid fucking bitch.'

His words, dripping with anger and contempt, came at her like high velocity bullets, smashing into her mind with almost physical force.

'I thought you might bottle it,' he went on, his voice low and menacing. 'That's why I've been keeping an eye on you.'

She knew then she'd been careless. She should never have told him that she had begun to have reservations about what was going to happen. It was a big mistake.

But at least she had her insurance. That would protect her. He wouldn't be expecting that. In his eyes she was just a naive bitch who was there to be exploited. But he was wrong. She'd known that one day she would probably need an exit strategy.

So she squared her shoulders and prepared to turn around and tell the bastard to go to hell. But she didn't get the chance because he struck without warning just as she started to move. She caught sight of a glint of steel as he thrust his arm forward and stabbed her in the back. The shocking impact caused an explosion of pain that suffused her entire body.

She barely felt the second blow, but it stifled a scream that formed in her throat and sent a wave of blackness washing over her. The last thing Genna Boyd was aware of before she died was a cold voice telling her that it was all her own fault.

1

I breathed a sigh of relief as the Boeing 777 from Houston, Texas made a bumpy landing at Heathrow Airport just after seven in the morning.

It had been an uncomfortable nine-hour flight, with a lot of unwelcome turbulence. My back was sore and my knee joints felt like they'd seized up; economy seats are not designed for men who are six feet tall. I'd managed to doze for only a couple of hours so I was jaded.

'Not long now, Jack,' Nicole said as she placed a reassuring hand on mine. 'You'll soon be able to have a good stretch.'

My wife was next to me in the window seat, looking tired and drawn. The lines around her large, mint-blue eyes were more pronounced than usual. Her brown shoulder-length hair was dishevelled and her cheeks were flushed. I felt a wave of affection wash over me. Today was her birthday. She was thirty-eight and this holiday was my gift to her.

I wanted it to be special because it had been a tough year. Back in March Nicole had miscarried the child we'd been desperately trying for. It had been a bitter blow, compounded by the fact that she wouldn't be able to conceive again because of damaged ovaries. Five months on and the sense of loss was at last beginning to fade. We'd finally come to terms with what had happened and had both accepted the need to put the pain behind us.

In the five years we'd been married we'd never been on a trip together to her native country. In fact, I'd never before been to England and I'd been looking forward to it for weeks.

We were going to stay in a secluded house in the ancient New Forest, close to where Nicole grew up. Her parents were dead and she had always wanted to return to the part of the forest where their ashes had been scattered. She had no other family there, no siblings and no uncles or aunts. I was Nicole's family now, along with Tina and Michael. Tina was my daughter by my first marriage. Her mother, Clare, had died nine years ago of an aneurysm at the ridiculously young age of thirty-two.

At fourteen my daughter was pretty, precocious, rebellious – and addicted to Facebook. That was one of the reasons she hadn't wanted to come on the trip. The house we were staying in apparently had no broadband connection and a poor cellphone signal. It suited me fine because I didn't want to be hassled by the office. But it was bound to give Tina withdrawal symptoms.

Michael was Nicole's ten year old son. His dad had left them when he was four and I'd worked hard at being a father figure to him. We got on well and he would often come to me with his problems, which thankfully paled into insignificance against the teenage woes that seemed to blight my daughter's life.

When Nicole and I got together we were worried about our kids, and how they'd take to being part of a new family. But our fears were short-lived because it turned out it was what they both wanted – and needed. There was no opposition, no resentment. And they'd grown to like, if not love each other. Tina was very protective of her younger step-brother and invariably leapt to his defence when he was in trouble. To be fair that wasn't very often. He was a polite boy with fair hair and big blue eyes that would one day melt more than a few hearts.

The pair of them were across the aisle from us looking pale and glum. They weren't used to travelling. For that matter neither was I. My job as a lawyer rarely took me beyond the city limits of Houston. Not that it worried me. Long haul flights were not my thing.

'Cheer up, kids,' I said, leaning across the aisle. 'The worst is over. In a few hours we'll be in the New Forest. And if it's even half as nice as we've been led to believe then you're in for a treat.'

Tina rolled her eyes at me, a gesture I was pretty used to.

'In your dreams, Pops,' she said. 'Forests are the same the world over. Green, dirty and boring.'

'Don't be so negative,' I said. 'We're only here for two weeks so try to have some fun.'

'I *was* having fun back in Houston, with my friends.'

I heaved an almighty sigh. 'Look, just try to enter the spirit of it, OK? I'm sure you're going to love it here.'

'And I'm sure I won't,' she said. 'In fact I've got a bad feeling about this trip. We should have gone to Florida.'

'We went there last year. And you did nothing but complain.'

'At least there were beaches and a pool.'

'Well here there are wild ponies and quaint little villages. And there's very little risk of getting sunburnt.'

She shook her head at me, unconvinced, and popped a stick of gum in to her mouth.

In the last year my daughter had developed a serious attitude; mood swings, temper tantrums, extreme bouts of bitchiness. She had threatened to leave home twice and when I banned her from dying her hair red she didn't speak to me for a week. But I was hopeful that this vacation would be good for her. I felt she needed to have a break from the toxic influence of her school friends.

At passport control we were in for a pleasant surprise – the guy behind the desk was actually civil. It's something we Americans aren't used to. Anyone who has visited the States will know how rude and unwelcoming the immigration officers can be. Some are even downright scary. For many of us they're a national embarrassment. But this Brit was friendly and polite. His smile was almost as wide as his red, chubby face.

'So you've come to England on holiday, Mr Keaton,' he said. 'Have you been here before?'

I shook my head. 'This is my first visit.'

'Where will you be staying?'

'In Hampshire. The New Forest. We're renting a house.'

His grin grew even wider. 'A beautiful part of the country. For a while the missus and I lived close by in Bournemouth. We used to go hiking in the forest.'

'My wife's from Burley,' I said, nodding towards Nicole.

'I know it well,' he said. 'The village famous for its witches and ghosts.'

'So I've heard. I'm looking forward to finding out more about that stuff.'

He laughed as he handed back our passports. 'Well be sure to have a great time and I hope the weather stays fine for you.'

Beyond passport control we followed the signs to the baggage reclaim area. It was a long walk, too long for Tina and Michael, who complained the whole time that they were tired. We had a twenty minute wait for our cases. Tina started frantically sending messages on her cellphone. Michael just stood to one side looking weary.

After we finally collected our cases we went to the car rental desk. There was no queue so within minutes I had the keys to a Land Rover Discovery – just the job for exploring our destination in comfort. Some of the forest roads were pretty rough, apparently, and even in September they were prone to flooding.

It took us ten minutes to locate the silver-grey Discovery in the car park and another five minutes to load our luggage in the back.

'All aboard the vacation express,' I said when we were done. 'The ancient forest beckons.'

2

The journey south from the airport was an experience in itself. I'd been warned about the notorious M25 motorway and I quickly discovered that its reputation as 'the road to hell' is well deserved. We hit it during the morning rush hour and the sheer volume of traffic led to a three-mile tailback.

Having never driven on the left I found it a struggle at first to hold my nerve. But before panic set in we turned onto the M3. This motorway, which veers down to the south coast, was, thankfully, much less busy.

The kids gave into fatigue and fell asleep in the back seat. Nicole, fearing I might do the same, produced her guidebook on the New Forest and began to read aloud facts and figures that I was already familiar with.

'The New Forest was created in 1079 by William the Conqueror as a hunting area for deer,' she said. Then she paused before adding, 'Do you know what's funny? When I lived there I never paid any attention to this historical stuff. But it's quite fascinating when you think about it.'

She was right about that. From what I'd been told, or gleaned from the internet, the New Forest was a unique area of historical, ecological and agricultural significance. It was hardly surprising, therefore, that the English regarded it as something of a national treasure.

As Nicole continued to read passages from the guidebook I detected in her voice a rising sense of excitement. She was looking forward to returning to the place of her childhood and her enthusiasm was infectious. This pleased me no end and gave me enormous satisfaction. For once I had been spot on with her birthday gift. This trip had been the perfect choice.

The idea had come to me a couple of months ago and I started doing some research. Nicole had lived in the New Forest with her parents before they were both killed in a road accident. She was twenty-six at the time and a stewardess with one of the major long-haul airlines. Nine months after the tragedy she met an oil company executive during a flight from London to Houston where he was based. Love blossomed and after selling the family home just outside Burley she crossed the Atlantic to marry him.

But it proved not to be the fairy tale she'd hoped for. Infidelity on his part ended the marriage and she found herself alone in the States with a young son and no intention of taking him away from his father by moving back to the UK.

But she still missed the place and had told me countless times that she'd like to go back for a holiday. So my search for accommodation began in the area around Burley. I soon discovered there was no shortage of places. Given that the forest attracts about a million visitors a year this was only to be expected. The house I finally settled on came up in a Google search. The owner had created his own promotional page and it was not part of a letting agency property portfolio.

The description immediately appealed to me: 'King's Manor is a charming Victorian house in a sought-after location within the New Forest National Park, two miles from the village of Burley. The renovated property is available for a holiday let and would be ideal for a family. It is utterly secluded with beautiful views of the surrounding heathland. It offers spacious accommodation with five bedrooms, large living room, dining room, fitted kitchen and separate garage block. The house is set in its own half-acre garden and enjoys the benefits of gas central heating, double glazing and a large gravel driveway ...'

There were several photographs of the exterior and interior and I knew it would be just the job. I sent an email to the owner inquiring about availability. His name was Nathan Slade and he responded almost immediately, asking me how many would be in the party and if we were a family. He also wanted to know the ages of our children. I then received an email explaining that the house was available only during September and because of the restriction on dates he offered a generous discount.

Once the house was booked I set about making arrangements.

Nicole worked part time as a kindergarten teacher at a school within walking distance of our home. I contacted her boss to make sure she could get the time off before I told her. She was absolutely delighted and had been talking about it ever since. She liked the look of the house from the photographs and thought the location was perfect. In fact, I could not have been happier with her reaction. I only hoped the house lived up to our expectations.

3

'Wow, it's gorgeous.'

That was Nicole's reaction when she saw King's Manor. It stood in the distance as we turned off the road onto a narrow, unmade track, a red-brick building nestling in a wide valley, backing on to a dense wood of conifers.

'It's in the middle of friggin' nowhere,' Tina said.

'That's why it's so cool,' Matthew enthused. 'We can make as much noise as we like and nobody will hear us.'

'Well I think it's just perfect,' Nicole said. Then she turned to me and flashed her ivory white teeth in a warm, grateful grin.

The track leading to the house was strewn with small rocks and potholes, but despite that it was fairly easy to negotiate. After about five minutes we crunched onto the gravel driveway and came to a stop in front of the house. It was big and square, with rustic brickwork and a high sloping roof of grey slate. There were six large bay windows at the front and a charming arched porch above the door. Over to the right was a double garage with a small skylight in the roof. A picket gate gave access to the rear garden and I could see a neatly cut lawn with a few mature trees and a substantial patio.

'The photographs don't do it justice,' Nicole said as she got swiftly out of the car. 'This is beautiful.'

The view from the front, facing north, was of the valley which gradually sloped down into a huge area of flat heathland. To the south, a wall of tall conifers rose majestically and formed a dramatic backdrop.

The setting was as remote as it was fabulous and there were no other properties in sight to share it with us. As I stared up at the house my spirits soared and finally blew away the irrational concerns I'd been having since that mystery phone call a few days ago. The woman caller – who had failed to identify herself – had told me that we should not come to the house, that it would not be safe. I might have taken her seriously if she'd bothered to phone back to explain herself. But she hadn't and so I'd assumed it was a prank, perhaps instigated by one of my colleagues. I'd been boring them for weeks about the trip and I could name at least two guys who would jump at the chance to have fun at my expense.

I hadn't mentioned the call to Nicole because I hadn't wanted to worry her, and although I'd more or less dismissed it as a stupid, callous prank, I'd still found it impossible to push it from my thoughts completely. But now I could because this was not the sort of place where bad things happened.

'Let's unpack the car after we've checked out the inside,' Nicole said. 'I can't wait to see what it's like.'

As she hurried towards the house, I said, 'Mr Slade told me he'd leave the key under the doormat.'

As Tina and Michael fell in behind Nicole I held back and just stood there, feeling pleased with myself and heaving a huge sigh of relief. I was confident now that this vacation was going to be special, particularly for Nicole. It was a while since we had spent quality time together as a family. I worked a lot of unsocial hours and at weekends the kids preferred to be with their friends.

The stress of the past five months had also put a strain on our marriage; we'd been arguing a lot lately and our sex life had become almost non-existent. This trip was hopefully going to help put the spring back into our relationship.

4

An hour and a half before Jack Keaton and his family arrived at King's Manor a gruesome discovery was made less than two miles away.

A man walking his dog on Cranes Moor stumbled across a girl's body. It lay in a shallow grave that had been disturbed by the creatures of the forest.

By the time Detective Chief Inspector Jeff Temple got to the scene, blue-suited technicians from the Scientific Services Department were already combing the area for clues.

It was 9.30 a.m. and the morning mist had lifted, allowing the sun to impart its warmth on a new day.

But the spectacular beauty of the moor was lost on Temple. As he stared down at the girl's crumpled body he felt an overwhelming sense of sadness. What a tragic waste of life, he thought. She could only have been in her twenties and she should have had a long and prosperous future to look forward to. Instead her life had been extinguished in a brutal fashion.

'Based on lividity patterns it's clear she was moved here within hours of being murdered,' Matherson said. 'Looks like she was wrapped in three plastic bin bags that got ripped apart, probably by animals.'

Dr Frank Matherson, one of the longest serving pathologists in Hampshire, was crouching next to the body. He was a big man with grey hair and bushy eyebrows. Temple had worked with him for years and rated him highly.

'She has two stab wounds to the back from a broad-bladed knife,' he said. 'Very deep. The blade must have been at least six inches long. Maybe a carving knife of some kind. It was thrust into her with considerable force.'

'So how long do you reckon she's been here?' Temple asked.

Matherson pursed his lips, said, 'The blowfly infestation and decomposition would suggest three to four days. But that's only a guess at this stage.'

'It's not much of a grave,' Temple observed.

Matherson nodded. 'Quite so. She was covered with a few inches of soil, then a bunch of twigs and some leaf mould. It wouldn't have taken long for an animal, perhaps a fox, to home in on the smell and dig her up. After that it was a wildlife free-for-all. You're lucky she was found today. At least she's still intact.'

Temple dragged his eyes away from the body and took in the wider scene – a vast expanse of moors and hills and patches of dense woodland. A road close by ran between Cranes Moor and Vales Moor and right now it was blocked off and packed with police vehicles. Temple couldn't see any properties so the chances of finding a witness to whatever had happened here were slim.

This girl's killer – or killers – had probably chosen this spot because it was near to a road. At night the area would be deserted and there were no lights. It would have been easy for someone to park a car at the side of the road and drag or carry the body a hundred yards or so onto the moor without being seen.

'Here's something that should help you identify her,' Matherson said.

The pathologist was holding the girl's right foot in his gloved hand and carefully scrutinizing it through his horn-rimmed glasses. Temple dropped to a squat beside him, saw the word *Genna* tattooed on the skin just above the girl's ankle. It wasn't a common name and if indeed it was this poor girl's name then it would be a crucial lead.

'I'll get this out to the media straight away,' he said. 'Anything on the other ankle?'

'No, I've checked. And there's no ID or money in her pockets.'

'Jewellery?'

'None.'

Temple stood up and tried to call the Major Crime Department office in Southampton to get things moving on the name, but there was no mobile signal.

'Shit,' he said. 'Any signal on your phone?'

Matherson took out his phone and tried it. 'No joy I'm afraid.'

Temple walked over to the road through the gorse and bracken. He finally managed to get a signal on his phone and called the office, asking to be put through to Detective Inspector Angelica Metcalfe, who was going to be his number two on the case.

'So what have we got, Guv?' she said, getting straight to the point as always.

He filled her in on the crime scene and told her to focus on the name tattooed on the dead girl's ankle. He said he wanted her to check missing persons and to arrange for more uniforms to be sent out to help search the area.

'I want the story carried in the lunchtime and evening news bulletins on both radio and television,' he said. 'Call in favours if you have to. Let's get as much publicity as we can before the day's out.'

'I'll sort it right away.'

'And get a team together. I'll be back in a couple of hours and we'll have a full briefing.'

'Will do, Guv. Anything else?'

'No, that's enough to be getting on with.'

Temple spoke to the sergeant in charge of the uniform contingent, told him to send some officers up to the village to find out if Genna was a local girl.

He then decided he needed a cigarette. He walked over to his car and retrieved a pack from the front seat, thankful that two weeks ago he'd abandoned his latest attempt at giving up. The grisly scene out on the moor had set off an emotional whirlwind inside him. He used to be less sensitive to the harsh realities of the job, but after his wife died, he'd found it increasingly difficult to remain detached. His own experience with death, the paralyzing effects of loss and grief, had made him more aware of how precious life is.

5

Nicole was the first through the door, followed by Tina and Michael. At least the kids had perked up a little and were demonstrating some enthusiasm. How long it would last remained to be seen.

I walked in after them. I didn't want anyone to be disappointed. If the place was a dump I would never be allowed to forget it. But thankfully it was OK. In fact, my first impression was a very favourable one based on the décor in the entrance hall. The bare floorboards were highly polished and the walls and ceiling were a subtle cream that extended up the stairs and made the place feel light and airy.

'I like it,' Nicole said. 'It's much cleaner than I thought it would be. I reckon it's just had a makeover.'

I thought so too and wondered if Mr Slade had spruced it up in advance of our visit. The kitchen had parquet flooring and all the mod cons including an electric cooker, a microwave and a smart breakfast bar with stools facing French windows that overlooked the back garden. There was a large American-style refrigerator with a note pinned to the door by a magnet in the shape of a New Forest pony.

Nicole came up behind me and we both read it.

Welcome to King's Manor. I've stocked up the fridge, freezer and cupboards with all the things you asked for. I've also added some wine, chocolates and other goodies with my compliments. On the table is a guest information folder with facts about the house and the area and various brochures. I'm afraid the telephone landline has still not been fixed, but I'm told it will be in the next day or two. One other thing – the garage is not available to guests as it's where my personal belongings are stored during lets. If you have any problems please don't hesitate to call me. I do hope you have a great time. It was signed Nathan Slade.

'He sounds like a nice man,' Nicole said.

I opened the refrigerator and was taken aback by the amount of stuff in there.

There were the things we had ordered and would be paying for, including bread, butter, cold meats, milk and various soft drinks. But there were also six bottles of white wine, a bottle of champagne and several boxes of chocolates. The freezer compartment was packed with pizzas, bacon, fries and fish, none of which we had asked for. When we checked the cupboards we found tins of soup, beans and a jar of coffee.

'I can't believe he's been so generous,' I said. 'This lot must have cost him a small fortune.'

There was a ring folder on the table. I picked it up and opened it. It contained a selection of brochures featuring various locations in the forest and one promotional leaflet on King's Manor dated 2010. It was described on the front as a 'stunning six-bedroom guest house with bed and breakfast accommodation and fantastic views over the moors.'

Nicole looked over my shoulder and said, 'So it used to be a B&B. How marvellous that we've got it all to ourselves.'

'Seems to have lost a bedroom in recent years,' I said. 'According to the website description there are only five.'

'Well thankfully we don't need more than four,' smiled Nicole.

The folder also contained laminated sheets of type-written notes on the history of the area and the house itself. It was built in 1895 by a man called Colin Maddox. There were two sepia photos of the house dated 1910. In the first, a man in a cloth cap was pouring coal into the cellar through a chute set in the ground up against the back wall. In another, a large plump woman in a black dress was standing in front of the house posing awkwardly for the camera. The caption beneath it read: *Elizabeth Maddox, widow of the original owner.*

'She looks like a tough old gal,' Nicole said. 'Life must have been hard in those days. Not like now.'

'It's amazing,' I said. 'The outside of the house seems hardly to have changed in all this time.'

'They sure knew how to build them to last in Victorian times,' Nicole said. Then she put her arms around me, pulled me close and gave me a gentle kiss on the mouth.

'That's for being so thoughtful,' she said. 'I know this is going to be the best birthday present ever.'

The kids chose that moment to come into the kitchen, having explored the other rooms on the ground floor.

'Jesus, guys,' Tina said, pulling a face. 'Can't you do that stuff in the privacy of your own bedroom?'

I laughed. 'Talking of bedrooms, this house has no less than five, so why don't you two go upstairs and stake your claims.'

'But steer clear of the master bedroom,' Nicole put in. 'That's ours.'

Nicole led me by the hand through the other rooms on the ground floor, beginning with the huge, cosy living room with French windows leading to the garden. There was a black leather sofa, coffee table and two comfy armchairs positioned in front of a flat-screen TV. The furniture was plain and simple and fairly modern, but despite that the house retained a rustic charm, thanks in part to the oak beams that festooned the ceilings.

Nicole could barely contain her excitement. I was reminded of the day we first explored our own house back in Texas. It was a new release in a suburban community. She'd just accepted my proposal of marriage and we'd set a date for the wedding. This was fourteen months after we'd met on a local dating website. Friends and family had convinced me to join, telling me that it was time I got my life back. Nicole was the second woman I went out with on the site and I was her fourth guy.

I knew on our first date that I wanted to spend the rest of my life with her. She was different in many ways to Clare, but they shared qualities that I felt were important like empathy, loyalty, a good nature and a self-deprecating humour.

So what made her choose me? A dentist's son with a boring job as a corporate lawyer and a shameful lack of ambition. It was a question I'd put to her on several occasions and she'd always given me the same answer.

'Because you're you, Jack. I'd have thought that was obvious.'

Back in the kitchen Nicole made straight for the refrigerator and pulled open the door.

'I think we should celebrate my birthday with the champers,' she said.

'But it's still officially morning.'

She took out the champagne bottle and placed it on the worktop. 'I don't care. Besides, I'm sure I read somewhere that champagne is a good antidote for jet lag.'

It was a moment to savour. The woman I loved was as she'd been before the miscarriage – bubbly, funny, sexy and extremely desirable. As she started searching the cupboards for glasses I felt my heart skip a beat. I decided that after we'd toasted the occasion I would take her up to bed and make mad, passionate love to her – in the privacy of our own master bedroom, of course.

But I never got the chance, because at that moment a loud, piercing scream came from upstairs. It sent a cold prickle of fear sweeping through my entire body.

My daughter was not one to overreact so I knew instinctively that something very bad had happened.

6

When we got to the top of the stairs, Tina was on the landing outside one of the bedrooms. She was still screaming and clearly distressed. Her hands were clenched into fists at her sides and the tendons in her neck looked as though they might burst through the skin. Michael was peering at her from another doorway, his pale face stricken with shock and bewilderment.

I rushed up to my daughter and grabbed her by the shoulders.

'Calm down, sweetheart,' I said. 'What is it? What's wrong?'

She raised an arm and pointed into the room.

'A snake,' she wailed. 'There's a friggin' snake on the bed. I pulled back the duvet and there it was.'

I couldn't see it from the landing so I let go of Tina and ventured into the room. I've never been scared of snakes but I don't like them and they make me nervous. Back in Houston they're pretty common in the hot summer months and I'd had a few unfortunate encounters on nature trails and in parks.

I approached the bed cautiously, my eyes flitting around the room, which had pink walls and pine furniture. It was a girl's room. Cool and fresh and feminine.

The snake was curled up on the white sheet next to the pillow. It was a grey-brown colour with a vague, zig-zag pattern on its scaly skin and a distinctive 'v' mark on the back of its head. No wonder Tina had gone into hysterics. It was a chilling, incongruous sight. The stuff of nightmares.

'It's an adder,' Nicole said from behind me. 'They're poisonous.'

'That's great,' I retorted.

I was now standing over the bed and looking down on it. Still it hadn't moved, so I guessed it must be sleeping. It was about two feet long. I couldn't see its eyes or its mouth. It was an ugly, scary creature.

'We have to get it out of here,' Nicole said, stating the obvious.

That was going to be easier said than done, I thought. The moment it woke up it would probably slither off the bed and lead us a merry dance around the house. Or crawl into a place where we couldn't reach it. Then where would we be?

'I need a bag or a sack to put it in,' I said, but a tremor in my voice betrayed my effort to remain calm. 'Someone go and empty my flight bag and bring it up to me. Quickly.'

Nicole relayed the instruction to a now sobbing Tina and I started looking around for something I could use to trap the snake. I spotted a large glass bowl on top of the pine dresser. It was half filled with pot pourri and it was close enough to reach without having to shift my position. I picked it up, emptied the contents onto the floor, and after a moment's hesitation leaned across the bed and dropped it over the immobile snake. It was a perfect fit. I took a long, deep breath and felt a wave of relief surge through me. Emboldened now by the glass barrier between myself and the snake, I placed my hands on the bowl and moved it around in order to wake it up. But still it didn't move, despite being shaken about so much that its long body began to uncurl.

'I think it's dead,' Michael said.

I turned and saw him standing at the foot of the bed, the colour having returned to his cheeks.

'Try prodding it,' he added.

'What with?' I said.

It was Nicole who supplied the answer. She opened the wardrobe and took out a wire coat hanger, which she handed to me. I immediately slipped it under the rim of the upside-down bowl and poked the snake. Once, twice, three times. It didn't stir, not even to flinch. I then lifted the bowl off completely, looped the hanger over the snake's tail end and moved it half way along its body. Then, with surprisingly little effort, I raised the snake off the bed so that it was drooped over the long section of the hanger like a length of thick rope.

A loud gasp came from the landing. Tina had returned and was standing in the doorway clutching my flight bag to her chest as though for protection.

'Relax, sweetheart,' I said. 'This snake is deceased.'

'So what the hell was it doing in the bed?' she yelled.

'It probably crawled under the duvet to keep warm,' I said. 'It's not uncommon for snakes to get into homes. It happens often enough in Texas, as you know.'

'But this isn't Texas,' she said. 'And besides, the door was closed. I opened it.'

'Well it must have sneaked in before the house was locked up,' I said.

She shook her head, unconvinced. And I didn't blame her. It was a complete mystery to me how the slithery fucker had managed to not only get into the house, but also up the stairs and into bed.

'Look, shall we have this conversation later?' Nicole said. 'I think we should get rid of that thing and check that there aren't any more.'

I walked slowly down the stairs with the family in tow, then out the front door and across the driveway to the edge of the heath. I laboured through bracken for about twenty yards. Before dropping the snake on the ground I looked closely at it for any wounds. I couldn't see any, which begged the question as to how it had died. Did snakes have heart attacks? I wondered.

I carried the hanger back to the house and dumped it in a wheelie bin around the side. Nicole and Michael then joined me in a careful and thorough search of the house. Tina stayed in the kitchen because she couldn't bear the thought of getting another nasty surprise.

After half an hour we were certain there were no more unwanted tenants. We gathered in the kitchen and Nicole made some coffee. A rush of anger prompted me to phone Nathan Slade. I wanted to ask him how in God's name such a thing could happen. But Slade didn't answer so I left a voice message, telling him I needed to talk to him as a matter of urgency. The experience had left us all feeling raw and edgy, especially Tina who still had a bad case of the shakes.

'Don't worry,' I said, rubbing her shoulders. 'It was a one off, a fluke. It won't happen again.'

Tina started sobbing again and I realized that she urgently needed something mundane to grip her mind and harness her imagination before it brought on another bout of hysterics.

'Let's go for a walk,' I said. 'Clear our heads and try to put this into perspective. After all, we're OK. That's the important thing. We can unpack later.'

The suggestion was well received. I think everyone was keen to get out of the house for a spell, if only to flush the adrenaline out of our bodies. As I closed the front door behind us I felt an easing of the tension that had seized me. The air was fresh and the sun was still shining. I put my arm around Tina and noticed with relief that she had stopped shaking. Nicole smiled at me and those familiar dimples appeared in her cheeks. But it was a half-hearted smile that required a degree of effort. And that made me feel guilty. OK, it wasn't my fault that the first day of our holiday had been ruined, but I couldn't help feeling responsible. I just had to hope that once the shock wore off we would all feel better.

As we started walking down the track we'd driven up, Michael suddenly began shouting excitedly and pointing up at the sky. He'd spotted a low-flying helicopter roaring towards us across the valley. Within seconds it was soaring above our heads and it was so close we could clearly see the word *Police* stencilled across the underside in large, black letters. It proved to be a welcome distraction because as it disappeared over a hill we were all left wondering if something awful had happened in another part of the forest.

And for a time we forgot about the snake.

7

DCI Temple watched the police helicopter swerve in low over Cranes Moor. The crew would be looking for anything unusual, an abandoned car, perhaps, or maybe someone observing the scene from a distance through binoculars.

The roar of the rotor blades shattered the plaintive silence of the forest. Most of the forensic technicians and police searchers stopped what they were doing to follow its progress.

Temple returned his attention to the dead girl. The team were in the process of erecting a small white tent over her to prevent further contamination of the area around the body. This was the most crucial phase of any investigation. Get lucky now and you could save yourself an awful lot of time and effort later on. Most killers were careless, even the ones who thought they were forensically astute because they had watched every episode of *CSI*. But criminals always leave something behind, be it DNA, fibres or fingerprints. And thanks to the latest technology it usually leads the police directly to them.

Despite the statistics, Temple was not confident that today's search would bear much fruit. Crime scenes that are out in the open, especially those on fields and in woodland, are notoriously unproductive. Weather, wildlife and body decomposition usually conspire to hinder the work of the forensic team. And today their job would be even more difficult. The girl hadn't died here, according to Matherson. And it hadn't rained lately so the ground was dry, which made it difficult to find useful tyre tracks and shoeprints. Nevertheless they would use their scientific wizardry to try to recreate the path that the killer took to reach this spot.

Temple already knew that the tattoo on the girl's ankle was going to be their best and possibly only lead at this early stage.

Genna. Who was she? What could she possibly have done to deserve such a fate? Was the killer her boyfriend or husband or perhaps someone she had rejected? Most times there's a connection between the victim and the offender. That's one reason the murder detection rate is so impressive. Quite often it's obvious who the perpetrator is. But Temple wasn't convinced that this was going to be one of those cases that would be easily solved.

He had a bad feeling about it. He called it detective's intuition, based on years of experience. And he was rarely wrong about such things. That was why he was so highly regarded by the Hampshire Constabulary's top brass. He got results and he never complained about pay and pension and the lack of promotion. There were those on the force who thought he should have made chief superintendent by now, but whenever they raised the issue with him he would tell them the truth – he was content with his job and did not want to become a pen pusher.

Temple walked back to the road, which was now a noisy car park: the crackle of police radios, raised voices, doors slamming. It was busy but not chaotic. TV crews and press photographers had gathered on the other side of the cordon. Normally at this point in a case Temple would have ignored them, but he was anxious on this occasion to stage an impromptu press conference. He wanted that name out there as soon as possible.

When he was standing before the media scrum he straightened his tie, buttoned his suit jacket and palmed back his receding brown hair.

'I'm only prepared to make a brief statement,' he said when everyone was ready. 'I'm not in a position to answer questions at this time. As you can appreciate we're at an extremely early stage in the investigation.'

He paused, swallowed hard, and began to wish that he had stood with his back to the sun so that he didn't have to squint.

'This morning just after eight o'clock a man walking his dog on Cranes Moor stumbled upon the body of a young woman,' he said. 'She'd been wrapped in bin liners and buried in a shallow grave that had been partially uncovered. The cause of death would appear to be two stab wounds to the back so we're treating this as a murder case and it will be investigated by Hampshire's Major Crime Department based in Southampton. We believe the girl's body had been here for three days or more. And it's likely she was brought here in a car or van that was parked on the nearby road.

'We don't yet know the victim's identity, but the name Genna is tattooed on her right ankle. So I'm appealing to anyone who believes they might know who she is to come forward without delay. Time is of the essence.'

He held up his hand to indicate that the press conference was over. He ignored the questions that were fired at him and walked smartly away.

8

We walked and we talked and we tried to forget about the snake in the bedroom. And we succeeded to some degree because the landscape all around us was so beautiful. We all relished the different scents of the trees and plants. We drew each other's attention to the ponies and wild flowers and the raucous sounds of the insects in the bracken.

It was still a bright day but some benign clouds had started to gather to the east. Tina remained subdued, which was understandable, but she made an effort to join in the conversation. I almost welcomed the fact that she wasn't being her usual precocious self. Normally she became detached and disinterested whenever we went out together as a family.

Michael, on the other hand, was embracing the moment. To him the experience with the snake was tremendously exciting and he couldn't see why the rest of us had made such a fuss. I could tell that Nicole had been unnerved by what had happened. During the walk she was quiet and pensive with a furrowed brow that didn't suit her. But by the time we got back to the house after about an hour, she was more upbeat and animated.

She took the key from me and unlocked the front door, telling us that she would make some tea before embarking on the task of unpacking our cases. But as soon as she stepped into the house her back stiffened and her face dropped.

'My God, what's that smell?' she yelped.

Tina and Michael responded with squeals of disgust that I would normally have considered completely over the top. But not this time. The heavy odour inside the house was truly awful. It hit us like a gust of putrid wind; thick and sickly and yet at the same time indefinable.

'Jesus, it didn't stink like this before we went out,' Tina said in a voice that was muffled because she had covered her mouth and nose with her hand.

The others hurried into the kitchen. I was about to follow when something else struck me. I suddenly realized that the smell was not the only thing that was different about the house. A deep frown settled across my forehead and I felt a sudden tightness in my throat.

All the doors on the ground floor were open.

Nicole and the kids would not have noticed because I'd been the last to step outside – after closing all the doors behind us. It was a habit of mine, almost an obsession. I always felt compelled to close doors before going out. It had been with me since I was a small boy and to this day I have no idea what sparked it in the first place. But I did know with absolute certainty that the doors had been shut when we left for the walk over an hour ago. I decided not to mention it to Nicole and the others. They'd been spooked enough by the snake and now by that harsh smell. If I told them it looked like someone had been in the house while we were out then that would surely mean the vacation would be over before it had even got started.

Besides, there might well be a reasonable explanation. Perhaps Nathan Slade had dropped by to welcome us and had let himself in with a key. The front door had definitely been locked, after all. But wouldn't he have left a note? And wouldn't we have seen his car on the track?

The odious, clinging smell gave me an excuse to rush around the house to see if it was secure. I told everyone to leave it to me and checked every window and the back doors. There were no broken locks or smashed windows. The house had been sealed and apart from us it was empty.

Meanwhile, Nicole, Tina and Michael went looking for the source of the foul odour. But even before their search was complete it had disappeared with a suddenness that surprised us all.

'I don't understand,' Nicole said. 'What the hell could have caused it?'

I didn't know. Just like I didn't know who had opened the doors in our absence. As I started to help Nicole make the tea I tried to play it down, even though an uneasy feeling settled in my abdomen.

'Maybe there's a sewage works nearby,' I said. 'If so the smell could get carried around by the wind.'

'There is no wind today,' she replied.

I shrugged. 'Then it could have something to do with the plumbing. Some rotting food stuck in a wastepipe or something.'

In truth there were many things it could have been. Strange smells that come and go are a feature in most homes. And it's not unusual for the cause never to be discovered. In fact, as bad as it was, it was not the smell that was troubling me. I was sure that would eventually be explained away, probably by the landlord. But the doors were another thing entirely. I just couldn't figure out how and why they'd been open on our return. It was a mystery.

Just like the snake. And the telephone call. And the smell. Coincidence? Or was some kind of pattern emerging? It was a far-fetched notion, of course, and it smacked of paranoia. But the thought had suddenly taken root inside my head like an unwanted tumour.

We had some tea sitting around the kitchen table. I tried to steer the conversation away from the snake and the smell by talking about what we were going to do over the coming two weeks.

We planned to go on lots of walks and visit tourist attractions like the famous motor museum at Beaulieu and the castle at Highcliffe. We were also keen to see the shops in Burley that sold souvenirs and books related to witchcraft and magic. According to Nicole you could buy such things as toy witches, wands, tarot cards and other pagan paraphernalia.

But trying to get the others to focus on our plans was impossible. They were tired, downbeat and shell-shocked. So I suggested it was time we went upstairs and unpacked.

Nicole and I made for the master bedroom which was big and bright, with a king-size bed, a dresser, and two stand-alone wardrobes with full-length mirrored doors. The room overlooked the front of the house with a view of the moor. There was also an en-suite bath and shower room which was fully tiled and had two wash basins.

The kids managed to decide which of the remaining rooms they were going to have without arguing over it. Nicole had much more stuff than I did so when my case was empty I slid it under the bed and went to check on the kids. Michael was lying on his bed reading a comic he'd brought with him. His room was already a mess with his belongings spread around like debris from a hurricane.

Tina was still putting her clothes away, neatly folded or on hangers. Jeans and blouses in the wardrobe; T-shirts and sweaters in the drawers. She took after her mother in that she liked things to be organized. I was the exact opposite, even in the office, which frustrated and sometimes infuriated the other lawyers in the practice.

'Are you feeling better?' I asked her.

'I've stopped shaking at least,' she said with a smile that did not quite reach her eyes.

'Well try to forget about what happened. I guarantee no more animals will be getting into this house. And that includes snakes.'

'I'll hold you to that, Pops.'

I put my arm around her. 'I love you so much, sweetheart. And I really want you to have a good time here.'

'I'll try,' she said. 'But I still think we should have gone to Florida.'

Tina had clearly been rattled by what had happened but I hoped that she wouldn't let it bother her for long. Although she was strong willed and assertive, she was also at that vulnerable age when behavioural problems can be triggered by traumatic events.

I left Tina to it and strolled around upstairs getting acquainted with our temporary home. It seemed like a good, solid property with fresh paint on the walls along with a collection of impressive watercolour paintings depicting scenes from the forest. The house was also spotlessly clean – which was probably why I noticed the large stain on the beige carpet in what was now the spare bedroom. I hadn't seen it before because I'd been otherwise engaged, but now I could see it clearly. It was circular in shape and about two feet across. It looked to me as though someone had spent a lot of time trying to get the stain out with carpet cleaner.

On closer inspection I saw that it had a reddish tint to it. So I wondered if perhaps a previous guest had spilled a drink or had even had some kind of accident which had resulted in him or her bleeding profusely onto the carpet. It was a shame because the carpet looked brand new along with the pine furniture in the room. It seemed that Mr Slade had gone to a lot of trouble to make the place comfortable and cosy.

After unpacking, Nicole suggested that we should all try to get some shut-eye so we could make the most of the evening. It sounded good to me because by this time my brain and body were aching from jet lag. Earlier I had intended to make mad, passionate love to my wife. But nothing could have been further from my mind when we finally slipped between the sheets. I could not stop thinking about the weird things that had happened to us today. The dead snake, the open doors and that awful, rancid smell. What a way to start a vacation.

9

I managed to sleep for about two hours. It was Michael who woke me by coming into the bedroom to tell us he was hungry. It never ceased to amaze me how often he said that – and how much he actually ate during the course of a day. It was a mystery why he was still as skinny as a garden hose.

Nicole was already awake so she was the one who responded by asking him to go downstairs and put the kettle on.

'I'll be down in five minutes to organize some dinner,' she said.

She turned on her side and looked at me. Her gaze was steady and the warmth of her breath was sweet. Then she smiled and it lit up her face and made me realize yet again how lucky I was to have her as my wife.

'You were restless,' she said. 'Were you dreaming?'

'I can't remember.'

'Well I slept like a log,' she said. 'And I feel much better now. In fact I'm looking forward to finally opening that bottle of champagne.'

I reached up, stroked her face with the tips of my fingers. Her eyes were sleepy and sexy, her lips soft and inviting.

'I was worried your birthday had been completely ruined,' I said.

She shook her head. 'Don't be daft. It'll take more than a dead old snake and a foul smell to dampen my spirits on the first day of our vacation.'

I pulled her close, buried my face in the nape of her neck. She put her arms around me and we stayed like that for perhaps a minute. I could hear a bird's repetitive melody outside the window and I was so comfortable and content that I didn't want to get up. But then Michael's voice reached us from downstairs. He was shouting something about not being able to find the tea and coffee.

Nicole rolled onto her back and expelled a sigh. 'I'll go down. Why don't you nip in the shower and freshen up?'

After she'd stepped out of the room I heaved myself up and looked out of the window. The sun was beginning to set, pulling the brightness out of the sky above the forest. My thoughts flashed back to what had happened earlier with the open doors and it caused my breathing to grow a little shallow. This wasn't good. I needed to unwind and accept that there had to be a straightforward explanation for it. I just didn't know what it was yet.

I stepped into the en-suite and fired up the shower. I got the water as hot as possible without burning my skin and stood under the scalding spray for endless minutes, letting it batter the paranoia out of me. Afterwards, I dried and dressed and went downstairs.

Nicole had raided the refrigerator and was preparing a dinner of chicken in breadcrumbs, fries and baked beans. Having laid the table in the kitchen she asked me to open the champagne. Tina appeared having slept in her clothes. Her hair was ruffled and her eyes looked dry and heavy.

'Would you like some bubbly?' I asked her.

She cracked a smile and I realized that she was feeling much better. I handed her a glass and half filled it with champagne.

'What about me?' Michael said. 'Can't I have some of that?'

'You're too young,' I told him. 'Help yourself to a soft drink. There are several bottles in that cupboard.'

He let the air out of his lungs in a long hiss and moaned under his breath that it wasn't fair. Then he went to the cupboard while I poured champagne into glasses for Nicole and me.

'Here's to the birthday girl,' I said, raising my glass.

I reckoned it was high quality plonk which would have set the landlord back a fair few pounds. It reminded me that I wanted to talk to Mr Slade. I tried the landline phone again but it still wasn't working. I found my cell and dialled his number. Once again it went through to his voicemail. I left another message for him to call me back and hung up.

The guy was beginning to annoy me. He should have returned my call by now. He was being totally unprofessional and inconsiderate. I wanted to know about the snake and the smell and whether or not he had dropped in unexpectedly. I resolved to give him a piece of mind when eventually he did get in touch.

I was famished by the time we all sat around the table for dinner. Eating together cheered us all up. We even had a laugh about that disgusting smell that had greeted us on our return from the walk. Michael said it was almost as bad as when Tina farted. Tina retaliated by saying that she was going to find a snake and put it in Michael's bed.

Nicole found a tub of ice cream in the freezer and served it up for dessert with strawberry sauce and crushed almonds. When we'd finished eating we retreated to the living room with a box of chocolates and what was left of the champagne.

Once I'd figured out how to work the television controls we settled down for a relaxing evening. Outside, the night had descended on the forest and we were all mesmerized by the unworldly silence of the moor. The moon had been swallowed up by gathering clouds and it was pitch black.

We found ourselves watching a news programme and I was about to channel hop with the remote when I heard the newscaster mention the New Forest.

'Listen up,' I said, raising a hand to silence the others.

'The girl's body was found in a shallow grave close to the village of Burley,' the newscaster said. 'It's believed she'd been stabbed to death. John Bradbury has just sent this report.'

I could hardly believe it. A young girl had been found murdered not far from where we were. She hadn't yet been identified but police believed her first name was Genna because of a tattoo on her right ankle. The reporter voiced over a video of Cranes Moor and there was a close-up of a small tent surrounded by people in pale blue overalls. The camera pulled out to reveal dozens of police officers searching the moor for clues and there was even a shot of a police helicopter.

'That must be the one we saw,' Michael said.

As I stared at the screen I felt a chill creeping through me, making the gooseflesh rise on my arms. This was the sort of thing that happened back home in Texas, where gruesome murders are an everyday occurrence. But not here in these beautiful, peaceful surroundings.

A middle-aged man identified as Detective Chief Inspector Jeff Temple was seen addressing the media. He had thin brown hair and was wearing a suit. His voice was deep and gruff as he appealed for anyone who might know the victim to come forward.

When the report was finished I muted the TV and turned to Nicole who was sitting on the sofa with her legs folded beneath her. Her face had suddenly become pinched and tense.

'How far away is Cranes Moor?' I asked her.

'About two miles, I think,' she said. 'It's over towards Burley.'

I shook my head. 'This is incredible. I thought we'd had our full quota of shocks for today.'

I sat next to Nicole and topped up our glasses. I felt like getting drunk. How else could I hide my darkening mood?

Predictably the news item had charged the atmosphere in the room and none of us felt much like talking afterwards. We desperately needed a distraction so I searched the channels for something to watch and found a movie starring Ben Stiller, which had only just started. Half an hour into the film I noticed that I was the only one still awake. Michael was lying on the floor in front of the TV and Tina was slumped in an armchair. Nicole was cuddled up to me and I could tell from her breathing that she was out to the world.

My own eyelids were heavy and had begun to droop. I was surprised at how tired I was considering I'd slept for a couple of hours earlier. My senses were dulled and I suddenly felt floppy and listless.

I hauled myself up off the sofa and woke the others.

'Come on,' I said. 'It's time we all went to bed. We can't sleep down here.'

All three of them protested but eventually I managed to herd them up to their bedrooms after switching off the TV and lights downstairs.

Nicole was so drowsy she didn't even bother to go to the bathroom. She just dropped her dressing gown on the floor and climbed quickly between the sheets. After cleaning my teeth, I checked that the kids were tucked up in their beds then shuffled back to the master bedroom and collapsed on the bed in a stupor of exhaustion. Nicole did not even stir. I switched off the bedside light and closed my eyes. The darkness closed in on me. My body went into lockdown as my muscles eased into a state of total relaxation.

It was a strange sensation – almost like being sedated.

10

Temple stood at one end of the incident room in Southampton's police headquarters overlooking the city's sprawling docks. On the board behind him were pinned maps of the New Forest and gruesome photographs of the dead girl lying in her shallow grave. There were close-ups of the tattoo and her wounds.

'OK, listen up,' he said above the buzz of conversation. He waited until he had the attention of the six detectives and four uniformed officers who were sitting on plastic chairs in front of him. Then he coughed to clear his throat before carrying on.

'As yet we don't have an ID on the victim,' he said. 'Her prints are now being processed and we should know soon if she's on the database. There's been a slight delay for some reason. In the meantime we have the ankle tattoo. Genna. It may or may not be her name but it's a distinctive mark so hopefully it will ring someone's bell.'

He pointed to one of two maps on the board. It showed the whole of the forest – all two hundred and eighteen square miles of it and the coastline to the south with towns and villages including Lymington, Barton-on-Sea and Highcliffe. To the west, close to Hampshire's county boundary with Dorset, were the towns of Ringwood and Fordingbridge. To the east the forest stopped a few miles short of Southampton, the nearest city to it.

The team knew the layout well enough. They also knew that there were probably more bodies buried in the forest and that it was sheer luck that had led to the discovery of this one.

'Here's where she was found,' Temple said, pointing now to the other map, which was a blown-up section of the first. 'It's an isolated spot close to a quiet road that runs between Burley and the village of Crow. So one possibility is that her killer – and for now we'll assume it's a lone male – drove there, parked up, and carried the body onto the moor at night.'

He paused to let them take in what he'd said and to dwell on the maps for a few moments. He wanted them to appreciate that this was probably not going to be an easy case. The forest was a desolate place, especially the area around Burley. Outside the villages properties were few and far between, with vast tracts of heath and large wooded areas.

Temple looked at DI Angelica Metcalfe, who was sitting at the front.

'Have you checked missing persons?' he asked.

'They just got back to me, Guv. But there's nobody named Genna on their list.'

'If she was killed three or four days ago she might not have been reported missing yet,' Temple said.

'But if she was local I expect she would have. Those forest communities are relatively small – even the towns. Everyone knows everyone else.'

DI Metcalfe – or Angel as she was fondly known – had recently become a DI. It was a well-deserved promotion. She was one of the sharpest and most efficient detectives Temple had ever come across. She was also the most attractive by far – with brown eyes, brown hair and a pretty, angular face. She was thirty-five and had served out her apprenticeship with the Met in London before moving south a year ago after a bitter break-up with her long-term boyfriend.

'So how goes it with the media?' Temple asked. 'Are we going to get blanket coverage or what?'

Another detective, DS Mark Bannerman, said, 'The press office has assured me that every national paper will be carrying the story tomorrow along with the appeal. The interview you gave at the scene has already gone out on TV and radio and they'll continue to run with it through the night.'

'Sounds good,' Temple said. He looked at his watch. 'The search of the area was called off for the night a while ago because of the dark. It'll resume at dawn and I want at least two of you there to monitor progress. We also need to canvas homes and commercial properties within a two mile radius of the murder scene.'

The team then started discussing every aspect of the case from the various theories to the detailed assignments and who would undertake them. Angel volunteered to go to the canteen for coffees and sand-wiches and insisted on paying for them out of her own money.

As she walked towards the door, a brash young detective named Paul Simmons, who had only been transferred to Southampton from Basingstoke CID a few days before, eyed her shapely bottom in a pair of tight grey trousers and said to the uniformed officer next to him, 'What a great ass. I'd like to have that bouncing up and down on me.'

He chose the wrong moment to speak because there was a sudden lull in the conversations around him and his voice carried across the room. Angel heard it and wheeled round on her heels, her face tight with fury. But before she could say anything Temple beat her to it.

'Listen here, you ignorant cretin,' he fumed across the large desk that separated them. 'If you ever make a remark like that again I'll have you booted off the force so fast your scrotum won't touch the ground. You got that?'

Simmons was so shocked by Temple's anger that it was several seconds before he was able to respond with a barely perceptible nod.

'And I think the lady deserves an apology, don't you?' Temple added in a tight, measured voice.

Simmons swallowed a huge lump and turned towards Angel who seemed as surprised as he was by their boss's outburst.

When he spoke it was in a tremulous, quavering voice. 'I … I'm sorry, ma'am. It won't happen again.'

Angel bit on her lower lip and Temple saw that she looked uncom-fortable. Had he overreacted? Was she embarrassed that he had leapt in to defend her honour in such a public way?

She gave him an unreadable look, then shrugged her shoulders and continued on towards the door.

The tension in the room was palpable during the next hour, espe-cially after Angel returned with a tray full of coffees and sandwiches. But she joined in the discussion as if nothing had happened and, to his credit, so did Simmons. But not once did Angel make eye contact with Temple and he assumed this was because she was pissed off with him.

He finally left the office at one in the morning and drove home to his small semi-detached house on the outskirts of Southampton. He'd bought the place after his wife Erin died because their former home held too many memories for him. The property was only ten years old and had two bedrooms, a large kitchen and a small garden with a concrete patio.

It was modest but nice. He'd bought a few new pieces of furniture from the Ikea store in Southampton. Cheap stuff, but solid enough, and the strange Nordic names of each product made him feel that he was buying something exclusive and personal. Never mind that the same furniture graced millions of other homes.

He took off his jacket and went into the living room to pour a whisky and light a cigarette. Then he dropped onto the sofa and switched on a TV news channel in the hope of catching himself being interviewed. He was still waiting for the report to come on when ten minutes later he heard his front door open and then close. He got up to pour another drink – this time a neat brandy with no ice, her favourite late-night tipple.

'Was that macho rant really necessary?' Angel said when she walked into the room and tossed her handbag on the sofa. 'I thought poor Simmons was going to have a heart attack.'

Temple handed her the brandy and said, 'The prick deserved it. He was out of order.'

'That maybe so, but I could have done without you drawing atten-tion to it in such a spectacular way. I felt like crawling under the nearest desk.'

'I'm sorry. What he said wound me up.'

'I can understand that, but you really don't have to fight my battles just because we're seeing each other.'

'I'm his boss. If he steps out of line it's my job to make sure he knows it.'

'Yeah, well if you went around bollocking every detective who drooled over me you'd be in a permanent state of hysteria.'

Temple shrugged. 'OK, I take the point. It won't happen again. So how cross are you on a scale of one to ten?'

She looked at him and couldn't suppress a smile. 'Nine and a half, but I'm sure I'll get over it after I've had a cuddle.'

She swigged back some brandy and walked into his arms. As always he felt the heat from her body surge through his own. The embrace lasted at least a minute and if they hadn't been so tired and it hadn't been so late it would almost certainly have been the prelude to sex. But they both knew that they needed to conserve their energy for the day ahead, so they finished their drinks and went upstairs. They had a quick shower together and towel-dried each other before jumping into bed and turning out the light.

Before dropping off to sleep, Temple once again reflected on their relationship – something he always did on the nights she came to the house to stay with him. He knew it was wrong on so many levels. She was a colleague. She was twelve years his junior. They were making love in the same bed he had shared with his wife. But he also knew that she had reignited in him the spark of life that was extinguished when Erin died. Angel gave him something to look forward to outside of work. She made him feel better about himself and she took his mind off the horrors he frequently encountered as part of his job.

She would eventually want a proper relationship with someone she could have a future – and a family – with. He didn't doubt that. Right now she was just filling in the time between the serious stuff. But although he knew he'd be devastated when she ended it, he also knew he should be grateful because the affair had already served a purpose. It had wrenched him out of the abyss of despair and self-pity that he had been drowning in for years.

And that, surely, had to be a good thing.

11

Something woke me from a deep, dreamless sleep. I had no idea what it was, but I was immediately alert and apprehensive. I felt utterly disoriented and it took a few seconds for me to realize where I was. I stared up at the dark mass that was the ceiling, only just able to make out the shape of the overhead fanlight.

I felt hot and sweaty. Dilated vessels pounded inside my skull and my eyes were stiff and heavy. I lifted my head and looked around the room, dim outlines of furniture giving some relief to the oppressive darkness. And then I heard something; muffled sounds coming from outside the bedroom. I felt my forehead tighten into a frown.

I strained my ears to listen, but at first I was only aware of Nicole's shallow breathing next to me, still lost in the comfort of sleep.

Then it came again and I felt an icy chill in my gut. Voices. Downstairs. Not loud enough to discern individual words, but loud enough to know that a conversation was taking place. Right below us.

I sat bolt upright and was gripped by a sudden bout of trembling. It was enough to wake Nicole. She stirred beside me and grunted something unintelligible.

'Shussh,' I whispered, touching her bare shoulder. 'Be quiet.'

I felt the duvet move as I held my breath and tried to make sense of what was happening. Was I dreaming? Were the voices part of that dream? I shook my head from side to side, took a deep breath and quickly concluded that it wasn't a dream. I was awake and the voices were real. They were coming up through the ceiling. Shit.

'What's up?' Nicole said sleepily.

'I think there's someone downstairs,' I said in a hushed tone. 'I can hear people talking.'

Nicole sat up and put a warm hand on my arm. As we both sat there listening I felt the hand start to shake.

After a moment, she said, 'Are you sure you didn't leave the television on?'

It was the obvious question and it hadn't even occurred to me. But now that I thought about it I distinctly remembered switching the TV off along with the lights.

'I'm sure,' I said.

'So maybe it switched itself on again. Could be on a timer or something. Like an alarm.'

I didn't think so, but of course I couldn't be certain. There was only one way to find out and that was by going downstairs. I threw back the duvet and flung my feet onto the floor. Nicole squeezed my arm and said, 'What are you doing?'

'I have to check it out.'

'But what if they're burglars? They might be armed.'

'Burglars wouldn't make such a racket. Besides, we can't ignore it and go back to sleep.'

'Oh, Jack, I don't like it. I'm scared.'

'Don't be. I won't let anything happen to you or the kids.'

'Shall I switch on the light?'

'Best leave it off for now. I can just about see.'

I managed to quickly pull on my jeans which I'd dropped over the chair next to the bed.

I could still hear the oddly muted voices as I tiptoed across the room to the door. They seemed to fluctuate from a murmur to a whisper. I gripped the handle in a sweat-soaked hand and eased the door open as quietly as possible. The voices at once became slightly louder and I felt a jolt of fear, a shot of adrenaline, as I stepped out onto the landing.

I was pretty sure the voices belonged to at least two people. I couldn't tell if the speakers were male or female. In fact even as I shuffled along the landing to the stairs I still couldn't decipher what was being said. They were talking quietly and maybe even in a foreign language.

I stood at the top of the stairs and looked down into the darkness below. I felt vulnerable suddenly and realized that I should have armed myself with a weapon of some kind, not that there was likely to be anything I could use in any of the bedrooms. So maybe the only thing I had going for me was the element of surprise. Perhaps that would be enough to scare the intruders into fleeing from the house.

I wasn't sure what to do next but I knew that I had to do something. Waiting for whoever was downstairs to come up and confront us was not an option. My heart was thumping loudly in my ears and sinuses, almost drowning out the sound of the voices. I came to a decision: I would switch on the light, then rush downstairs and try to make it into the kitchen before they realized what was happening. There I would grab a knife and do whatever was necessary to protect my family.

I knew roughly where the light switch was so I groped for it. My heart clenched as I flicked it on and braced myself for action. But nothing happened. The lights failed to come on. The bastards must have switched the electricity off at the mains.

Just then I heard a floorboard creak behind me and I almost jumped out of my skin.

'It's only me,' Nicole whispered nervously. 'Are you all right?'

I momentarily lost the power of speech so I couldn't respond. My chest started to hurt. It was tight and hot and I couldn't catch my breath.

'Take this,' she said. 'They're my scissors.'

She thrust them into my hand and I experienced a tremendous sense of relief that I now had a weapon. They were large hair-dressing scissors that Nicole always kept in her toiletry bag. They gave me the confidence to press ahead even though I didn't know what to expect. The intruders must have known by now that they had woken us. They were probably watching me from the shadows, waiting to pounce as soon as I ventured down. But what choice did I have? Our phones were down there and so too was our only means of escape.

A rush of anger propelled me forward down the stairs. I had to tread carefully because even though my eyes had adjusted to the dark I still couldn't see that far ahead.

Fear gave me courage. I held the scissors out in front of me and started shouting in the hope that it would spook our unwanted visitors.

'Whoever you are you'd better leave this house right now before you get hurt. I've got a fucking knife here and I'm going to use it.'

As threats go it wasn't very convincing. But it did psych me up so that by the time I got to the bottom of the stairs I was ready to take on the world. But I didn't have to, because nothing happened. I stopped in the hallway and searched the darkness, but there was nobody waiting to jump on me. The voices continued, though, and it became immediately obvious that they were coming from the living room.

I walked, weak-kneed, towards the living room door, which was open. Had I closed it last night? For the life of me I couldn't remember. I'd been that tired. When I reached the door I went straight in without hesitating, waving the scissors in front of me in a fierce defensive arc. I halted just inside the door, arm outstretched, heart thumping, wondering why I hadn't been attacked. I noticed straight away that the television was not on. That came as no surprise. What did surprise me was the fact that the room appeared at first glance to be empty.

And yet I could still hear the voices. They seemed to be coming from all around me, but at the same time they were distant and distorted. How the hell could that be happening?

'Where are you?' I shouted. 'Show yourselves, you fucking cowards.'

And that's when the voices suddenly stopped. Just like that. One moment the muted chatter of incoherent conversation, the next a profound silence. As I stood there feeling totally freaked out my gut tightened another notch. The silence that pressed against my ears seemed strangely watchful, filling me with a deep sense of dread. After a few moments I heard Nicole coming down the stairs. She called out to me but I was still too wary and confused to respond immediately. Instead, I turned my full attention to the shapes and shadows in the living room. I squinted into the dark, trying to see if there was something I'd missed when I entered the room.

And that's when I became aware of the figure in the armchair. A small black shape outlined against the light fabric of the furniture. Someone – or something – was sitting not six feet away from me. Motionless. Featureless. And yet terrifyingly real.

A cold prickle of fear swept through me. I tried to say something, anything, but the words wouldn't form in my throat. So I continued to stare at the eerie apparition, feeling sick and shaky and wondering what the hell was going to happen next. But I didn't have to wait long to find out because the lights suddenly came on and behind me Nicole let out an ear-splitting scream.

12

The figure in the chair was not an intruder. Or a ghost.

It was Michael.

And that was why Nicole screamed. It was an instinctive reaction to the shock of seeing her son like that and thinking he was dead. I thought so too at first. He was slumped back in the chair in his pyjamas with his head tilted back and his mouth wide open. It wasn't until I rushed over to him and grabbed him by the shoulders that I realized he was alive and unharmed and in a deep sleep.

'He's OK,' I quickly reassured Nicole. 'He's breathing. He's fine.'

She knelt on the floor in front of him and took his hands in hers.

'Michael, wake up,' she said. 'It's Mommy.'

I stood up and rubbed knuckles into my eyes. It was surreal. Michael sitting there unconscious when he should have been in bed. The voices that had woken us up and had carried on even though there was nobody in the room. What the hell was I to make of it all?

'Did you switch on the light when you came in here?' I asked Nicole.

'Yes, of course,' she said without looking round.

While Nicole tried to wake her son I went into the hall. Sure enough the light was on. I looked around for the fuse box, found it high up on the wall next to the front door. All the switches were in the ON position. So why had the upstairs light not come on?

I hurried around the house checking doors and windows. They were all closed. And locked. It seemed as though nothing had been disturbed. I even went outside. The night was black and still and there were myriad bright stars in the sky. A soft wind blew, chilling the air. I saw nothing unusual. No signs of life, no lights and no unnatural shapes in the dark. Back in the house I checked all the cupboards and wardrobes. Tina, bless her, was still fast asleep in her room, undisturbed by the events of the night. In the living room I checked the television to make sure that the sound hadn't come on without the pictures, which might have accounted for the voices. But even the standby button was off. I then looked to see if there were any radios or CD recorders in the room, but there weren't.

I told Nicole that I was satisfied there was nobody else in the house.

'Are you absolutely sure?'

'I'm positive,' I said. 'The place is secure. And both the front and back doors were locked from the inside. I can't see how anyone could have got in.'

So who had those voices belonged to? And if intruders had indeed been in the house then where were they now? They couldn't have just vanished into thin air.

Not unless …

No, I didn't want to entertain the notion that what we had heard and experienced had something to do with the supernatural. I'd never believed in ghosts or poltergeists or any of that mumbo jumbo. It's all bullshit. I've always been convinced of it. Which means there had to be an earthly explanation for everything that happened.

So what had happened in this house on this night? Who the fuck had been having a conversation in the living room and why hadn't I been able to see them?

'It must have been Michael,' Nicole said.

I looked down at her and wondered if she was serious. Michael had opened his eyes and Nicole was stroking his forehead.

'What do you mean?' I said.

'Well you know how restless he is at night. He often talks in his sleep and there was that time about a year ago when he went through that sleepwalking phase. Don't you remember? He woke us up one night and said he was late for school.'

'But there's no way it was Michael. There was more than one voice and they belonged to adults.'

'But you've said that nobody could have got in. We can't even be sure what we heard. I mean, it was all a bit muffled and we couldn't make out what was being said.'

I stared at her, slack-jawed, unable to accept that the explanation was that simple. Surely I would have known if it was Michael who'd been speaking.

'We were both confused and disoriented, Jack,' Nicole said. 'Maybe we just thought we heard more than one voice.'

I wasn't sure if she really believed what she was suggesting or if it was her way of dealing with something she couldn't explain. Like me, Nicole had never believed in the paranormal or the supernatural or whatever people chose to call it, so she'd be anxious to come up with a down-to-earth explanation, however unlikely it seemed.

Michael groaned and suddenly seemed to become aware of his surroundings.

'Hi, sweetheart,' Nicole said. 'Are you all right?'

He looked around, licked his lips, scratched his nose.

'I want to go to bed.'

'You were in bed,' Nicole said. 'Why did you come downstairs?'

He stared at her, perplexed. 'I don't know. I had a bad dream.'

'What about?' Nicole pressed him. 'What did you dream about?'

He sat up straighter, said he was thirsty, so I went into the kitchen and brought him back a glass of water.

After he'd gulped some down Nicole repeated the question.

Michael furrowed his brow, said, 'I'm not sure. I remember being scared, though.'

'What was there to be scared of?' Nicole asked.

'It was dark and there was a man leaning over me and I felt him lift me up. At least I think it was a man.'

'What did this man look like?'

He shook his head. 'I don't know. It might not have been a man. He had something over his face. That's why I was scared. I thought it was a ghost. So I shut my eyes and he went away.'

The boy was clearly confused by the remnants of his nightmare. And who could blame him? It sounded pretty scary.

'It was just a dream,' Nicole reassured him. 'There's no man in the house and there're no such things as ghosts.'

But Michael wasn't listening. In fact he could barely keep his eyes open.

'We should put him back in bed,' Nicole said, standing up. 'He's still half asleep.'

I carried him upstairs and by the time we tucked him under his duvet he was out cold.

'What time is it?' Nicole asked.

I was still wearing my watch so I held it up for her to see. It was 3 a.m.

'I'm going to have a cup of tea,' she said. 'You want to join me?'

I opted for something stronger than tea – a large, neat whisky, compliments of our landlord. I felt I needed it. My thoughts were still burning like a fuse and I couldn't shift the unease in the pit of my stomach. Nicole sat at the kitchen table. She was pale and glassy-eyed, but she did not seem as troubled as I was.

'Try to relax, Jack,' she said. 'Michael is OK and so are we. I'm a hundred per cent convinced that he was talking in his sleep having wandered downstairs. And because he was rambling on about nothing it sounded to us like there was more than one voice.'

'You reckon that's all it was?' I said, incredulous.

She nodded. 'Think about it for a minute, Jack. We know now that nobody has broken in. The house is all locked up. We also know we're all suffering from jet lag and that's bound to affect our sleep patterns. Plus, you and I had a fair amount to drink before we went to bed. We polished off a bottle of champagne between us.'

'I suppose you could be right,' I said.

'Of course I am. I can't in all honesty see that there can be any other explanation – unless we're prepared to accept that the house is haunted and we've experienced some paranormal event.'

'Do you think that's possible?'

A tight smile twisted on her lips. 'Don't be ridiculous. It'll take more than one weird night to change my views on that particular subject.'

I fired down the whisky and felt it bite into the back of my throat. Nicole was probably right, I decided. In any case, there was no point staying up for the rest of the night fretting over it. In the morning the whole episode would no doubt seem far less alarming.

So we finished our drinks and I did one more tour of the house before we went upstairs. We got into bed. I kissed Nicole and turned off the light. Then I listened hard for any signs of life downstairs. But there were no voices or faint vibrations. And no sense of any other presence in the house.

Nicole was asleep within minutes, but it took much longer for me to drop off. My mind was awash with all the strange things that had happened to us since that morning. The snake. The doors. The lights. The voices. Michael's curious dream.

And once again I found myself asking that same, disturbing question: *Could these events somehow be connected?*

13

Temple woke up just before his alarm went off. It was 6 a.m. He'd had a restless night, taunted by vivid images of the dead girl out on Cranes Moor. He would have to see her again today in the mortuary and the prospect filled him with dread. It was an aspect of the job he detested and he always found it hard to suppress his emotions.

He would have been quite happy to stay in bed and spend the day snuggling up to Angel. She had that effect on him when she stayed over. Made him realize that the job did not have to be all-consuming; it *was* possible to become detached from it, however briefly, without feeling guilty.

It was to his eternal shame that he hadn't discovered this sooner so that he could have spent more quality time with his late wife. But during their years together he'd been a workaholic, devoting too much time to catching criminals. Not that Erin complained. She remained loyal and supportive right up to the end when the cancer finally claimed her. But she missed out on an awful lot because of his obsession with the job. They'd had relatively few holidays and little in the way of a social life. After their daughter Tanya moved out, Erin spent most of her days – and many of her nights – at home alone.

Knowing that he should have been a more thoughtful husband was with him all the time, gnawing at his conscience. It was one of the reasons he'd found it difficult to move on after she died. He just didn't think that he deserved to. Which was why, when he felt himself being drawn towards Angel, he tried to resist.

It happened gradually over a period of months. He sensed there was a mutual spark as soon as they started working together. But the relationship took on a personal dimension when she got all emotional one day in the car after hearing that her ex had got engaged. She told Temple that all the men in her life had been total shits and she was fed up being by herself. Like any understanding boss he listened and he sympathized. He saw himself as a shoulder to cry on and nothing more.

But the next day she asked him about his own life outside the office. Did he have a girlfriend? Would he ever marry again? How did he manage to cope after his wife's death? He wasn't sure how to react at first because nobody had ever dared to broach these subjects with him. But he was touched by her interest and he found himself opening up to her.

It wasn't long before they were meeting for drinks in the evenings, unbeknown to their colleagues, and a quiet intimacy developed between them. Even so, Temple got the shock of his life when Angel said after one too many gin and tonics, 'Here's the thing, Guv. I fancy the pants off you and I know you like me. But I also know you won't make the first move. So let me be the one to suggest that we take this relationship to a new level. I'm sure it will do us both the world of good.'

It took Temple three days to take up the offer and invite her over for drinks. During that time he wrestled with his conscience and spent hours looking at photographs of Erin. Feelings of guilt and betrayal weighed him down, but in the end he asked himself a simple question: *Would Erin really want me to go on punishing myself for not being a better husband?* Of course she wouldn't. She'd want him to get on with his life and stop feeling sorry for himself. And so that's what he decided to do. And five months on this was where he was at – waking up next to a sexy young detective whose only flaw seemed to be that she had questionable taste in men.

Temple sat up and looked down at her. Not for the first time he felt like pinching himself. She had a natural beauty, with soft, gentle features and a slightly upturned nose with a dash of freckles. She also had a body to die for – toned and shapely and with not a single blemish. How could he be so lucky?

'What time is it?' she groaned, without opening her eyes.

'Just after six,' he said. 'I'll jump in the shower first and then fetch you a cup of tea.'

He switched off the digital alarm and then leant over to give her a kiss on the forehead.

'You spoil me,' she said.

He smiled. 'That's so you won't be in a hurry to end our little arrangement.'

Her eyes flickered open. 'What makes you think I will? You have only to say the word and I'll move in.'

He stared at her, dumbstruck.

'That's right, boss,' she said. 'I did say what you think I said. And I mean it too. It's about time we took this relationship to another new level.'

His breath lodged in his throat and he struggled to find his voice. He was caught totally off guard. It was the last thing he had expected her to say.

'Why look so surprised?' she said, touching his face. 'Isn't it bloody obvious that things have got serious between us?'

He started to speak but she put a finger against his lips and grinned.

'I don't expect you to respond right now,' she said. 'You need to think about it and we need to talk about it. But it ought to wait until after this latest case because that's what we should be fully focused on.'

Temple was rarely lost for words, but on this occasion he could not think of anything to say. Angel had completely thrown him. His heart was beating furiously and there was a tingle in his eyes. He decided his best bet was to say nothing. Play it cool and be non-committal. That way he wouldn't mess things up by blurting out something that was stupid or inappropriate. She was right. He needed to think this one through.

'Tell you what,' he said. 'I'll get you that cup of tea *before* I have a shower.'

Temple's mood was buoyant as he drove into the city. He still couldn't believe that Angel wanted to move in with him. He'd convinced himself that the affair would fizzle out; that when it came right down to it they weren't a particularly good match. But before they left the house she had made a point of telling him that she was being sincere.

'I really do think we're great together,' she'd said, and he was sure she'd meant it.

He glanced in the rear view mirror at her little grey Corsa. She waved at him through the windscreen and he waved back. Jesus, he thought, I feel like a loved-up teenager. He did have strong feelings for her, of course. He had known it for some time but hadn't wanted to face up to it. And he was pretty confident that she wouldn't lead him on. Come to think of it, hadn't she dropped enough hints in recent weeks? She'd told him she didn't want to have any children, and when he'd pressed her on this she'd been adamant that she did not want to bring a child into a world as shitty as this one.

She'd gone on to say that when she finally settled down it would be with a mature man who was kind, considerate and financially secure. She could have said the man of her dreams would have to be young, handsome and incredibly virile. But she hadn't – and now he couldn't wait to talk it through with her. It promised to be a life-changing conversation for both of them.

With a degree of effort he managed to switch his mind away from his personal life and focus on the case. Whilst having breakfast he had received a call from the incident room and been informed that the murdered girl's fingerprints were not on the database.

However, they got a result shortly after Temple and Angel arrived at the station. A female viewer of Sky's morning news programme saw the appeal for information and called the number that was given out. The woman claimed she lived in Southampton and was a friend and neighbour of a girl named Genna Boyd who hadn't been seen for several days.

The description she gave matched that of the girl found in the forest.

14

I snapped awake in a panic, my face and body drenched in a cold sweat. But the air in the room was warm and heavy – claustrophobic.

I pushed back the duvet and stared up at the ceiling, wondering why the electric fan wasn't working. I was sure it had been on when we got back into bed last night. So maybe it was something else that couldn't be explained, along with the snake, the doors and that terrible smell. Not to mention the muffled voices downstairs that Nicole had attributed to Michael.

Daylight filtered into the room through a narrow gap in the heavy drapes. I craned my neck to check the clock. The digital display read 09:15. I managed to get up without waking Nicole. I slipped on my jeans and a T-shirt and crept quietly out of the bedroom. I used the bathroom at the end of the landing to relieve my bladder and then went downstairs.

Thankfully there were no unwelcome surprises waiting for me. No snakes. No bad smells. All the doors were still closed and it seemed like nothing had been disturbed. I felt a surge of relief. In the kitchen I made myself a mug of coffee and carried it through to the living room. The day revealed itself when I drew back the curtains across the large bay window at the front of the house.

The sight that greeted me lifted my spirits. It was another magnificent morning, the sun climbing ever higher into a pristine blue sky. Its rays poured molten light over the rolling heathland, igniting bursts of colour, from the burnt orange of the dying bracken to the striking purple of the heather blooms.

'That's what I call a sight to behold.'

Startled, I whirled round and spilled some of my coffee on the floor.

Nicole was standing right behind me in her dressing gown, a broad smile on her face.

'Oops. Sorry,' she said. 'I didn't mean to spook you.'

I swallowed an expletive and took a deep breath to regain my composure.

'I didn't hear you. Thought you were still sleeping.'

'I woke up and you weren't there. So I thought I'd come down and join you. It's a beautiful morning.'

'How did you sleep?'

'Not bad considering all the excitement last night. What about you?'

I shrugged. 'I was on edge so I struggled.'

Her arm encircled my waist. 'Well I'm not surprised. But the more I think about it the more I'm convinced that it's nothing to get worked up about. Michael was walking and talking in his sleep. And the so-called voices must have been him having a conversation with himself.'

'I suppose that does kind of make sense,' I admitted.

She gave a short laugh. 'We could tie him to the bed frame tonight so that he doesn't do it again.'

I was glad Nicole was able to make light of it. No doubt it was due to her sheer contempt for the so-called supernatural. For her there had to be a simple, straightforward explanation for everything.

I made her a cup of coffee and we sat in the kitchen and talked about the day ahead. She wanted to go into Burley to check out the shops. She also wanted to drive over to the spot where her parents' ashes were scattered. I knew it meant a lot to her, but I did wonder how she would handle it emotionally.

Michael surfaced half an hour later. He shuffled into the kitchen in his PJs with tousled hair and a face so pale it was like wax.

'What's for breakfast?' he asked.

It turned out he had absolutely no recollection of what had happened during the night. Couldn't even recall telling us he had dreamt about being lifted off his bed by a man – or was it a ghost?

'Sounds funny,' he chuckled. 'Wish I could remember.'

And that was that. He didn't ask questions and he didn't seem in the least bit perturbed. I suppose I'd expected him to wake up this morning feeling confused and even distraught. I'd been hoping he would shed some light on the conversation he supposedly had with himself.

'I'm really hungry,' he said.

I got up and ruffled his hair.

'I'll go wake lazybones,' I said. 'And then I reckon we should all have a slap-up breakfast before we go out and see what this fantastic forest has to offer.'

I went upstairs to Tina's room and tapped lightly on the door.

'Time to get up, sleepyhead,' I said. 'Breakfast will soon be on the table.'

There was no response so I twisted the knob and eased the door open. Light from the landing cut into the pitch blackness of the room, revealing a piled-up duvet on the bed. I grinned. My daughter had always been a messy sleeper.

'Wakey, wakey,' I said as I stepped into the room and headed for the window. As I did so I noticed a crack of light under the door to the en-suite. At the same time I heard the toilet flush which told me that Tina was already up. That was good because coaxing her out of bed was never an easy task, particular when she didn't have to go to school.

I opened the curtains and then the window to let some fresh air into the room. When I turned back towards the bed I saw an arm and a leg poking out from under the duvet. It immediately struck me as odd. If Tina was still in bed then who the hell had flushed the toilet? I felt a cold shiver as I went straight over to the en-suite door and wrenched it open. But the tiny room was empty – not a bogeyman in sight. The fluorescent light was buzzing overhead and I could hear water flowing back into the cistern, which was concealed behind the tiled wall.

I went back into the bedroom. Tina wasn't moving but she had covered her head with a pillow to shield her eyes from the light.

'Did you just go into the bathroom?' I asked her.

She stirred, moaned, pulled the duvet up over her shoulders.

'Talk to me, sweetheart,' I said. 'Have you just been to the toilet?'

She moved the pillow and peered at me through half-closed eyes.

'No, I just woke up,' she groaned irritably.

I went back into the en-suite to check the toilet. There was nothing special about it: white porcelain pan, plastic seat and a normal domestic push-button flush control fitted to a tile.

'Have you finished messing around in there, Pops? I'm bursting to go.'

Tina had dragged herself out of bed and was standing behind me in her PJs with her legs crossed and her arms folded.

'Did you sleep OK?' I asked her.

She gave me a funny look. 'Yeah. Why?'

'You didn't wake up in the night or have any nightmares?'

'No. Should I have?'

I shook my head. 'I just wondered. Only your brother had a bad night. He went walkabout in his sleep.'

'Well that's not so unusual,' she said. 'I'm only glad he didn't come in here and freak me out. Now can I get in there before I pee over the floor?'

Nicole was already preparing breakfast when I got back downstairs. Eggs, bacon, tomatoes and a loaf of bread had been assembled on the worktop.

'Where's Michael?' I asked.

'In the living room watching television. Do you mind laying the table?'

As I got to work, I said, 'Something weird just happened upstairs in Tina's bedroom.'

Nicole stopped what she was doing and gave me a long searching look.

'What now, for heaven's sake?'

I told her about the toilet flushing whilst Tina was in bed.

'Is that it?' she said.

'What do you mean is that it? Don't you think it's strange?'

She shrugged. 'Well it's an odd thing to happen, I suppose. But so what? It's probably a mechanical fault or something.'

'But on top of everything else …'

She rolled her eyes. 'Jack, you're making it sound like this is some kind of horror movie – one of those cliché-packed classics where the family move into a lovely house and nasty things start to happen. Eventually they realize the place is haunted and they all get possessed or worse. Is that what you think – that this house is haunted?'

'I didn't say that.'

'No, but you're hinting at it. Christ, a couple of unusual things have happened since we got here. That's all. It's no big deal.'

'Well I'm not so sure,' I said. 'We've had the snake, the smell, the light, the doors, those voices—'

'Hold on a sec,' she said, interrupting. 'What's this about doors?'

Shit.

'Come on, Jack. Explain.'

So I told her about finding all the doors open on our return from the walk. She was unimpressed.

'So, not content with letting your imagination run riot, you've also decided to keep things from me,' she said.

I felt a pang of guilt. 'I'm sorry. I didn't want to worry you – not after the scare with the snake.'

'I'm a grown-up, Jack. Not a child. You don't have to keep things from me. Especially nonsense like that.'

'It won't happen again.'

'I should hope not. Is there anything else you're not telling me?'

Oh, yeah. A crazy woman phoned me a few days ago and warned me not to bring you here. She said it wouldn't be safe. But I decided you didn't have to know about it.

'No, there's nothing,' I lied.

'Thank God for that.'

She turned and started putting bacon strips into a frying pan.

'So how do you explain all the stuff that's happened?' I said.

She turned back to me, annoyed. 'Oh, come on, Jack. You're being silly.'

'But it's bugging me. I can't help it.'

'OK, let's start with the snake,' she said evenly. 'It obviously managed to get in at some point when a door was left open. It then crawled onto the bed to keep warm and nobody realized it was there. I've no idea why it died and frankly I don't care. As for the smell, well who knows? Probably something to do with the drains.'

'And the lights? Who switched them off and then back on again?'

She shrugged. 'Maybe there was a power cut while we were sleeping. Then coincidentally the power came on again when you walked down the stairs. Or it could have been a faulty wire. Who knows? What we do know is that nobody tampered with the fuse box. If someone had we would have seen them.'

'OK, so explain the doors?'

'That's an easy one. You only *thought* you closed them. We all make mistakes, Jack. And don't forget we'd all just had a massive shock and we couldn't wait to get out of the house.'

'But it's a bit much don't you think?'

She drew a breath. 'Oh, come on, Jack. Reason imposes its simplistic logic on everything. You should know that. Unless you really believe we've been experiencing paranormal activity. In which case you're a moron.'

'Of course I don't believe that. You know I'm as sceptical as you are about that stuff. But something isn't right. I'm sure of it.'

'Well if you're that concerned maybe we shouldn't stay here. We could pack up and go home. Or book into a hotel and incur a huge amount of expense.'

'Now who's being silly? No way are we doing that.'

'Then stop trying to make something out of nothing. You're starting to creep me out and I don't like it.'

I stepped forward, held her shoulders. 'Look, I'm sorry, hon. It's just that I'm uptight because I want us all to have a great time. I'm worried that the vacation is being spoilt. It's been one thing after another.'

She rested her head against my chest and sighed. 'The only reason it'll be ruined is if you don't keep things in perspective. Stop assuming that there's something sinister behind every little thing that happens. This is so out of character for you. Normally it takes a lot to ruffle your macho feathers.'

My mind flashed back to that damned telephone call. It was suddenly clear to me that the warning from the girl was the sauce of my anxiety.

You have to stay away from this place ... your family will not be safe here ... Please cancel your plans and go on holiday somewhere else.

A knife of guilt twisted in my stomach. I should at least have tried to find out what she was going on about instead of dismissing the call as a hoax. And I should have told Nicole about it. Then she'd know why I was so uneasy.

'Look, the last thing I want is for us to fall out over this,' I said. 'So let's start over and pretend that none of the weird shit has happened. OK?'

She looked up at me and gave an impish smile.

'OK,' she said. 'It's a deal. Now go and shower while I make break-fast.'

15

At least one of the little mysteries got solved when I came back downstairs. Nicole mentioned that she'd woken up just before dawn because I'd stolen the duvet – as per usual – and she was cold. So she'd switched off the ceiling fan before prising the duvet away from me and going back to sleep.

I was tempted to tell her that I'd wondered why it hadn't been working when I woke up. But I decided not to because I didn't want her to think I'd added it to the contentious list of 'weird incidents'.

Tina appeared as we were dishing up the breakfast.

'I'm famished,' she announced. 'I could eat a horse.'

'What about a dog?' Michael said in all seriousness. 'Would you eat a dog if you were really hungry?'

'Grow up, you idiot,' she said. 'Nobody eats dogs.'

'They do in China. My teacher told me.'

'Well your teacher doesn't know what she's talking about.'

'My teacher's a man.'

'So what?'

'Well you called him a she.'

Tina raised her eyes and dropped into one of the chairs at the table.

She was wearing tight jeans and a T-shirt – her usual attire – and her hair was tied back. Her skin was flushed from the heat of the shower.

'You look very nice this morning,' Nicole told her. 'The New Forest air must agree with you.'

'I don't think I've ever slept so deeply,' she said. Then she threw a glance my way. 'And I'd still be zoned out now if Dad hadn't come in shouting his head off.'

'Don't you think that's an exaggeration?' I said, taking a seat next to her.

She shrugged. 'Whatever.'

And so everything was back to normal. Tina had slipped into obnoxious teen mode, Michael had begun attacking his food like a pig at the trough, and Nicole and I chatted about our plans for the next two weeks.

It was good to talk about ordinary, mundane things. It had an immediate – and positive – affect on my mood. I started to chill out and every fibre and sinew in my body seemed to relax. It was hard to believe that so much tension had built up inside me since we arrived in England.

I offered to clear the table while Nicole and Michael went upstairs to get ready. Tina sloped off to the living room to watch television. When the kitchen was clean I tried again to contact Nathan Slade. But, frustratingly, the house phone still wasn't working. So I searched out my cell, found it on the table in the hall, and decided to step outside to make the call. As I punched in his number I felt the autumn sun on my face. It was already gathering strength and looked set to stay with us for the rest of the day. It came as no surprise that there was no response from Slade, except for the same generic answering service asking me to leave a message. So I said I was anxious to speak to him and would he call me back straight away.

Since I was outside I took the opportunity to stroll around the house and have a closer look at it. It was certainly an impressive property and had been well maintained. The window frames, roof and brick-work were all in excellent condition. Even the small back garden was well kept, with neat, colourful flower beds and a couple of apple trees.

Beyond the rear picket fence there was a narrow stretch of grassland dotted with blackberry bushes and shrubs such as dogwood, hawthorn and heather. Then came the brooding woodland, a great dark wall of timber and foliage stretching for miles to the east and west of us. As I walked around to the front of the property the detached garage seized my attention. It was like a mini version of the house, with the same brickwork and pointed slate grey roof. There was an up-and-over door made of steel and painted brown. I guessed there was storage space in the loft area and that's why the skylight had been fitted in the roof.

I walked around the building. There was a door at the rear and another window. Out of curiosity I peered through the window, but the glass had been painted black on the inside and my own reflection stared back at me. I then tried the door but it was locked. That was only to be expected, since Nathan Slade had said in his note that the garage was out of bounds because he was using it to store his personal belongings.

As I stepped away from the door something on the ground caught my eye – a collection of cigarette butts, some of which looked as though they hadn't been there long. Since I'm a non-smoker the sight of cigarette litter always makes me cringe. And this lot was no exception, even though it was a secluded place where few people would ever venture. It was my guess that a member of the family who had rented this place before us had come here to have secret smokes. Or perhaps it was Nathan Slade, hiding away from a disapproving wife.

The acrid stench of tobacco still lingered in the air – or maybe that was just my imagination. Anyway, it was more than a little unpleasant so I quick-stepped away from there and went back into the house.

16

For the first time in years DCI Jeff Temple saw the future as something other than an empty road littered with loneliness and
disappointment. There was now the promise of good times to come; a
glimmer of hope in all the gloom.

And he had DI Angelica Metcalfe to thank for it. Even her name
pressed his buttons: Angelica – it was poetic and strangely beautiful.

He was still reeling from the shock of what she'd told him; it was as
though his world had been rocked on its axis. He was desperate to talk
to her about it, to ask her if she was absolutely sure she wanted to
move in with him, despite the age difference and the fact that he was
her boss, which would inevitably cause some complications.

But even though they were sharing a police pool car he knew that
now was not the time. The case took priority. They were detectives
before they were lovers. So during the fifteen minute journey across
the city of Southampton he didn't once raise the issue. Instead he
talked about the investigation and what would need to be done after
they confirmed the identity of the murder victim. But the conversation
was somewhat stilted and he was relieved when they finally arrived at
their destination, a small block of flats overlooking the Itchen River
which flowed through part of the city.

'It's the block on the left,' Angel said, referring to her notes.
'Christine Faber lives at number ten. Genna Boyd is her next door
neighbour. She says Genna's single and lives alone, but hasn't been
around since the weekend.'

'So let's go see if Miss Boyd is the girl with the ankle tattoo,' Temple
said.

The entrance to the block had an access control system. On the wall
speaker panel there were names against some of the buttons. Temple

spotted Faber against number ten and Boyd against number nine. He pressed ten and a high-pitched voice responded after fifteen seconds. 'Yes? Who is it?'

'It's the police, Miss Faber. Can you let us in?'

The block was just as grim on the inside, with more graffiti and a threadbare carpet that was badly stained.

Christine Faber was waiting for them on the first floor landing. She was tall and willowy, with long straw-coloured hair that was stretched away from her face with a ponytail. Temple guessed she was in her early thirties. Her face was pallid and tight; her cheeks narrow, showing off her delicate bone structure. She wore a short mini skirt and a halter-neck top that revealed the tops of her large breasts.

Temple and Angel showed their warrant cards and introduced themselves.

'Thank you for calling us, Miss Faber,' Temple said.

'That's all right,' she replied. 'When I saw the news I knew who it was. It was the tattoo that did it. I spotted it when she moved in.'

'When exactly was that?' Temple asked.

'Oh, about fifteen months ago.'

There were three doors on the landing. Temple gestured towards number nine.

'Is that her flat?'

She nodded. 'I rang the bell again this morning but there was no answer. But I've already contacted the landlord. It's Mr Patel. I phoned him after I called you and he's on his way over. He can let you in.'

'That's great, Miss Faber,' Temple said. 'So while we wait what can you tell us about Genna?'

Christine Faber shrugged. 'Well we weren't close friends. Only neighbours. But she was nice enough, and quite pretty. I invited her in a few times for tea or a drink, but she never returned the gesture. She liked to keep to herself.'

'Do you know her age?'

'Twenty-six. She told me once.'

'You said on the phone that she lived by herself.'

'That's right. But she did have a lot of male visitors – if you know what I mean.'

Temple felt a low thud jar through his thoughts.

72

'Can you spell that out for me please, Miss Faber?' he asked. 'What exactly do you mean?'

Another shrug. 'Well she was on the game – along with some of the other girls in this street.' She said it like it was no big deal – the same as any other job.

Temple and Angel exchanged uneasy glances. It was the kind of revelation that could have a significant impact on the investigation.

'Are you sure?' Temple asked.

'Well she never came out and said it,' Christine explained. 'She told everyone she was a model, but it was bloody obvious what she did. As far as I know she didn't have a proper job and yet she could pay the rent on this place and afford a car. But don't get me wrong. I've never complained. I resorted to escort work myself a few years ago.'

Temple felt a frisson of disappointment. He didn't want to believe that Genna Boyd and the young woman buried in the forest were one and the same. He knew what it would mean if they were. As a victim she would attract much less sympathy, both from the public and from his own officers. The general feeling would be that she had brought it upon herself.

'You mentioned a car,' Angel said. 'Where it is?'

Christine shook her head. 'It's usually parked in front of the block, but the last time I saw it was the last day I saw her. That was Saturday. She drove away in it.'

'What time?'

'About three in the afternoon. I saw her from my window. But I have no idea where she was going.'

Temple took out his notebook. 'Can you give me any details about the car? Make, colour, registration?'

'It was blue and I think it was a Mazda. But I never noticed the number plate.'

'What about her relatives? Can you help us there?'

'She told me once that her father was dead but she had a mother living in Portsmouth. She didn't say where exactly. But I got the impression they didn't get on.'

'And what about friends? Did she have many?'

Another shrug. 'Well if she did she never talked about them. I asked her a while ago if she had a boyfriend. She said she was too busy trying to get some money behind her to bother with a relationship.'

Just then a small, bald Asian man in a crumpled brown suit came bounding up the stairs. He was out of breath and shiny with sweat, but he managed to introduce himself as Rashid Patel, the owner of three flats in the block.

'I do hope that the body you found is not Genna,' he said. 'That kind of thing is never good for business.'

Temple bristled at the man's crass insensitivity. But then, to him, Genna Boyd was merely another source of income.

'Have you got the key to the flat?'

The landlord took a bunch of keys from his pocket, unclipped one and handed it over.

'You'll have to wait out here,' Temple said. 'If we need you we'll shout.'

Christine Faber invited Patel into her flat for a cup of tea. As he followed her in he started dabbing at his forehead with a hanky.

Temple waited until they'd closed the door behind them before inserting the key in Genna Boyd's lock.

'OK, gloves on,' he said to Angel.

A moment later they were inside the flat.

'Oh my God,' Angel said. 'What the hell has been going on here?'

The flat had been ransacked. Every room was a mess. Drawers had been pulled out and dumped on the floor. The carpets were littered with clothes and other personal belongings.

The trail of destruction began in the hallway where the contents of an airing cupboard had been emptied. Sheets and towels were piled against the wall and the door had been left open. In the kitchen it seemed as though nothing had been left untouched. Every drawer and cupboard gaped open. The linoleum floor was half covered with tins, packets, saucepans, crockery and food from the fridge, including butter and eggs.

Temple and Angel trod carefully, anxious not to contaminate the scene. But it was necessary to have a good look around the entire flat to make sure that it was empty. And it was. From the stench of the rotting food it had been for some days. In the living room the cushions had been pulled off the two-piece suite and the contents of a low-level unit had been turned out – CDs, glasses, candles, a few bottles of spirits.

It was an otherwise small, bland room with cinnamon coloured walls and a door leading to a balcony that overlooked the road out front. The room contained an oversized flat-screen TV on a stand and a smoked-glass coffee table. There was a bedroom with a double bed and a tiny bathroom with shower and toilet. In the bedroom the walls were light green and there was a fitted wardrobe with sliding doors.

'There's no trace of blood anywhere,' Angel said.

Temple had noticed this too. 'Seems unlikely she was murdered here then. But we'll know for sure after the techies have worked it over.'

As Angel started picking her way through the debris Temple took out his mobile and called the incident room. He asked for a scene-of-crime team to be sent to the flat; he wanted the pros to subject the place to another search. When he hung up, Angel drew his attention to something she had picked up off the floor.

'It's a photo album,' she said. 'Take a look at this.'

She held the book open at a page containing two pictures of a dark-haired girl standing in front of a large caravan. She was wearing snug jeans and a white blouse and she was smiling for the camera.

'That's our girl,' he said.

Angel arched her brow. 'You sure? You said her face was pretty messed up.'

Temple nodded. 'Even so I'm ninety-nine per cent certain.'

'So what do you think happened here, Guv?'

Temple mulled over the question before answering. 'Someone was desperate to find something,' he said. 'In all probability it was whoever killed her. What I'd like to know is what he or she was looking for.'

'We also need to find out if this happened before or after the murder,' Angel said.

Among the stuff on the bedroom floor they found some personal documents: utility bills, a council tax demand, bank statements – even a mobile phone contract, which would come in useful. As a matter of priority they'd be requesting a call list from the service provider to find out who she had been in contact with in the days and weeks before she was killed.

Temple glanced at a Barclays bank statement dated only a couple of weeks ago. It was an ordinary savings account and the then balance was £5,500. There had been regular deposits over the previous months of between £200 and £300 on each occasion.

Temple gave a little whistle. 'Seems Miss Boyd was making quite a bit of money. We'd better check to see if anyone has been accessing her accounts over the past few days.'

But the money wasn't the only surprise.

Under a pile of clothes in the wardrobe they found something that gave them a vivid insight into Genna Boyd's life. And it also confirmed what Temple had begun to suspect – that this investigation was going to be anything but simple.

1 7

'This is the place,' Nicole told us. 'I can still remember the day I brought them here. It was cloudy and cold, with the hint of a breeze.'

By contrast today was warm and bright. The sky was bleached a pale blue and the air was filled with the subtly sharp scent of wild flowers. We were standing on the bank of a narrow, clear-running stream a few miles east of King's Manor. On our side of the stream the open grassland dipped into a valley in which nestled a tiny hamlet. We'd driven through the hamlet before parking the car and following the stream on foot. Nicole had shown us where she used to live – a lovely period cottage set back from the road with a thatched roof and a large chimney.

I'd tried to persuade her to knock on the door and speak to the new owners. She hadn't been keen, though. Said it would be too upsetting to be invited inside. But she was upset now, of course, as she pointed across the stream to a small clearing in front of some woods. It was where her parents had often come to picnic and it was where she had scattered their ashes after they were killed when their car was struck by a lorry on the A35 near Lyndhurst.

I stood with my arm around my wife as the tears gathered in her eyes. Michael and Tina sat a few feet away on the decaying remains of a huge tree trunk. It was an enchanting spot. The clearing was shel-tered by tall, ageless trees that broke up the sun's reflection on the water. The rich brown of beech and sweet chestnut leaves formed a striking canopy above the damp woodland floor. Wild flowers clung to the banks of the stream and I could see shoals of tiny minnows swimming over the gravel on the bottom.

I held Nicole close as she began to cry, her shoulders heaving with every sob. Tina followed suit and to his credit Michael put his arms around his step-sister and held her head against his chest.

I blinked back my own tears. It wasn't easy. Never had I experienced such an overwhelming surge of emotion. It was a moment of sheer, unbridled sentiment that reinforced the love I had for my family. God forbid that any harm should ever come to them. I wasn't sure that I would want to go on living if I lost what I had now. So beguiled was I by the intensity of my feelings that it was some moments before I noticed something truly amazing at the edge of the wood. Not fifty yards away two brown fallow deer had entered the clearing and were watching us.

'I don't believe it,' I blurted. 'Take a look at that.'

I let go of Nicole and she followed my gaze, her eyes wet and red-rimmed. When she saw them she gasped out loud and her face lit up.

'My God,' she said. 'They're beautiful.'

One was a buck deer, with antlers that were broad and shovel-shaped rising above his head. The other was a doe, or female, and her back was covered with a sprinkling of white dots. You don't have to be an expert to know that fallow deer are shy creatures and rarely make an appearance when there are people around. So we were immensely privileged. Even the kids were awestruck and I watched Tina scramble to get her camera out of her mini rucksack. Nicole broke away from me and took a step towards the water's edge. It was as though she was suddenly in a trance. She stared at the two deer and they stared back, without moving and without showing any fear.

'It's a sign,' Nicole said. 'It has to be.'

I knew instinctively what she was thinking before she came out with it. Nonetheless her words filled me with a wondrous sense of elation.

'Mum and Dad sent them,' she said. 'I know it. I can feel their presence. They're here with us now and that makes me so happy.'

I was happy too, even though I knew that this was just a coincidence and not some strange, spiritual event. Nicole's joy made me feel better about bringing her to England and swept away all my misgivings. I knew that this moment would live with her for years to come – long after she'd forgotten about all the weird and unpleasant stuff that had happened to us.

We were all still on a high by the time we got to Burley. Nicole was positively glowing. She couldn't stop talking about the experience with the two fallow deer. As far as she was concerned her parents had sent them into the clearing to let her know they were there.

I said nothing to discourage her from believing this fantasy, but the irony wasn't lost on me. My wife professed not to believe in ghosts and demons and anything supernatural, and yet she was suddenly convinced that her mother and father had communicated with her from beyond the grave.

The village of Burley is a popular tourist attraction. It was once an Anglo Saxon settlement and during the fifties and sixties was known as the home of a famous 'white witch' named Sybil Leak who eventually moved to America.

We left the Discovery in a car park behind The Queen's Head pub, which Nicole informed me was a notorious meeting place for smugglers and highwaymen in the sixteenth century. Armed with our cameras, and looking very touristy, we strolled into the tiny village, which consisted of a few streets lined with gift shops, cafés, a post office and a couple of pubs.

It was surprisingly busy, but not only with day-trippers. The police were very much in evidence. Two patrol cars were parked up in the centre of the village and several uniformed officers were standing around with clipboards talking to passers-by. We were approached almost as soon as we left the car park but once the officer established that we were not locals he didn't bother to ask us any more questions. But he did confirm what I already suspected, that it was all part of the investigation into the murder of the young woman whose body was found in a shallow grave near the village.

We tried not to let it unsettle us, but that was difficult because everyone seemed to be talking about it. There were enough things to distract us, however, including the gift shops selling occult paraphernalia. Their names were as intriguing as their products – The Coven of Witches, The Sorcerer's Apprentice, Witchcraft, Wizzydoras. Their shelves were cluttered with such things as spell books, magical concoctions, witches' broomsticks, pot-bellied stoves, tarot cards, toy dragons and wands.

A book about the ghosts of Burley was prominently displayed in one shop. I glanced through it and discovered that the village was supposed to be well and truly haunted. There was the boy in ragged clothes who wandered around the lanes crying, the mysterious rider who had apparently been spotted roaming the heath outside the village and a knick-knack store, which apparently had its own ghostly cat. All bullshit, of course, but the kids were fascinated.

After visiting the witches' shops I was ready for some lunch and suggested we pop into one of the pubs or cafés. But the others wanted to carry on exploring the rest of the village shops.

'Why don't you go and have a drink,' Nicole said. 'We can meet you in an hour or so.'

'Are you sure?'

'We all know you don't like shopping so if you come with us we'll feel obliged to hurry up.'

I laughed. 'In that case I'll go and sample a pint of your famous English beer.'

Nicole pointed across the road to a small café called the Black Cat Tea Rooms.

'I'd like to have lunch there,' she said. 'It was my dad's favourite place.'

I kissed her on the cheek. 'So be it. Meanwhile, try not to burn a hole in your credit card.'

Of the several pubs in the village I was closest to one called The White Horse. It looked like a typical British pub, with a half-timbered exterior and wooden benches out front.

I crossed the road and went into the public bar. The interior was charming and traditional, as I'd hoped it would be. There were stout oak beams criss-crossing the low ceiling, a huge inglenook fireplace, horse brasses and thick leather belts mounted on the walls. The public bar was tiny but that was OK because I was the only customer. The barman was in his fifties with a downturned mouth and sagging cheeks. His red, bulbous nose suggested a fondness for drink.

'So what can I get for you, sir?' he asked in a smoker's husky voice.

'I'd like to try a pint of your best beer,' I said.

His eyes brightened and he let loose a grin that revealed a set of unsightly yellow teeth.

'So you're a Yank,' he said. 'That's marvellous. I can't remember when we last had an American in here. We used to get loads of you, but I reckon the recession and the exchange rate has made our little corner of the world less appealing.'

I warmed to the guy immediately and when he served my pint I offered to buy him a drink. He thanked me and poured himself a large brandy. I sipped at my beer which was warm and heavy. But I liked it. It slid smoothly down the back of my throat.

So we got talking. He told me his name was Ray Turner and that he'd been the pub landlord for twenty years. He asked me where I was from in the States and who I was with. He was intrigued to learn that I was married to someone who had lived locally and he actually remembered Nicole's parents and what happened to them, describing it as an awful tragedy.

'I didn't know them personally,' he said. 'But I saw them in the village from time to time, along with their daughter. A pretty young lady as I recall. Such a shame.'

He moved the conversation on and explained, in case I hadn't heard, why the police were in town.

'Dreadful business,' he said. 'The poor girl's body was found over near Castle Hill – that's a ten minute walk from here.'

'Is she a local girl?' I asked.

He shook his head. 'Don't think so. They say her name's Genna and I've never come across it before.'

He then asked me if we were staying in the forest. When I told him we were renting a house called King's Manor he arched his brow, 'That's Nathan Slade's place. I didn't know he was still letting it out.'

'It was advertised on the internet. It looked perfect so we booked it. Arrived yesterday.'

'Have you met him yet?'

'I've been trying to reach him, but he's not answering his phone. I haven't actually spoken to him. All our dealings have been by email.'

'He used to pop in here occasionally, but I haven't seen him in a while. That's no bad thing because he's a bit strange.'

'What's strange about him?'

Ray sipped his brandy, smacked his lips together. 'Well to say that

Nathan Slade is an eccentric would be an understatement. I reckon he's just plain weird. In fact he's always given me the creeps.'

'Any particular reason?'

'His appearance for one thing. He's in his mid to late fifties but he has this thick mane of grey hair that he wears in dreadlocks. And he has glasses with yellow-tinted lenses. They look daft. And he looks daft.'

'That doesn't sound too weird to me,' I said. 'Just, well, unconventional.'

'But that's not all. There's other stuff too – like the way he makes women feel uncomfortable. It's happened here in the bar a couple of times. He ogles them and makes smutty remarks. One of my female customers took offence one time and called him a pervy old sod. He laughed in her face.'

'And is he? A perv, I mean.'

'That's how he comes across. In fact, rumour has it that's why his second wife left him. She found something out about him and scarpered. They'd only been married a couple of years.'

'What did she find out?'

He shrugged again. 'Who knows? He's never talked about it. But his wife told a friend before she went that he was sick in the head and she wanted to get as far away from him as possible.'

'So where is she now?'

'Living in Poole apparently. That's along the coast from here. She's with her son from a previous marriage.'

'All very mysterious.'

'And so is what happened at King's Manor earlier this year.'

'What happened?' I asked, not sure I really wanted to know the answer.

He leaned on the bar and I could smell the brandy on his breath.

'As you probably know, this area of the forest has long been associated with the occult and the paranormal.'

I nodded. 'I've seen the shops. Almost bought a book of spells.'

'Yeah, well these legends about ghosts and witches are good for business. They attract thousands of visitors every year. It's why we have more than our fair share of so-called haunted properties – and that includes this pub as well as King's Manor.'

'You've got to be shittin' me,' I said. 'King's Manor?'

'The story goes that it's haunted by the ghost of a woman named Elizabeth Maddox. She lived and died there years ago.'

'There's an old photograph of her at the house,' I said. 'She was apparently the widow of the original owner.'

'Well I shouldn't worry about it. Nobody really takes all that stuff seriously. And I'm pretty sure that the only scary thing ever to walk the corridors of the manor is Slade himself.'

I was about to tell him what we had experienced in the house, but suddenly thought better of it. I didn't want him to think I was another gullible tourist.

He downed some more of his brandy and carried on. 'Anyway, a local teenage lad went to the house late one afternoon back in June. He wanted to ask Slade if he could take some photos of the house for a school project he was working on about haunted Burley.'

'Don't tell me he saw a ghost,' I said.

He shook his head. 'For this boy it would have been less of a shock if he had. You see, Slade opened the door with a live snake around his neck.'

An image of the adder on the bed reared up in my head and my chest tingled. A wave of questions followed, fizzing and spitting inside me like frenzied bubbles in boiling water.

'It was a grass snake apparently so it would have been harmless,' Turner said. 'But that's not the point. It gave the poor lad a fright because he's apparently terrified of reptiles. It's like a phobia with him. So he took to his toes and bolted away from there.'

'Jesus, it must have been awful for him.'

'It was. But Slade got a shock himself a couple of hours later when the boy's father turned up at his house ranting and raving. I know the guy. His name's Ned Parker. He went ballistic, calling Slade potty and dangerous.'

'Did Slade explain why he had the snake around his neck?'

'He said he was clearing a nest of them from his back garden. But the father said that was no reason to scare people who called at his house. He wanted a grovelling apology but Slade told him to piss off. That's when it turned nasty. The guy threatened him with violence and suddenly two blokes appeared from inside the house. They dragged the father back to his car and told him that if he came back they'd punch his face in.'

'Who were the guys?'

'Nobody knows and when I asked Slade he told me to mind my own business. But according to Ned they were really unpleasant and not from around here.'

'Did he go to the police?'

'Of course not. What was the point? He was the one who started making threats.'

I took a swig of my beer; felt I needed it. 'And there was me thinking that nothing much happens in sleepy little Burley,' I said. 'Houston is tame by comparison.'

I then told Ray about our own weird encounter with the adder. His reaction surprised me.

'It's not uncommon for the little bastards to get into a house,' he said. 'Especially if they're nesting close by. But you were lucky it was dead. Live ones pack a poisonous punch.'

I stayed chatting to Ray Turner for another half an hour. I had a second pint of beer – on him this time – and the more we spoke the more uneasy I began to feel.

I was pretty sure he'd embellished his account of Nathan Slade's behaviour, and probably the story of the snake too, but it was still pretty macabre.

I left the pub after promising to come back with Nicole later in the week. He was keen to meet her and bring her up to date on what life had been like in Burley since she'd moved to Texas. The village was even busier now. I noticed a couple of TV news trucks parked up in the main street and there were more police officers wandering around. I also spotted a few press photographers and a television camera crew. The girl's murder had clearly become a major national news story and it was my guess the village had never seen anything quite like it.

As I walked towards the Black Cat Tea Rooms my mind tried to process what I'd been told. But I really wasn't sure what to make of it. Or whether it was in any way relevant to my family and me. After all, we were only renting King's Manor for a short period. Sure, I had a strange feeling about the place – more a wary instinct that something was slightly and deliberately out of kilter there. But so what? We'd soon be returning to the States and no doubt another family would be moving in.

So how much should I tell Nicole and the kids? Did they really need to know that the house was said to be haunted and that the owner was, according to his wife, sick in the head? Wouldn't it just alarm them? Make them feel uncomfortable staying there? It was a real dilemma and one I hadn't resolved by the time I stepped into the café. Luckily I was there before the others so I had time to think about it over a cup of coffee.

When they finally turned up, weighed down with gift-shop bags, I'd come to a decision. And that was to say nothing, except that my first pint of real English beer had gone down a treat.

18

Temple stared at the photograph. It was in high quality colour and showed a naked girl in her twenties suspended from a ceiling by ropes tied to her wrists and ankles. There was a red ball gag in her mouth and a brown leather strap around her head to hold it in place.

Another girl about the same age stood to one side holding a long, thin cane. She was also naked except for a pair of nylon stockings. This girl was facing the camera and Temple recognized her at once. She had the same long dark hair and high cheekbones as the girl in the album that Angel had just shown him … Genna Boyd.

The photograph was on the sleeve of a pornographic DVD entitled *Bondage Heaven*. It was one of five DVDs they'd found at the bottom of the wardrobe in Genna's bedroom. In another cover photo she was standing astride a young man who was lying on the floor having been 'hogtied' with ropes that rendered him helpless and immobile. The other three DVDs featured less painful forms of sexual activity – a lesbian threesome, solo performances with sex toys, various encounters between well-endowed men and women. Genna Boyd appeared on all the covers.

Temple was no prude when it came to pornography. But in the context of a criminal investigation – especially one involving murder or rape – his attitude shifted somewhat, became less tolerant and more wary. Porn was often the motivational factor behind serious sex crimes. And the discovery of the DVDs meant that this was an avenue of inquiry they would have to pursue.

Genna Boyd was obviously part of that vulgar and dangerous world; a world in which the boundaries of moral decency did not exist. The moment she stepped onto the set of a porn movie or became a sex worker, she set herself up as a potential target. It wouldn't have taken long for any number of sexual predators to spot her on their radar screens.

'Have you noticed that all the DVDs were produced by the same company?' Angel said. 'And it's based in Southampton.'

Temple flipped over the one he was holding. On the back cover was a crude montage of images showing Genna doing nasty things to various girls who were bound and gagged. Underneath that a small box containing the production credit – *Filthy Films, Southampton UK*. There were no other details, but it wouldn't take the team long to find out all they needed to know about the company and who was running it. It would be a small outfit, for sure. Maybe a one-man operation. It didn't take much in the way of manpower and resources these days to tap into the lucrative porn market. You no longer needed expensive equipment and crews. New high-tech cameras and PC-based editing meant that top quality material could be produced on a shoestring – and most performers came cheap.

As for distribution – well that was the easiest part of all. Footage could be uploaded onto internet pay sites or sold directly through virtual adult DVD stores. And the audience for porn was enormous. Temple had seen the statistics and they were shocking. More than twenty-five per cent of all search engine requests were porn related. Nearly forty per cent of all internet downloads were pornographic material. And every taste was catered for. He didn't doubt that the films they'd found were already out there in cyberspace and probably on sale in sex shops across the UK.

He viewed this as a disturbing development. Partly because it dramatically increased the possibility that Genna Boyd was murdered by a complete stranger. And partly because the tabloids were going to turn the whole thing into a media circus once they got wind of what kind of girl she was.

The scene-of-crime team arrived at the flat along with a contingent of uniforms. Temple organized the bagging of some of the priority evidence that he wanted rushed back to the incident room so it could be collated and followed up. This included the DVDs and all Genna Boyd's personal documents. Her mobile phone details had already been passed on.

He and Angel then talked to Christine Faber in more detail about her neighbour, but she added very little to what she had already told them. She was shocked to learn that Genna's flat had been ransacked and said she hadn't heard any unusual noises or seen any suspicious people over the past few days.

As the uniforms started door-to-door inquiries in the block, and along the rest of the street, Temple told Angel to hang around and oversee things.

'Speak to Genna's landlord,' he said. 'And get someone to check on CCTV cameras. There are none covering the block but we might strike lucky if nearby streets are covered.'

'And where are you going, Guv?'

'The mortuary, to check on the post mortem results. Get one of the patrols to give you a lift back to the station. We'll have a briefing session this afternoon.'

As soon as Temple entered the chilly hospital mortuary his thoughts snapped back to the investigation. Coming here was a necessary evil, and he hated it: the smells, the insipid colours, the suffocating air of misery that hung in the air like an invisible cloud.

He only ever stayed as long as he had to. He wasn't one of those detectives who liked to witness autopsies. He just wanted to get the results, ask a few questions and be on his way before the stench of death and decay turned his stomach.

The pathologist, Dr Matherson, knew better than to try to interest Temple in all the gory procedural details. So when Temple walked into the autopsy room, having put on a hospital gown, there was no long, drawn-out preamble.

'It'll come as no surprise that the victim died from the stab wounds,' he said. 'I can't be precise with the time of death until I've done more tests, but I'd say it was four days ago based on what I've found so far. It's my guess she was buried within hours of being murdered. The killer did a piss poor job of covering the body. No doubt he rushed it.'

The murdered girl lay supine on the stainless steel table. The blood and muck had been washed away and her skin had taken on a green-grey tinge. As Temple stared at her his complexion grew ashen. Matherson had already started the post mortem examination. He had opened up the torso with a Y-shaped incision to get at the organs. Some had already been removed and placed in trays.

'Both wounds are approximately five inches deep,' Matherson continued as he turned the body on its side with the help of his young assistant, whose name was Samuel. He then pointed at one of two gashes in the flesh. 'With this one the blade travelled between two ribs and perforated the right lung, leading to an accumulation of two hundred millilitres of blood. As you can see, the second wound is located lower down the back and this perforated the left lung, with just over a thousand millilitres of blood accumulation. Both wounds would be considered fatal.'

Matherson and his assistant lowered the body to its original position.

He went on, 'The blade used has one cutting edge which is serrated. Most likely a form of kitchen knife. Both wounds show hilt marks at point of entry, which gives an indication of the sheer force behind each thrust of the weapon.'

'What about angle of entry?' Temple asked.

Matherson nodded. 'Both wounds are angled slightly upwards, which suggests her killer used underhand thrusts. That's the favoured technique of males. Women prefer the overhand method.'

Temple averted his gaze from the corpse and started making some notes.

'There was a great deal of blood,' Matherson said, 'so the murder scene would have been pretty messy. We found various carpet fibres on the clothes and the bin bags. I think you'll find that some of the fibres are from the boot of a car.'

'Which is consistent with our theory that she was driven to the spot and dumped,' Temple said.

The pathologist nodded. 'Absolutely.'

'So what else can you tell me?'

Matherson spoke as he peered at the dead girl's face through a large magnifying glass.

'As you can see I'm not through here yet and I'm still waiting for the results of routine toxicology tests. However, I've found no evidence that she was sexually active immediately before she was killed. And there's no indication of sexual assault – there are no vaginal lesions.

There are some unsightly bite marks but they were put there by animals. And there are no defensive wounds, which tells me the killer took her by surprise.

'She's never had a child and she doesn't seem to have any congenital abnormalities. There are no significant distinguishing marks apart from the ankle tattoo. But there are faint bruises and scars on her buttocks consistent with being struck over a period of time. So maybe the lady was into sadomasochism.'

'Spot on,' Temple said.

He told Matherson about the DVDs they had found.

'I think it's safe to assume that she preferred to give punishment rather than take it,' Matherson said. 'Otherwise I'm sure there would be more evidence of old injuries.'

Matherson confirmed that DNA swabs had been taken. He said he'd send a full report to the incident room as soon as it was ready. That was all Temple needed to know. He gave a sigh of relief and hurried back outside.

The day had become overcast and dark clouds were gathering at the edges of the grey sky. He walked to his car and got in. His eyes felt like they were burning in the corners; a sure sign of tiredness. He checked himself in the rear-view mirror and saw that they were bloodshot. The skin around them was coarse and lined. He looked every bit his age and for the umpteenth time he wondered what the hell Angel saw in him.

He was about to start the car when he took a call from Detective Constable Neil Buchan in the incident room. The DC wanted Temple to know they'd received the phone records from Genna Boyd's mobile service provider. The call list covered the past month.

'What's interesting is that the very last call was made four days ago and it was to a number in the United States,' Buchan said. 'The call was timed at 5 p.m. GMT and lasted less than a minute.'

'That was most likely the day she was murdered,' Temple said, intrigued.

'That's why I'm alerting you, sir. It could be significant.'

'Do we know where in the States?'

'Sure do. It was Texas. The phone is registered to someone named Jack Keaton.'

'Have you tried ringing the number?'

'I have, but there's no answer.'

'Well keep trying. And find out all you can about this guy. I want to know what his connection is to Genna Boyd.'

19

We spent the afternoon exploring the forest around Burley. We did it at a leisurely pace because everyone was feeling tired and ragged.

We drove slowly along winding lanes and stopped at beauty spots to take photographs. I managed to snap a few grey squirrels, some rabbits and dozens of those ubiquitous little ponies. We checked out the famous Rufus Stone, an iron monument marking the spot where King William II – whose nickname was Rufus – is said to have been killed by an arrow during a hunt in the year 1100. After that we went to see the largest tree in the forest, the Knightwood Oak, which has a girth of over seven and a half metres and is six hundred years old.

By five o'clock we were ready to call it a day so we headed back to King's Manor. I entered the house with some trepidation, having failed to suppress a mounting paranoia. All afternoon I'd been reflecting on what the pub landlord had told me about the property and its strange owner, Nathan Slade. His words had resurrected my anxiety; made me edgy and suspicious.

It came as a relief to find that the house was as we'd left it. I made sure I was the first up the stairs to check the rooms. They were all empty. Even so, uneasy thoughts continued to tug at my mind. And it wasn't just because of what Ray Turner had told me. There were still those things that had happened that couldn't be explained, despite Nicole's best efforts to do so.

I went into the bathroom, locked the door and sat on the toilet. I needed some quiet time to rein in my scattered thoughts. They were making me tense, and that was a shame. I should have been relaxed, focused on making sure that the vacation was a great success. But in truth I would have been happy to pack up and go back to Texas on the first available flight. The lawyer in me told me to get a grip, that I was not being at all rational. But there was another, louder voice telling me I should have listened to the girl on the phone and cancelled the trip.

You have to stay away from this place ... Your family will not be safe here ... Please cancel your plans and go on holiday somewhere else ...

Questions whirled around inside my head. Who the hell was she? Why did she call me? Why did she not ring back? How had she got my name and number? And how had she known we were planning to come here? But these were questions I should have asked myself when I took the call.

I was conscious of an agonizing build-up of guilt inside me. I should have told Nicole about the warning. We could have then decided together whether or not to come. And I should have told her about my conversation with Ray Turner. Christ, I was digging a hole for myself and I feared that at some point the walls were going to collapse in on me.

After a couple of minutes I heard Nicole calling my name. I stood up, flushed the toilet, washed my hands and face.

As I stepped out onto the landing she was coming up the stairs. 'There you are,' she said. 'I've been calling you.'

'What's up?'

'It's the landlord. Mr Slade. He's on the phone. I thought it best if you spoke to him.'

I felt my jaw clench. 'At fucking last.'

I followed Nicole down the stairs and into the living room.

She pointed to the house phone. The hand piece was resting on the side table.

'At least it's working now,' Nicole said.

I picked up the phone, pushing down the rage that was threatening to overwhelm me, said, 'This is Jack Keaton.'

'Hello there, Mr Keaton. It's Nathan here. Nathan Slade. I'm so sorry I haven't been able to call you before now.'

His words and his softly spoken voice took the wind out of my sails.

'I had some urgent business to attend to in London,' he said. 'And I forgot to take my mobile phone. I only just got your messages.'

He sounded sincere; both an apology and an explanation. What more could I reasonably ask for? I felt my anger subside.

'I wanted to talk to you about some problems we've had,' I said.

'What kind of problems?'

I cleared my throat. 'Well when we arrived we found a dead adder in one of the beds. It gave my daughter a real fright.'

'Oh dear. I'm really sorry. That's never happened before.'

'Well luckily no harm was done,' I said. 'But if it hadn't been dead my daughter might well have been bitten.'

'Then please accept my apology,' he said. 'This time of year there are a lot of them around. Sometimes they manage to get into properties if doors are left open. That must be what happened.'

'But that's not all,' I said. 'Yesterday we went for a walk. When we got back there was this awful smell. It didn't last long, but it was very unsettling.'

'I have no idea what that could have been,' Slade said. 'But I'll come out to the house and check all the pipes. It might be a blockage in the sewage outlet.'

'Did you happen to drop by yesterday?' I asked.

'No, why?'

'Well, we went out for a walk and wondered if we'd missed you.'

'Like I said, I only just got back from London.'

I suddenly couldn't remember what other questions I'd wanted to ask him. That was probably because in the light of what he'd said so far they no longer seemed so important. Nicole caught my attention. She'd been sitting on the sofa listening to my side of the conversation and was now signalling for me to thank him for the food and drink.

'By the way we'd like to thank you for all the goodies you left for us, especially the champagne.'

'You're most welcome,' he said. 'It's important to me that my guests are comfortable when they stay in King's Manor. In view of the problems you've just mentioned I intend to give you a significant discount on the cost of your accommodation.'

'Well that's not what I'm asking for,' I said.

'I realize that, Mr Keaton. But I insist. It's the least I can do.'

'Well, thank you.'

'My pleasure. Now, are there any other issues you would like to raise?'

'I don't think so,' I said.

'In that case I'll leave you to enjoy your stay and look forward to meeting you later in the week.'

I hung up the phone and told Nicole what he'd said.

'Well I think he's being more than reasonable,' she said. 'I hope he's put your mind at ease.'

'I guess so.'

She stood up and headed for the kitchen.

'So why don't you open a bottle of wine and I'll sort dinner? I think we should have a nice relaxing evening.'

'Sounds good,' I said.

I trailed after her and went to the refrigerator. Took out a bottle of Pinot. The seal on the screw top was already broken, so I wondered if Slade had helped himself to a tiny tipple before leaving it for us. I thought about what he'd said on the phone. Nicole was right. He was being pretty reasonable, and what's more he had come across as rather pleasant. He certainly hadn't sounded like a sick in the head pervert or a man who would be abusive to women in pubs. And that made me feel less tense and more relaxed during dinner.

'I have to go to bed,' Nicole said. 'If I don't I think I'll collapse.'

She was pale, glassy-eyed. Her shoulders were slouched and she looked dead on her feet. But she wasn't the only one. Tina and Michael had already gone upstairs because they could barely keep their eyes open. And I felt floppy and listless. My eyelids had begun to droop. Yet it was only eight o'clock.

I couldn't figure out why we were all more tired than the hour would normally have made us. It had been the same the previous evening. Exhaustion had come upon us suddenly, dulling our senses and making our movements slow, almost sluggish. Maybe it was the country air. Or maybe our bodies were still out of sync with the local time due to jet lag.

As Nicole retreated upstairs I closed all the doors on the ground floor. I also made sure that everything was secure. I flicked off the TV standby switch and checked that all was in order inside the mains fuse box.

Nicole was coming out of the en-suite bathroom as I entered the bedroom. I could smell the toothpaste on her breath. A ghost of a smile crossed her face and she said, 'Don't worry, hon. Everything will be all right tomorrow. You'll see.'

I pulled her to me, squeezed her gently. Her body felt tight and knotted.

'I love you,' I whispered.

She breathed out a slightly ragged breath. 'I love you too – very much.'

A couple of minutes later, after I had brushed my teeth, we were snuggling up in bed under the duvet. I allowed sleep to roll over me quickly, just letting go into the darkness.

20

The team were still waiting to find out why the last call made on Genna Boyd's mobile phone was to a man named Jack Keaton in the States.

He hadn't answered his phone despite repeated attempts to contact him, so they'd requested help from the Houston Police Department. Now they were waiting for them to get back. It was a slow process because Texas is six hours behind GMT and for the cops there it was low priority.

But the team had better luck tracking down the company that produced the DVDs found in Genna's flat. It turned out that Filthy Films was a limited company with an address in the Sholing area of Southampton. Two registered directors were named as Damien Roth and Belinda Wallis. The company, which had been trading for three years, also had a website.

Temple checked this out and found it was little more than an online store for selling their pornographic DVDs. There were links to other porn sites, including those set up by the people who appeared in their movies. Five of these so-called 'artists' were listed. Two men and three women – one of them Genna Boyd. Her own site contained a short bio section which described her as a 'talented actress and model who worked exclusively for Filthy Films.' It listed her interests as reading, swimming and TV history documentaries. Yeah right, Temple thought. There were also freeze frames from the various movies she appeared in.

At the top of the screen was a sign-up icon and below it a list of ways to contact Genna including 'send message', 'instant message' and 'friends' comments'. Temple clicked on the 'friends' comments' icon and noted that Genna had over two thousand so-called friends. More than three hundred comments were displayed.

The first, from someone calling himself Wacko Will, said: 'Hello beautiful. Can't wait to see your next movie. You have the best ass in the world.'

Cool Bobby from Brooklyn in New York wrote: 'I really got off on your solo scene with the bottle. What a fucking turn on babe.'

Steve-the-Stud from Birmingham wrote: 'Keep up the good work Genna. I love you and my dream is to one day lick you all over.'

Temple read a few more comments and then closed the site. Not for the first time it occurred to him that there were a lot of people out there leading sad, lonely lives.

After a quick ciggy he went out into the incident room for the evening debrief. He began by telling the team that he and DI Metcalfe would shortly be interviewing the two directors of Filthy Films.

'We've spoken to Damien Roth on the phone and he's expecting us at seven,' Temple said. 'But before we go I want to summarize where we are and decide what needs to be followed up by the night crew.'

There were perhaps fifteen people in the room – detectives, uniforms and auxiliary civilians. They'd all been working their socks off. After learning the identity of the victim, the pace of the investigation had accelerated. There were suddenly innumerable lines of inquiry to pursue. Information was piling up.

'We now have confirmation that the dead girl is indeed Genna Boyd,' Temple said. 'There's a match between the victim's fingerprints and those found in the flat.'

'We still haven't traced her next of kin,' DC John Reagan said. 'But we understand her mother lives locally and we're following up various leads.'

'We can also assume she wasn't murdered in her flat,' Temple said. 'Forensics found no trace of blood and the pathologist reckons there would have been plenty of it. For now we also assume that it was the killer who ransacked the flat. We can rule out robbery because her jewellery and other valuables are still there. So we need to find out what he was looking for. We've checked her bank accounts and they're intact. No one has tried to access them in the past few days.'

'What about a computer?' DC Reagan asked.

'That's a good question,' Temple said. 'There wasn't one in the flat.

But she must have had one because she had her own official website. So we assume that it was taken by whoever trashed the flat.'

Temple told them about Genna's website and how it put Genna into contact with her fans.

'Check it out and see what turns up,' he told no one in particular. 'You'll find that she has lots of admirers. See if you can track down those living in the south of England.'

'Why just the south of England, Guv?' someone asked.

'Because we have to start somewhere. She's got over two thousand registered friends and they're all over the world.'

Temple then asked for reports from the detectives.

DC Neil Buchan was the first up. 'We've drawn a blank in Burley, Guv,' he said. 'No one we've spoken to has heard of Genna Boyd. And you won't be surprised to learn that we haven't found anyone who saw anything suspicious on the day she was killed. We've had teams searching the moor all day but they've come up with sweet fuck all.'

'What about CCTV?'

'Cameras are few and far between in the forest and none within a mile of where the body was buried,' Buchan said.

Another detective explained that cameras within a half mile radius of Genna's flat were now being checked, but without knowing what they were looking for it was going to be a long haul.

'We've put out a country-wide alert for Genna's car,' Angel said. 'There was tax and insurance paperwork in the flat so we have all the details.'

Angel then said that all the numbers on Genna's call list were being checked out and they'd already discovered that three of them belonged to guys who'd used her as an escort.

'But going through the list is going to take time,' she said. 'We really need more officers.'

'I've spoken to the super,' Temple said. 'He's got a meeting with the chief constable in an hour and he's confident we'll get more help. The media are getting excited about this so he won't want to be accused of skimping because the victim was a girl of dubious character.'

Mention of the media prompted a question from Wayne Fuller, the press officer assigned to the case. 'When will you be ready to stage a press conference?' he asked.

'I'll do it tomorrow,' Temple said. 'By then we should know more. How much do they know about Genna?'

'They've got wind that she was into porn and prostitution if that's what you mean,' Fuller said. 'I gather one of the nationals took a call from the neighbour, Christine Faber. She was after money.'

Temple nodded resignedly. He'd been hoping to keep a lid on that aspect of the case, at least for a while, but it didn't surprise him that the information was already out there. People were quick off the mark to cash in on anything these days – including murder.

21

The two directors of Filthy Films lived and worked in a large detached bungalow opposite a primary school. Temple couldn't have imagined a more unlikely base for a pair of hardcore porn peddlers.

The street was clean and quiet, with neatly trimmed privet hedges and speed bumps in the road. He wondered if the neighbours knew what the couple got up to.

It was Damien Roth who answered the front door to Temple and Angel. His friendly smile revealed a set of gleaming white teeth, with a large gap at the front.

'You must be the two detectives,' he said. 'So who's who?'

'I'm DCI Jeff Temple,' Temple said. 'This is DI Angelica Metcalfe.'

'Then please come in. I'm Damien.'

Roth was not what Temple had expected. He looked like a respectable teacher, or doctor, and not a producer of dirty movies. He was maybe six feet tall with broad shoulders and a rugby player's build. But he had a thin, hollowed-out face that didn't seem to match his body. His fair hair was shoulder length and neatly combed, falling over the collar of his white button-down shirt.

As he closed the door behind them, he said, 'The living room is through the door on the right.'

A woman in a tight green sweater and jeans was waiting for them. She was about five six and lean, with straight auburn hair cut into a bob, the fringe resting below her brow. There were too many hard lines in her face for it to be pretty, Temple thought. Her eyes were black and hard, like chips of coal. And they homed in on Angel.

'This is Belinda,' Roth said. 'My fiancée and business partner. Belinda, this is DCI Jeff Temple and DI Angelica Metcalfe.'

Belinda Wallis smiled, but it didn't sit right on her face.

'Angelica is a lovely name,' she said. 'You share it with a girl I used to know. We called her Angel.'

Angel shrugged. 'That's what my friends and colleagues call me.'

'And why not?' Wallis said. 'It suits you. You have an angelic face. Perfect bone structure.'

Angel blushed and gave a little cough.

'Belinda's right,' Roth said. 'Yours is a natural beauty, unlike most of the girls who come to us. They try too hard and it shows.'

'We can't stand false boobs and Botox faces,' Wallis explained. 'All the girls who appear in our movies are one hundred per cent real.'

'That's good to know,' Angel said.

Temple noted with amusement that his DI looked distinctly uncomfortable. He was going to pass comment but then caught her eye and the look which told him: *Don't you dare.*

Roth motioned at one of two chunky sofas positioned either side of a smoked-glass coffee table.

'Please, sit down.'

The two detectives planted themselves on the sofa and Roth and Wallis sat opposite. Wallis chewed on a thumbnail and continued to stare at Angel. Roth leaned forward, giving them his full attention.

Temple took in the room. It was bland and anonymous. No personal touches, no pictures, no plants. There was a wall-mounted TV and a cabinet with a glass front. Inside, a DVD machine and a Sky satellite box. The carpet was the same dull cream as the walls, the curtains dark brown and heavy.

'Thank you for agreeing to see us at such short notice,' Temple said.

'It's a shocking business,' Roth replied. 'We still can't believe it. Are you certain the girl who was found is Genna?'

'Ninety-nine per cent,' Temple said.

Roth shook his head. 'I can't imagine why anyone would want to harm her. She was such a lovely person.'

'How long had you known her?'

Roth pursed his lips. 'Just over a year. She answered one of our ads in the local paper. We were looking for models to take part in our adult productions.'

'You mean porn films?' Angel said.

Roth nodded, unabashed. 'As you know, that's what we do. And we've been very successful at it.'

Angel raised her brow. 'Is that so?'

Wallis got in before Roth could respond. 'There's a big demand for the type of high quality hardcore material that we produce,' she said. 'We're a small company with a growing reputation.'

'What's so special about your stuff?' Angel asked.

'We're both passionate about what we do,' Wallis said. 'Our production values are high and appreciated by porn aficionados the world over.'

Angel bit down on her lower lip and Temple could see that she was trying not to grin.

'When was the last time you saw Genna, Mr Roth?' Temple asked.

'We checked before you came,' he said. 'She was here for some filming eight days ago.'

'Did you speak to her after that?'

'Belinda did. Two days later. She rang her with an offer of more work. That would have been the fifteenth.'

Temple turned to Wallis. 'Was she OK when you talked to her, Miss Wallis?'

'She was fine,' she said. 'But then Genna was always so – well – together. She never turned down work. But for some reason on this occasion she did.'

'Do you know why?'

'She didn't say and I didn't ask. It was really none of my business.'

Temple mulled this over, said, 'Who else was here on the fifteenth with her?'

'There were two other performers,' Roth said. 'Jordan Cash and Bev Stuart. They're both regulars with us. We shot a few scenes for a new DVD.'

'We'll need their contact details,' Temple said. 'Along with the details of everyone else who worked with Genna.'

'That won't be a problem, Inspector. We use a small band of freelancers and I'm sure they'll be only too happy to help.'

'Did she have a special relationship with any of them?' Angel asked.

'I very much doubt that,' Roth said. 'It was work and they were colleagues. As far as we know, Genna didn't have a serious boyfriend. And she kept her private life to herself.'

'I take it you knew she was an escort,' Temple said.

Roth nodded. 'She was upfront about that at the start. But it wasn't an issue with us. We've used other girls who were sex workers.'

Temple thought about that. He wasn't surprised. Sex was big business – even in this neck of the woods. The rate at which young girls were getting involved was quite alarming. It was why the detectives who worked in the Hampshire vice squad were so overstretched.

'Do you know if she worked for someone?' he asked.

'If you mean did she have a pimp then the answer is no. But she worked the street sometimes, around the St Mary's area of the city.'

'Is this where you do your filming, Mr Roth?' Angel asked.

'Mostly in the spare room at the back,' Roth said. 'But we're very discreet. The neighbours have no idea what we do. They think we run an export business.'

'It must be quite restrictive here. I mean, it's not very big.'

'Depends what we're filming,' Roth said. 'If its bondage with lots of equipment we often go to other locations. It's pretty difficult to transform the third bedroom into a dungeon.'

'I can imagine it is,' Angel said.

Temple cleared his throat and took out his notebook.

'Have you been to her flat?' he asked.

'A couple of times. We had to pick her up once when her car was off the road. And then another time she let us film her there in a solo scene.'

'Have you been to the flat in the last few days?'

'No we haven't. There was no need. And besides, we've been very busy.'

Temple scribbled down a few notes. After a moment, he said, 'Do you know if Genna was in contact with her mother? We understand she lives in the area.'

Roth shrugged. 'I don't know if they were in touch. But I do know that they didn't get along. There was history there, apparently. Genna mentioned it once but refused to elaborate.'

'Tell me,' Temple said. 'Have you any idea who might have carried out this murder?'

Roth shook his head emphatically. 'None at all. Genna wasn't the kind of girl to have enemies. But I suppose that through her work as an escort she would have come into contact with some unsavoury men.'

'No question about it,' Temple said. 'But it's going to take time to trace her clients, especially if their numbers don't come up on her phone records.'

'Do you have any clues?'

'A few, but it's early days. We're still going through her flat. It was in a bit of a mess.'

He watched Roth's face closely for a reaction. When there wasn't one, he added, 'For your information someone ransacked the flat. They were obviously looking for something.'

Now Roth did react with what appeared to be genuine shock. 'Bloody hell. Do you think it was connected with her death?'

'We're not sure yet. Any thoughts on what they might have been looking for?'

'I haven't a clue. Why would I?'

Temple didn't bother to answer. Instead, he changed tack, said, 'How many of your films did Genna appear in, Mr Roth?'

Roth had to think about it. 'Ten or twelve,' he said. 'We paid her well and she seemed to enjoy the work. Told us she was saving to buy her own house abroad.'

'And these DVDs – where were they made available?'

'On our website, for one thing,' he said. 'Also on Genna's own site. In addition we have a distribution arrangement with a wholesaler who sells them on to sex shops here and abroad. They also appear on internet pay sites from where they can be downloaded.'

'Do you know if Genna had any stalkers?'

'She never said.'

'But what if someone fixated on her as a result of watching her in action? Would that individual have been able to find out where she lived?'

'Not from us. We never give out any information and I'm sure that Genna wouldn't have divulged anything about herself to a stranger. She wasn't stupid.'

Temple then explained that they would need to take their finger-prints and DNA samples so they could be eliminated from those found in Genna's flat. And he asked to see copies of all the movies that Genna had appeared in. The detectives were invited into what the couple called their studio. The room, with a window overlooking the small back garden, was typical of those in brothels the world over. It exuded an air of sleaze and sex. The walls were painted black and the carpet was a morose shade of grey. There was a double bed with a red silk throw on it and a shelving unit packed with DVDs and an array of sex toys.

At the foot of the bed was a digital video camera on a tripod. Another camera rested on one of the bedside tables along with a pair of pink handcuffs and a blindfold with a frilly edge.

Temple felt uncomfortable in the room and he didn't want to dwell, so he asked to see the DVDs in which Genna had appeared. Roth got them down from the shelves and Temple noted the titles. Several alluded to sadomasochism; at least four contained violent sex scenes, according to the blurbs. One jacket description included the phrase 'simulated rape'.

'Do you specialize in rough sex?' Temple asked.

Roth's gaze flickered briefly to Angel, then back to Temple.

'There's a growing demand for edgy material,' he said. 'But I can assure you that everything we produce is within the legal parameters. We're very careful about that. You see, we're essentially film makers, Inspector. These movies present us with a challenge and allow us to extend ourselves artistically.'

Back in the living room Angel used her small forensics kit to take their prints and DNA. Roth then produced a computer print-out listing the people who'd worked with Genna.

'You've been really helpful,' Temple said as they were shown to the door. 'I have one last question. Did Genna ever mention a man named Jack Keaton? He's possibly an American.'

Roth looked at Wallis and they both shook their heads.

'The name doesn't ring a bell,' Roth said. 'Is he a suspect?'

Temple shrugged. 'At this stage everyone is a suspect. But we're interested in this man because the last call on Genna's phone was made to his house in America.'

Roth frowned. 'It's a mystery to me, Inspector. But I'm sure Genna would have had a sizeable fan base in the States. They're the world's biggest consumers of internet porn. And as you probably know, she was in contact with her admirers through her website. Perhaps Jack Keaton is one of them.'

Temple handed Roth his card. 'If you can think of anything else that might help us then please give me a call.'

'You can count on it,' Roth said.

As Temple and Angel walked down the front path the couple disappeared inside the bungalow.

'So what did you make of them?' Temple asked when they were seated in the car.

'They're creepy and full of bullshit,' she said. 'I didn't like them. I felt they were putting on an act. And I didn't like the way that woman stared at me. It was as though she was undressing me with her eyes.'

'I can hardly blame her for that,' Temple said. 'But you're right. There was something out of whack about them. We'll check them out first thing in the morning. Now what about tonight? Are you coming back to my place or do I have to take you back to the nick so you can pick up your car?'

'Your place,' she said without hesitation. 'All this talk about sex has got me feeling horny.'

He laughed. 'I'm glad I'm not the only one.'

22

It began as it did the previous night – with the voices. But this time they woke Nicole.

'Jack, can you hear that? Wake up.'

She nudged me out of a deep sleep. My eyes flickered open and I was blinded by the overhead light.

'Jesus,' I said. 'Why'd you turn the light on?'

'I didn't. It was on when I woke.'

My brain was still fuzzy with sleep. And my senses had yet to fully kick in. But what she said hit me like a hard slap across the face. I sprang into a sitting position, rubbed fingers into my eyes.

'What's happening?' I croaked.

Nicole was sitting up with her back against the headboard, one arm curling protectively around her waist. The other was resting across my lap and I could feel it trembling.

'Voices,' she said. 'Downstairs. Listen.'

I strained my ears. Heard them. Louder than the night before, but muffled. My mouth went dry and a deadbolt twisted in my stomach. I forced myself out of bed and into my jeans. Padded barefoot over to the door. The light switch was still in the OFF position as I suspected it would be. But how was that possible? I looked at the clock on the bedside table: 0:2 a.m.

'Where's your cell?' I whispered.

'Downstairs,' Nicole said. 'In my bag.'

For several seconds I stood there, feeling sick with fear and apprehension. The lights. The voices. Two nights in a row. What the fuck was happening?

'You think it's Michael again?' Nicole said.

I wanted to tell her that I didn't think it was Michael the first time. But instead I said, 'I'll check.'

I eased the door open. The landing light was on but that switch too was in the OFF position. In fact the whole fucking house was probably lit up like a Christmas tree even though it should have been dark and silent and asleep. I could still hear the voices, but they continued to be faint. Like the sound of a conversation behind a closed door where the people involved don't want to be overheard.

I stepped up to Michael's room and opened the door. I was surprised to find that the room was in darkness. I stepped up to the bed and saw that Michael was fast asleep. He was lying on his back, breathing heavily through his nose. My heart began to thud. I backed out of the room, closed the door. Nicole was waiting for me on the landing. I might have known she wouldn't stay in the bedroom. She had slipped on her dressing gown and was hugging herself, her eyes soulful and afraid.

'Michael's in bed,' I told her.

'Oh shit,' she said.

The air suddenly felt heavy around me. I found it hard to breathe. My thoughts were a vortex of fear and confusion. I didn't know what to do. How to react. Whether or not to go charging down the stairs to confront the intruders.

And then Nicole said, 'It's gone quiet.'

I hadn't realized, but she was right. The voices had stopped and the silence was unexpectedly profound.

But not for long. We both jumped at the sudden sound of breaking glass from downstairs.

'Oh my God,' Nicole cried, grabbing my arm.

An urge to vomit rolled through my stomach. I felt vulnerable and helpless and totally defenceless. Who was downstairs? How many of them were there? Why had they come back? What were they doing? My brain leapt from one bad thought to another. My body froze and my beating heart thumped loudly against my ribs.

'I'll get the scissors,' Nicole said.

As she retreated to the bedroom, I steeled myself, convinced that any second one or more of the intruders would come tearing up the stairs to attack us. And I'd be unable to protect myself and my family. Our screams would go unheard because we were in the middle of nowhere.

'Here,' Nicole said as she emerged from the bedroom and handed the scissors to me.

A sense of déjà vu swept over me. We were re-living the events of the night before and once again I had no idea what was going to happen next. But I knew it was time to find out.

'I'm going down,' I said. 'Stay here.'

'Not on your life, Jack.' She held up a thin, glass vase that had decorated the dressing table in our room. 'We're in this together, so let's get on with it.'

There was no time to argue. No time to give thought to whatever other options we might have.

We descended the stairs slowly, me in front. The only sound now was our own heavy breathing. The hallway light was on – the wall switch in the OFF position. No surprise there. I pressed on towards the living room, Nicole close behind me. The door was open, yet I distinctly remembered closing it before going to bed.

I was ready to strike out at the first thing that moved. But as I stepped into the living room I saw immediately that it was empty. The overhead light was blazing and everything seemed to be in order. Nothing had been disturbed. Nothing was broken. It was just how we'd left it before we retired to bed.

But it was a different story in the kitchen.

Someone had made a mess. Most of the kitchen drawers and cupboards were open. The wine bottle that Nicole and I had emptied over dinner was in pieces on the floor.

The fruit bowl had been upended and apples, oranges and grapes were scattered across the worktop. A chair was on its side and the sink was filled to the brim with water. Nicole was speechless, her expression one of terrified disbelief. As I stared into the kitchen the hairs on my arms stood up and I could feel the pounding of panic in my head. My immediate thought was that intruders had broken into the house and had seen fit to wreak havoc. But why only the kitchen? And for what purpose? More importantly where were they now?

I left Nicole standing in the doorway and checked the rest of the ground floor, but nothing had been disturbed. I then checked all the doors and windows. They were all locked – from the inside. There was no evidence of a break-in.

Nicole was still standing in the kitchen doorway, her eyes popping against their sockets.

'There's no one here,' I said. 'And everything is locked up.'

'So who did this? I don't understand.' Her voice was high with hysteria.

'Me neither,' I said.

'What about the other rooms?'

'Untouched.'

She raked a hand through her tousled hair.

'We should call the police, Jack.'

'And tell them what?'

'That we've been burgled.'

'But I don't know if anything has been taken.'

'Then tell them that someone broke in and trashed the kitchen while we were sleeping.'

I put a hand on her shoulders, held her gaze, said, 'Sweetheart, I don't see how anyone could have got into the house. And there's no way they could have got out without us knowing because all the doors and windows are locked from the inside.'

'So what are you getting at?'

I held up my hands. 'In all honesty I don't know. I can't for the life of me explain it.'

As if on cue, the lights went out, plunging the house into darkness.

Nicole grabbed my hand and I pulled her against me. Her body was rigid with fear.

'Oh, Jack. What's going on?'

Before I could respond the lights came on again, along with the TV. We could hear it from where we stood in the kitchen doorway. We moved as one into the living room. On the television, an old black and white movie was playing.

'This is fucking ridiculous,' I said.

I stamped across the room and pressed the power button on the TV, but it remained on. With a rush of anger I reached for the cable and wrenched the plug from the wall socket. That did the trick. Silence once again.

I looked at my wife in the harsh light. Her eyes were glazed and haunted. A great fit of shivering suddenly overcame her, and her teeth clattered. I took her in my arms, held her close enough to feel her heartbeat.

'I'm scared, Jack,' she said.

'I know, hon. This is weird shit. If I didn't know better I'd have to believe that what they say about this place is true.'

I felt her stiffen. 'What are you talking about?'

I was slow to respond; a sure sign of guilt, which my wife picked up on. She wriggled out of my embrace and looked up at me.

'What else haven't you told me, Jack?'

I heaved a sigh. 'Well, according to local legend King's Manor is haunted. At least that's what Ray Turner told me. I assumed it was bullshit for the tourists.'

She frowned. 'Well it's news to me. I heard all kinds of ghost stories when I lived around here, but King's Manor was never mentioned.'

'I'm just telling you what he said.'

'So why didn't you tell me before now?'

'It slipped my mind.'

She stared at me with barely controlled fury.

'You're lying, Jack. You made a conscious decision not to tell me and I'm fucking pissed off.'

'Look, let's not get into this now.'

'I don't intend to,' she said. 'But I'm not going to—'

At that moment the phone rang, a startling burst of sound that stopped Nicole mid-flow.

I launched myself across the room. Picked up the handset.

'Hello?'

The line was dead. No dialling tone.

I slammed the handset back in its cradle.

'This is madness,' I yelled.

Nicole immediately forgot that she was angry with me. She came over, gripped my arm, said, 'We ought to get out of here, Jack. Let's wake the kids and go to a hotel.'

'But why should we?'

'Because whatever's happening, it's out of control. And as much as

I hate to admit it I don't have an explanation for what's going on and that terrifies me.'

'So now you know why I've been freaked out since we got here. All the stuff. The doors, the toilet cistern, the snake—'

'OK, so you were right and I was wrong. But now is hardly the time to say I told you so.'

I broke away from Nicole and started pacing the floor, chewing my lip.

'We should think about Tina and Michael,' Nicole said. 'They're not safe here. We're not safe. Something sinister is going on.'

I stopped pacing, dragged in ragged gulps of air.

'It'll be daylight in a few hours,' I said. 'Maybe we should wait until then. It'll take us that long to pack.'

She shook her head. 'We should go now. We can find somewhere to stay or even drive around in the car. Then come back later in the day for our things.'

I dropped onto the sofa. My whole body felt like it was humming with electricity.

'We have no choice, Jack. If we hang around here then sooner or later one or more of us is going to get hurt.'

I thought about it for a few seconds, then nodded. 'You're right. Go get the kids and I'll start sorting things.'

Nicole went upstairs and I got up and stepped into the kitchen. I emptied the water from the sink, then started closing drawers and cupboards. I still couldn't get my mind around what was happening. I'd watched countless episodes of those TV reality shows where a bunch of ghost hunters explore so-called haunted buildings with night-vision cameras. I'd read hundreds of 'real-life' stories about poltergeists and ghostly sightings. Yet I'd never been persuaded that ghosts really do exist. I'd always assumed it was wishful thinking by people who wanted to believe in life after death. But was what I'd witnessed tonight evidence of the paranormal? The lights, the drawers, the cupboards, the phone … the voices? How else could it be explained? I was still trying to grasp this disturbing notion when Nicole came bursting into the kitchen, her face a rictus of terror.

'Tina's not in her room, Jack,' she gasped.

'What?'

'I can't find her. I've looked everywhere.'

My spine went rigid. 'You're mistaken. You have to be. We know she isn't down here.'

She shook her head vigorously and tears formed in her eyes. 'I'm not mistaken. I've checked every part of every room and I swear to God she isn't there.'

'Then where is she? She can't have just vanished.'

'But she has, Jack. That's the thing. Tina has disappeared.'

23

I dashed past Nicole and up the stairs. Michael was on the landing, rubbing his eyes and looking confused.

'Have you seen Tina?' I asked him in an unintentionally sharp tone.

He gave me a puzzled look. 'No. Mom already asked me.'

I went into Tina's room. The bed was empty, the duvet on the floor. I checked under the bed, in the wardrobe, then the en-suite. No sign.

Her trainers were under the dressing table alongside her flip-flops. Her dressing gown was hanging from a hook on the back of the door. The denim jacket she had worn on her outing to Burley was draped over the chair. I rushed downstairs, went through every room, but there were very few places a person could hide. Nicole was in the kitchen, her face pale and gaunt.

'I don't get it,' I said. 'Where the hell could she be?'

I started shaking all over, uncertain what to do. Bile rose in my throat and I swallowed it back down. I wanted to close my eyes and find that it was all some terrible nightmare. Except that I knew it wasn't. This was real. Tina was missing and I had no idea where she was.

'You should look outside,' Nicole said.

'But I told you – everything is locked up from the inside.'

She shrank away from my raised voice. I was in too much of a panic to feel guilty about that. So I turned away from her and went to the front door. Outside, the night was dark and heavy. The air smelled of pine and damp, decaying leaves.

'Are you out here, Tina?' I called. 'Can you hear me?'

Nothing.

I stepped onto the gravel driveway. In the starlight I could make out the garage block over to the left. And beyond it the wall of trees. To the right was the Discovery and beyond that the track that eventually led to the road.

'Tina, sweetheart. Are you there?'

I heard the hoot of an owl, the rustle of trees in the slight breeze. But my daughter did not respond. I hurried back into the house and told Nicole I needed a flashlight. We both started looking and she found one in the kitchen. Back outside, I went in search of my daughter. I walked around the house, shining the flashlight at everything. All the windows on both the ground and upper floor were closed. The garden gate was shut. There was nobody lurking behind the bushes. I went over to the garage, tried the window and door. They were both locked. Nicole was waiting for me back in front of the house, Michael beside her.

'I'm going to check the woods and moor,' I said.

'Where's Tina gone?' Michael asked.

'We don't know,' I said. 'Are you sure you didn't see her after we went to bed?'

'I went straight to sleep,' he said. 'I only just woke up. Why is the kitchen in a mess?'

'I'll tell you later, sweetheart,' Nicole said. 'I want you to go upstairs and put some clothes on.'

'Can I help look for Tina?'

'It's too dark out there. Go and get dressed. Please.'

Michael stomped off reluctantly. When he was out of earshot, Nicole said, 'If Tina, for whatever reason, ventured out onto the moor or into the woods then she could be lost. And you could get lost too if you go out there.'

'But what do you expect me to do?'

'We have to call the police. They'll find her.'

'But I still don't see how she's managed to—'

She put a finger to my lips. 'Don't try to make sense of it, Jack. At least not yet.'

'OK,' I said. 'But first I want to drive down to the road. Maybe she took off along the track.'

I was sure I had left the keys to the Discovery on the small occasional table in the hall. But they weren't there. They weren't in my jacket pocket either. Or anywhere in the kitchen.

'They must be here somewhere,' I said.

But after searching for them for another ten minutes we gave up.

'The police,' Nicole said. 'We have to call them.'

I half expected to find that my cell phone was also missing. But fortunately it was on the kitchen table where I had left it. As I picked it up I saw that I had a text message. From Tina. I felt my chest contract as I opened it up and read the message.

Gone for a walk. Don't worry. Back soon.

But I did worry. I worried enough to call 999.

A patrol car turned up thirty minutes later. Two uniformed officers came into the house. One was bald and in his late forties. The other was a lanky twentysomething. But talking to them proved to be a waste of time. After they read the text from Tina the bald one said, 'So what's the problem? She says she'll be back soon.'

I pointed out that it was pitch black out in the forest and Tina did not know her way around. She was probably lost and might get hurt.

'Have you tried ringing her mobile?' the bald one asked.

'Of course, but it's switched off.'

'So she doesn't want to talk to you. Did you have an argument with her?'

'No, not at all. If I had I would have told you.'

He shrugged. 'Well I don't need to tell you that teenage girls are apt to do crazy things on the spur of the moment. And I should know. I have two of my own.'

He then said that the most they were prepared to do at this stage was keep an eye out for her and if she wasn't back by mid-morning they would consider mounting a search.

'But that's not good enough,' I said. 'My daughter is out there in bare feet and pyjamas and God only knows what might happen to her.'

'Are you sure she didn't put some clothes on?'

'Well I can't be certain,' I admitted. 'But all her clothes are still upstairs.'

'So you know exactly what she packed to come here, do you?'

'Well not really. She did it herself.'

'So she could be wearing shoes and jeans that you didn't know she brought with her.'

'It's possible, but that shouldn't make any difference.'

'She probably hasn't gone very far, Mr Keaton. It's a warm night so I'm sure she'll be all right. Plus, there aren't many dangerous animals in this forest.'

I then made the mistake of telling them about the other stuff that had happened. The lights, the mess in the kitchen – how Michael had dreamt about being lifted out of his bed by what he thought might have been a ghost. Even as I spoke I realized how absurd it sounded. Both officers listened, the young one making copious notes. But I could tell from their expressions that they thought I was talking nonsense.

'So you're saying you've got a poltergeist here,' the bald one said.

'I'm just telling you what we've been experiencing,' I answered.

'But you're suggesting it could have something to do with why your daughter has gone walkabout in the early hours.'

I didn't like his tone. But I kept my temper in check and said, 'I don't know why she's gone out, officer. And I don't know how she managed it, seeing as the doors are still locked on the inside. But she's out there somewhere and it's fucking dark and I'm fucking worried.'

'All right, calm down, Mr Keaton. Sounds to me like you've all had a rough night. Are you sure that you didn't have more than one bottle of wine before going to bed?'

I would have lost it then if Nicole hadn't stepped between me and the bald moron.

'Look, officer, we did not get drunk last night,' she said. 'And we did not imagine the things that have happened. So we expect you to take what we're saying more seriously.'

He heaved a sigh, said, 'I'm trying to, Mrs Keaton. I really am. And trust me if your daughter doesn't show within a reasonable time we'll do all we can to find her. But she's only been gone a short time by the sound of it and she told you by text not to worry. As for the weird things that have happened – well, it's hard to see how they're matters for the police. Maybe you should contact a priest.'

I thought Nicole was going to hit him. And she might have done if he hadn't said that he and his partner would have a look around the house and the grounds before leaving. I joined them outside but they merely did what I'd already done and I couldn't persuade them to venture into the woods and onto the moor. When they drove off I went back into the house. Michael had got dressed and was lying on the sofa, too upset to go to sleep. I sat down at the kitchen table with Nicole. She poured me a coffee. I was still trembling with fear and anger, the adrenaline swirling at the base of my spine, so badly it was making my head ache.

'I'm sure she'll be all right,' Nicole said.

We might have been a family, but when it came down to it, Tina was my daughter. My flesh and blood. So I could not expect Nicole to be as strung out as I was. But then maybe I was being unfair. Maybe Nicole was as cut up inside but better able to stay composed.

I slumped back in the chair despairingly. My brain felt like it was going to explode. I tried not to imagine Tina in a vulnerable state. When I did it made things worse. Something had happened to my little girl. Something that could not be explained. I was not reassured by her text message. It wasn't like Tina to wander off. Sure she may have threatened to leave home a couple of times, but that was usually after a huge argument or during one of her low moods. Earlier she had been fine. No sign of tension at all. I could not imagine what would prompt her to take off in the middle of the night, in the middle of nowhere.

'As soon as the sun is up we'll go and look for her,' Nicole said. 'It shouldn't be long now. And who knows – she might even come back before then.'

I wasn't able to find comfort in my wife's words or in her delicate tone of optimism. Instead, I sat there feeling hollow inside, sucking air into my lungs like a drowning man waiting to be rescued.

Dawn was a long time coming.

24

There had been two significant developments during the night. Temple was told about them when he received a call from the incident room at 6 a.m.

His alarm had already gone off minutes before and he was in the process of trying to interest Angel in some morning sex. In fact she had just begun to respond to the touch of his fingers when the phone trilled.

'You can't ignore it,' she said. 'It's bound to be important.'

It was DC Buchan, who had been the officer in charge of the night shift.

'We've heard back from Houston Police Department,' he said. 'They've been to Jack Keaton's house.'

'Terrific. So what have they got for us?'

'Keaton's a lawyer living in a community development with his wife and two children. They weren't there when the officers called but a neighbour who's looking after their place said they're on holiday.'

'Where?'

'Well that's the interesting thing, boss. They're actually renting a house near Burley.'

'Really?'

'That's what she said. I've already checked with immigration. The family flew into Heathrow two days ago.'

'Did the neighbour have an address for them?'

'She did. The place is about two miles from where Genna Boyd's body was found. You want me to send someone?'

'No, I'll go myself. But I'll come into the office first for the debriefing.'

'Fair enough, Guv,' he said. 'The other development is Genna's car.

It's been found in a street near the city centre. I've arranged for it to be towed to the forensics lab.'

'Give me the details when I get in,' Temple said.

He hung up and gave Angel a nudge.

'I think we'd better postpone the nooky,' he said.

She rolled onto her side and issued a sigh.

'What's going on then?' she asked.

He told her about Genna's car and then about Keaton.

Angel frowned. 'So Genna called him on his home phone on the day she was murdered. And then a few days later he flew into the UK with his family.'

'That's right. But I can't think what connection there might be between a lawyer from Texas and a porn star from Southampton.'

'Maybe they know each other. He might even have been one of her fans.'

'It's possible, I suppose. They might have made arrangements to meet up.'

Temple threw back the duvet and got out of bed.

'We'd better get a move on,' he said. 'I'll go make the tea while you jump in the shower.'

Her face cracked around a smile. 'Is this what life will be like when I move in here?'

Temple looked at her. 'What do you mean?'

'Well is it always going to be business before pleasure?'

He thought about it, said, 'Not at weekends.'

She laughed. 'Oh well, that's all right then.'

There was a full house for the handover session at 7.30 a.m. The incident room was buzzing and the smell of coffee and sweat was almost palpable.

The detectives who had worked through the night were in their shirt-sleeves. They had tired eyes and stained armpits. The others were suited up and raring to go, spurred on by the fact that this was the biggest case many of them had worked on.

The session started with the news about Jack Keaton and his family coming to stay in the New Forest. But even as DC Buchan was reading his report, there was a bizarre update from the uniform division. In the early hours of the morning a patrol car had gone to the house the family were renting in response to an emergency call from Keaton himself. He was in a panic because his 14-year-old daughter had wandered off. According to the officers she had sent a text message to her father telling him not to worry and that she would be back soon. But Keaton was apparently convinced that her disappearance was linked to poltergeist activity in the house. He had told them about the lights going on and off, the mess in the kitchen and doors opening and shutting of their own accord. He also claimed he did not know how his daughter had got out of the house, since all the doors and windows were locked on the inside.

'So Jack Keaton is a nutter,' one of the detectives said. 'Someone should tell him to call Ghostbusters instead of wasting police time.'

Temple called for order but had to wait almost a full minute before the team got serious again.

'Let's not judge this bloke until we've had a proper chat with him,' he said. 'What concerns me is that whatever weird stuff is going on in that house might have some bearing on this case.'

He then asked DC Buchan to finish reading his report. Buchan told them the house was known as King's Manor and was owned by a man named Nathan Slade.

'I did a web search and found that it's being advertised as a holiday let,' he said. 'That's probably how the Keatons came across it. According to the site it used to be a guest house but is now rented out as a single unit to families.'

'What else have you got on Keaton?'

'Houston police say he works for a legal firm in the city and has never been in trouble with the law. An upstanding citizen as far as they're concerned. The neighbours think very highly of him and his wife. Her name's Nicole. She's English and used to live near Burley. That's why they chose to come here on holiday. There are two children – Tina and 10-year-old Michael.'

'It's hard to see what the connection is between the family and Genna Boyd,' Temple said. 'We'll go straight over to the house after this meeting. Get to the bottom of it. Meanwhile, what else have we got?'

Forensics were still examining the carpet fibres on Genna's clothes.

A report would be available later. The night crew had managed to trace Genna's mother, whose name was Patricia Boyd, to a terraced house in Portsmouth. But a uniformed officer who called there got no answer and neighbours said they hadn't seen her for several days. According to one, she had a serious drink problem and once collapsed in the street.

'Check the hospitals,' Temple said. 'Maybe she's sleeping off a hangover.'

The discovery of Genna Boyd's car in the city threw up another possible lead even before the forensics team had examined it.

'I went to see it,' Buchan said. 'It was locked and there was nothing inside belonging to Genna. The boot was also empty. But the call about the car came from a resident in the street – an old guy who lives across the road from where it was found. He saw the appeal on the news and went to check the licence plate. He told us it struck a bell with him because he remembered it being parked there on Saturday evening.'

'Did he see who got out?'

Buchan nodded. 'He says he was putting his bin out when the car drew up. The driver got out, locked the door and walked off in the direction of the central railway station. It was dark, but he reckons the driver was wearing trousers and a coat with a hood. Plus, he's sure it was a woman.'

'Why's that?' Temple asked.

'The way she walked. He says he's old enough to know the difference between the sexes when it comes to how we walk.'

Temple nodded. 'So this raises the question as to whether it was Genna who parked it there before she was murdered.'

Buchan agreed. 'Or was it left there *after* she was killed and dumped on Cranes Moor?'

Temple scratched his chin. 'If that's what happened, then who the hell was the woman driver? If indeed it was a woman.'

'I'll talk to the old guy again,' Buchan said. 'But he was pretty sure of himself.'

'I don't suppose there are any CCTV cameras in the street?' This from Angel.

Buchan shook his head. 'Not that particular street. But we're checking others in the area.'

'We need to come back to this,' Temple said. 'Meanwhile, what about Genna's phone records?'

'We're still working through them,' DC Reagan said. 'Most of the numbers have been identified and are being followed up. But again it's time consuming.'

Temple then turned his attention to the day ahead, saying he wanted to know more about Damien Roth and Belinda Wallis.

'And chase up all their freelance performers,' he said. 'I'm guessing that those people were as close to Genna as anybody – and I don't just mean in a physical sense.'

They discussed ideas and tactics for another twenty minutes. The press officer, Wayne Fuller, drew their attention to the first editions of the morning papers. All the tabloids had splashed on the news that the girl found murdered in the forest had appeared in porn films. Fuller said he thought it was time Temple held a formal press conference.

'Organize something for this afternoon,' Temple said.

At the conclusion of the meeting Temple and Angel got into a pool car and set off towards King's Manor to interview Jack Keaton and his wife, Nicole.

25

The sun had started raking through the early morning mist several hours ago. The moor in front of King's Manor was a blaze of green and purple. Behind the house the woods loomed high and proud, the autumn tones sombre and subdued.

I wondered if my daughter was lost in those woods. The thought that she might be scared or hurt filled me with dread. Since dawn, we had all been looking for her. I'd searched the woods and Nicole and Michael had trudged across the moor, calling out her name.

I had also walked down the track to the road because I still hadn't found the keys to the Discovery. God only knew what had happened to them. But there was no sign of Tina anywhere. I'd tried ringing her cell but it continued to be switched off. An hour ago I'd called the police again and was informed that two officers would soon be coming out to the house. It was time they launched a full-scale search of the forest. If they refused to do so I intended to kick up an almighty fuss.

Michael was now in the house having some cereal. He was distraught. Twice he'd broken down in tears. Nicole was holding up well, but the strain was evident in her mournful expression and down-turned mouth. She hadn't looked so distressed and hassled since the miscarriage.

I'd just emerged from my latest walk into the woods. I'd discovered a footpath close to the house and followed it, but about fifty yards into the woods the path merged with two others and they went off in three different directions. I followed one, which went to the east, but after about fifteen minutes I turned back and concluded that it was a hopeless endeavour. The woods were so big and dense that you could wander for hours without seeing another living soul. Nicole was standing behind the detached garage block. She had put on jeans and a sweatshirt.

'Have you seen these?' she asked as I approached.

She was pointing at the cigarette butts on the ground in front of the rear door to the garage.

'I noticed them yesterday,' I said. 'Figured they were left there by the previous tenant – or by Slade himself.'

She crouched down and picked one up.

'They're pretty soggy,' she said. 'That's the dew. But don't you think they would look even more weathered if they had been out here more than a few days?'

I reached down and picked up two of the butts. The slightest pressure caused one of them to disintegrate between my finger and thumb.

'Do you think someone's been here since we arrived?' I said.

Nicole motioned to the garage door.

'I don't know, but maybe we should look inside.'

'I tried yesterday. It was locked.'

'Well perhaps the keys are in the house. Let's check.'

After a fruitless ten minute search of drawers and cupboards we returned to the garage door armed with a hammer and chisel I'd found in a tool box.

It was an old wooden door and it did not look very sturdy. But it proved more difficult to open than I expected. However, I eventually managed to break the rusty lock and push the door inwards.

The light switch was next to the door but when I flicked it on nothing happened. It was difficult to see much in the gloom, but we could tell that the garage was packed with Slade's personal belongings. Most of the stuff was in cardboard boxes, but a lot of it had been left in piles on the floor, including clothes, bed linen and towels. There were also half-empty tins of paint that matched the colours inside the house, some moth-eaten cushions, a threadbare rug and a mangled mountain bike.

The two side walls were lined with shelves on which rested tools and other junk that had been accumulated over the years. My heart slumped with disappointment. There was no sign of Tina in the garage, but I hadn't really expected there to be.

26

'Now that's my idea of a haunted house,' Angel said when she saw King's Manor. 'You can scream till the cows come home and nobody will hear you.'

'Don't tell me you believe in all that rubbish,' Temple said.

'I'll have you know that my Great Aunt Edith is a medium. I'm serious. She's been talking to ghosts for years.'

'And conning gullible people out of their hard-earned cash at the same time, I don't doubt.'

'She's the genuine article. Even performs before an audience.'

'Yeah, and I bet she makes a tidy packet from it.'

'That's not why she does it.'

'Of course not. She does it because out of the goodness of her heart she wants to reunite people with their dear departed.'

'Exactly.'

Temple rolled his eyes. 'Please tell me this is a wind-up.'

'Absolutely not,' Angel said. 'I've believed in the spirit world since I had a paranormal experience at the age of twelve.'

Temple gave her a look. 'Now I know you're getting me at it.'

She shook her head. 'It's true. I swear. I was sleeping at a friend's house. I woke up and saw the figure of a woman standing next to the bed. I was too terrified to scream. So I stared at it. After a couple of seconds it faded away.'

'Ever thought you might have been dreaming?'

'No, because I wasn't. I know what I saw and I'll never let anyone persuade me otherwise.'

'So I'm going to be sharing my home with a woman who thinks she sees dead people,' Temple said.

Angel chuckled. 'That's right, boss. Aren't you the lucky one?'

*

An attractive middle-aged woman was standing in front of the house, holding the hand of a small boy.

'That must be Nicole Keaton and her son, Michael,' Angel said as their car drew to a halt on the gravel driveway.

Temple's first impression of Mrs Keaton was that she was pretty, but not in the way of a beauty parade contestant or model. She had a pleasant, open face with full lips and high cheekbones. But as he stepped from the car and walked up to her, Temple was struck by how stressed out she looked. Her eyes were wide and solemn, her complexion almost grey. He showed her his warrant card and introduced himself and Angel.

'You must be Mrs Keaton,' he said.

She nodded. 'We've been expecting you. This is Michael, my son.'

Temple smiled at the boy, who did not smile back. He looked forlorn. His eyes were dull and opaque, as though someone had switched off the light.

'Has your daughter turned up yet, Mrs Keaton?' Temple asked.

'I'm afraid not. And please, call me Nicole.' Her words sounded pained and filled with anguish.

'Jack's in the kitchen,' she said. 'Come in.'

In the hallway she bent towards her son and whispered something to him. He responded by disappearing through an open doorway on the right. Temple peered in and saw that it was the living room.

The bright, modern decor of the house surprised Temple. He had been expecting the interior to be old and gloomy – like any stereotypical 'haunted house'. But the walls looked as though they had recently been painted and the rooms smelled of lemon air freshener.

Jack Keaton was sitting at the kitchen table. He was hunched over a mug of tea or coffee. It looked to Temple as though he had been crying. His eyes were bloodshot, the skin beneath them red and puffy.

'Hello, Mr Keaton. I'm DCI Jeff Temple. This is my colleague, DI Metcalfe.'

Keaton was tall and lean, with a tanned face and stooped shoulders. He had light brown hair cut short, the grey just finding its way around his ears.

'Tina's still missing,' he said.

Without being asked, Temple pulled out a chair from under the table and sat opposite him. Angel remained standing, her back against the worktop.

'Actually we didn't come here to talk about your daughter, Mr Keaton,' he said. 'The uniformed officers who were here last night told us she had been in contact with you. That's why they didn't feel it necessary to launch an immediate search of the forest.'

'But I think it is,' Keaton snapped. 'My daughter is only fourteen. She's not safe out there.'

'Well she probably hasn't gone far,' Temple said. 'I'm sure she'll be back soon.'

Keaton shook his head. 'It's not that simple. She wouldn't have gone off like that. Not alone and in the dark.'

'She's a teenager, Mr Keaton. They can be unpredictable.'

'This is different. I'm sure it has something to do with all the other crazy things that have happened.'

'Are you talking about the poltergeist activity you mentioned to the other officers?'

'I didn't actually use that word,' Keaton said. 'And you're making us sound like head cases. Some weird shit has happened here.'

Temple did not know what to think. Keaton's distress seemed genuine enough and he didn't appear to be on drugs.

'Why don't you start by telling me what's been going on then?' Temple said. 'Maybe I can help you make sense of it.'

27

I started at the beginning and told them everything. How we found the dead snake in the bed. The open doors. The bad smell. The voices. The lights. The mess in the kitchen. The text message from Tina. The conversation with Nathan Slade. The fact that my daughter had somehow got out of the house even though the doors had remained locked on the inside.

It took about fifteen minutes, but putting into words everything that had happened served only to increase the sense of despair that was bearing down on me.

The two detectives listened attentively, but I sensed that DCI Temple remained unconvinced. It was the way he looked at me. And the way he asked his questions; his tone conveyed the scepticism he felt, I was sure of it. But the female detective appeared enthralled. She leaned across the table, her eyes dilated, hanging on to my every word.

'That really is strange,' she said. 'I can understand why you're so upset.'

I watched her boss sit back and clear his throat. I could tell from his eyes that he wasn't so sympathetic.

'I agree that what you've told us is very odd, Mr Keaton,' he said. 'But I'm sure there must be a rational explanation for what's been happening. There always is.'

'Don't you think we've racked our brains trying to figure it out?' I said sharply. 'My wife and I have never believed in the paranormal. But how else can you explain the lights and the voices?'

Temple shrugged. 'I can't explain it, I'm afraid.'

'Exactly. But what you *can* do is mount a search of the forest. We need to know what's happened to Tina.'

'Is it possible she's still in the house somewhere?' he asked. 'You said the doors and windows were all locked on the inside. Could she be hiding?'

I shook my head. 'We've checked all over. Even the loft. But she's gone. There's no trace of her.'

'Has she ever done this before back home in Texas?'

'Never.'

'Has she threatened to?'

I hesitated and he seized on it.

'So she has threatened to,' he said.

'She's like any teenager, Inspector,' I said. 'She can be moody. A couple of times she told us she was going to leave. But of course she never did.'

Temple paused before continuing and I could see that he was choosing his words carefully.

'Very well, Mr Keaton,' he said. 'In view of your concern I'll arrange for some officers to come and take a formal statement. They can then decide what action to take in respect of your daughter.'

I glared at him. 'Are you serious? Isn't that why you're here?'

'No it isn't,' Temple said. 'We came to ask you about a separate matter. I did point that out to you when we arrived. But understandably you were anxious to tell us about Tina.'

Now I was even more confused. I drew in a sharp breath. 'So what the hell did you come to see us about?'

Temple reached into his pocket for his notebook and placed it on the table in front of him. 'We'd like you to tell us what you know about Genna Boyd,' he said.

I gave him a blank stare.

'Who is Genna Boyd?' I asked.

'Are you saying that you have never heard of her?'

'Should I have?'

Nicole reached over and placed a hand on my arm.

'Isn't that the name of the girl found murdered on the moor?' she said.

I felt a prickle of unease. I suddenly recalled seeing Temple on the TV news talking about the murder.

'That's right,' he said. 'Her body was discovered not two miles from here.'

'So what's it got to do with us?' I asked.

'We believe Miss Boyd was murdered four days ago,' he said. 'Her mobile phone records reveal that the last call she made was to your home phone number in Houston.'

I stared at the detective, slack-jawed, unable to move.

You have to stay away from this place ... Your family will not be safe here ... Please cancel your plans and go on holiday somewhere else ...

The girl's voice boomed inside my head. I felt a sheen of sweat accumulate on my face.

'Do either of you remember taking the call?' Temple asked. 'It was about midday Texas time. It lasted less than a minute.'

After several long beats I nodded slowly and felt Nicole's gaze snap on to me.

'I answered a call from a girl – or young woman,' I said. 'Nicole was out at the time. The girl didn't give her name. The line was pretty bad so she said she would ring back and hung up. But she didn't call back. I decided not to tell anyone because I thought it was probably a prank. So I pushed it from my mind.'

Temple scowled at me, his lips pursed together.

'Did you not wonder how she knew you were coming here?'

'A lot of people knew we were coming here,' I said. 'Colleagues at the office and our neighbours. It wasn't a secret.'

'So what did she want?'

I glanced at Nicole and a shudder of guilt ran through me.

'She told me that we should cancel our holiday,' I said. 'She said we should stay away from this house. That if we came here my family would not be safe.'

Nicole's head reared back. 'My God, why didn't you tell me? I don't believe it. You were actually warned that something would happen if we came here?'

I blinked uncomfortably. 'But I thought it was a practical joke. That maybe someone at the office was trying to be funny. The girl didn't elaborate before hanging up and when she didn't ring back I decided not to take it seriously.'

My wife's body trembled, her eyes watered and she seemed poised to explode. I reached for her hand but she snatched it away from me.

'You lied to me, Jack. Again. You said you'd told me everything.'

'I'm sorry. I thought it would worry you unnecessarily.'

'That's a feeble excuse. I might have decided we should heed her warning, however vague it was. Then we wouldn't have come here and been plunged into this awful fucking nightmare.'

I felt my heart slump, tried to hold down my emotions. She was right, of course, and the litany of guilt was gnawing at my gut. Tina was missing because of me. Our lives had been ravaged because I had made a terrible mistake. If only I had tried to find out who the caller was. If only I'd told Nicole. If, if, if …

'I'd like to know exactly what Genna Boyd told you, Mr Keaton,' Temple said. 'I realize it was a brief conversation and so it's important that you try to remember as much as possible.'

It was hard to concentrate. I closed my eyes, tried to empty my mind and focus on the call. But Tina's face kept intruding, causing me to falter.

'I asked her who she was and she told me that her name was not important,' I said. 'She then said I should take my family on holiday somewhere else. That it wouldn't be safe in this house. She said I would regret it if I didn't do it. But the signal was awful so she told me she would ring back. But I heard no more.'

'This might sound like a silly question, but have you any idea what she meant?' Temple asked.

'Not at all. Like I said, I thought it was someone's idea of a joke.'

'It's strange that her body was found not far from the house she warned you not to come to.'

I nodded. 'And stranger still that she knew that bad things were going to happen to us.'

'How much do you know about Miss Boyd?'

I shrugged. 'Absolutely nothing – except what we heard on the news.'

'So you weren't aware that she appeared in pornographic films?'

'Of course not,' I said, shocked. 'Why would I know something like that?'

'Her films and photos are on the internet and we suspect they've been seen by millions of men around the world.'

'And you think I'm one of them?'

'Are you?'

'Of course not. I haven't looked at porn on the web since I was at college.'

Temple made a note. 'So you have no idea why she called or even how she knew you were coming to this house on your holiday?'

'I wish I did, but I don't.'

Temple fell silent as he thought about everything I had told him, his face inscrutable.

I looked at Nicole. She was now standing over by the sink, her hip against the counter, watching me. I could tell she was still furious but she was managing to control it.

Temple then asked if they could look around the house. I escorted them. They checked all the exterior doors and windows. They found nothing untoward. I showed them the spare bedroom where we found the dead snake and the en-suite bathroom where I heard the toilet flush. Finally, back downstairs, Temple asked us some more general questions about ourselves and made notes. He wanted to know about Nicole's life in the area before she moved to the States. He wanted details about my law firm and about Tina and Michael.

Temple then explained that they would talk to the uniform division about Tina. They would also be tracking down Nathan Slade and they agreed to keep us informed of any progress.

'We will probably want to talk to you both again,' Temple said. 'If you decide to move to a hotel then contact me.' He placed his card on the table.

The next thing that happened I didn't see coming. As I walked towards the front door with the two detectives, my cell phone bleeped with an incoming message. I whipped it out of my pocket, looked at it, said, 'Sweet Jesus. It's from Tina.'

All four of us stood in a huddle in the hallway as I opened up the message. It read:

Don't involve the friggin' police, Pops. I'll come back when I'm ready.

28

Temple studied the couple's reaction to the text message. It seemed to him to be a mixture of relief and bewilderment.

'I don't get it,' Keaton said, his brow knitted. 'This is beyond weird.'

'But at least we now know that she's OK,' his wife said. 'Thank God.'

Keaton immediately tried to phone his daughter, but the call did not go through.

'She's already switched the damn phone off,' he said.

Temple asked to look at the message so Keaton handed over his phone.

'Is this the sort of language your daughter would use?' Temple asked.

Keaton nodded. 'She calls me Pops. And the word "friggin" has become part of her vocabulary this past year. We pick her up on it but she insists it's not a swear word.'

'Sounds to me like she's in a huff. Are you sure she wasn't upset over something?'

'We're positive,' Keaton said. 'She was fine when she went to bed. In fact we were all so tired I'm surprised she woke up at all during the night.'

Temple handed the phone back.

'She might have gone outside to work off steam,' he said. 'In all probability she didn't go far and is watching the house. Maybe from the woods at the back. That might be how she knows we're here.'

Keaton did not seem convinced. 'It doesn't explain how she got out of the house when the doors were still locked.'

'Well maybe there's a hidden door or window somewhere.'

'I don't think so, Inspector. Even if there were I don't see how Tina would have known about it.'

Temple glanced at his watch, said, 'Look, the text you just received should ease your mind somewhat. Hopefully Tina will turn up soon and she'll be able to explain how she got out and why she went.'

He made a note of their contact numbers and took the number Keaton had for Nathan Slade.

'We'll be in touch,' he said. 'And be sure to let us know when your daughter comes back.'

The two detectives then showed themselves out. They left the Keatons standing in the hallway looking tired and shell-shocked.

'This is turning into one of the strangest cases I've ever worked on,' Temple said when he and Angel were in the car and driving away from King's Manor. They had sparked up cigarettes and were blowing smoke out of the open windows. 'I mean, what are we supposed to make of all that?'

'I know one thing,' Angel said. 'You couldn't pay me to spend a night in that place. Not after hearing about all those eerie things that have happened.'

'So you don't think they're making all or some of it up?' Temple said.

'No I don't. Why would they?'

'Who knows? But I do know we've spent nearly an hour inside and nothing seemed to be out of kilter. No doors flew open and the lights didn't keep going on and off.'

Temple, who was driving, slowed the car to let a couple of New Forest ponies cross the track in front of them.

'So what about Genna Boyd's call to the Keatons in Texas?' Angel asked.

'Now that's where it gets interesting. She knew the family were coming here on holiday, but why would she be privy to that information?'

'Nathan Slade might have told her – assuming there's a connection between them.'

'So then we have to ask why she told Keaton to change his plans and go elsewhere. What exactly did she mean about it not being safe?'

'There are a lot of unanswered questions,' Angel said. 'But for me the big one is whether the call and what's been going on with the Keatons has anything to do with her murder.'

'We need to talk to this Nathan Slade,' Temple said. 'Try calling his number now.'

Angel took out her phone, consulted her notebook, made the call.

'It's switched off,' she said.

'Then call the office and get them to check the number. And tell them to run a background on Slade.'

Angel rang the incident room and relayed Temple's instructions. Then she asked if there had been any developments. There had been and she jotted down the details in her notebook.

When she came off the phone, she said, 'They've traced Genna's mother. She's in Southampton General Hospital of all places – apparently she had an accident whilst drinking. She's not serious, though, and has asked to talk to the police.'

'In that case that'll be our next port of call.'

29

After the detectives left I stood in the hallway feeling dazed and disoriented. My heart drummed frantically and my thoughts sprang first one way and then the other.

Nicole had slumped into a sitting position on the stairs. She too was struggling to cope with what was happening. I watched her tugging nervously at her earlobe, saw a glimmer of tears in her eyes. We were both immensely relieved that Tina had sent another text, but the relief was tempered by confusion and uncertainty. A simmering unease eroded my optimism. Why would Tina go off for no reason? Why the indignant tone in her message? How did she know about the cops?

But there were other questions, other mysteries, all of them seemingly interlinked. I now knew that the girl who called me was Genna Boyd. The same girl who was found murdered on the moor. So how did she get our number? Why did she warn me not to come? Did she know there was something odd about King's Manor; that we would become victims of something sinister? And, more worryingly, who had murdered her? Did her death have something to do with King's Manor and Nathan Slade? And did it have anything to do with us? The questions were rolling around inside me, stuck in my head, not going away. I sagged against the doorway, closed my eyes, fought for clarity. But it was no use. Chaos reigned inside my mind.

'Are you all right?' Nicole's voice sounded tired and strained. I looked at her. Her blue eyes gazed at me with intensity.

'I want Tina back,' I said. 'And then I want to take you all away from here.'

The tension seemed to slide from her face. She came over to me. I swallowed a well of emotion as she slid her arms around my waist. I could feel her heartbeat, slow spasms in her chest.

'Have faith, hon,' she said. 'I've got a feeling that Tina will walk through that door at any minute.'

I did not feel so confident. The creeping sense of terror and help-lessness would not go away. Something far bigger than my own fear was at work here and I was powerless to do anything about it.

'We have to stay strong and focused,' Nicole said. 'We've got to hold it together for the sake of our children.'

I swallowed, trying to moisten my throat. 'I'm so sorry that I didn't tell you about the call,' I said. 'I should have. It was unforgiveable.'

She tightened her grip on my waist.

'Don't beat yourself up over it, Jack. We can talk about it when this is over. We've got too much else to think about.'

My eyes welled and her words served to reinforce the guilt that weighed heavily on my mind.

'Come on,' she said. 'I'll make some coffee. Maybe we should also have something to eat.'

She took my hand, led me into the kitchen. I sat at the table and rubbed a palm across my face. Nicole put on the kettle.

I dug out my cell and read Tina's messages again. They caused the skin to tighten on the back of my neck. I switched the phone to the photo viewing mode – I was the only one in the family who did not have a separate camera. I scrolled through the most recent photos of my daughter, including those I took in and around Burley. She seemed relaxed and untroubled. In a few of the pictures she was smiling. In one she was posing with me close to a group of New Forest ponies. So what had happened during the night to upset her and make her run off? It was something I couldn't fathom.

And this, along with all the other inexplicable events, was starting to distort my perception of reality.

30

Genna's mother had only learned about her daughter's death a few hours before Temple and Angel arrived at the hospital to interview her.

'Patricia Boyd has been admitted here on three previous occasions,' her doctor told them. 'She has a serious alcohol addiction and at the same time appears to be accident prone. I fear she'll eventually have an accident that will be fatal.'

'So what happened this time?' Temple asked.

The doctor, a cadaverous man with unruly blond hair, referred to his clipboard notes.

'She stumbled into the road and was struck by a cyclist,' he said.

'How badly hurt is she?'

'Broken left ankle, two fractured ribs and various contusions to the head and face. She was lucky, though. If it had been a motorcycle or car she'd be dead.'

'So how did she find out about her daughter?'

'The patient in the next bed had a newspaper this morning. Miss Boyd asked to read it. The discovery of the body is on the front page.'

'How did she react?'

The doctor shrugged. 'She was upset for a bit and had a little cry. But she appears to have recovered amazingly well. That's partly due to the fact that she sees everything through an alcoholic haze.'

'I gather she wants to speak to us?' Temple said.

'Indeed she does, Inspector. She's fully awake at the moment and quite lucid so now is a good time to talk to her.'

Patricia Boyd was sitting up in her hospital bed, her head swathed in bandages, her face a swollen mass of bruises and cuts. The doctor introduced Temple and Angel, then retreated, leaving the two detectives standing either side of her bed.

'Thank you for getting in touch with the police, Miss Boyd,' Temple said. 'We came as soon as we could. And let me say at the outset that we're very sorry for your loss. It must have come as a terrible shock.'

'It wasn't a shock,' she said, her voice surprisingly strident. 'I knew something like it would happen sooner or later. I told her enough times to find a proper job and stop doing that sex stuff, but she wouldn't listen.'

Temple found it difficult to determine her age because of the damage to her face, but he guessed she was in her late fifties or early sixties. Her skin had a waxy pallor and her body, under the thin hospital gown, looked almost skeletal. She had a tight mouth with vertical lines above her upper lip. Her eyes were bloodshot and watery and they did not seem fully focused.

'How much do you know about the circumstances of your daughter's death?' he asked.

'Only what I read in the paper,' she replied. 'They said she was stabbed in the back. I knew it was her from the tattoo.'

She closed her eyes briefly and grimaced as though in pain. Temple wondered if it was the pain of grief or a reaction to her injuries.

'Can you tell us about Genna?' Angel said. 'We need to build up a picture. It will hopefully help us find whoever killed her.'

Patricia Boyd opened her eyes and looked at Angel as though for the first time. 'We always had a strained relationship,' she said. 'Genna was a problem child from an early age. When she was fifteen she spent several months in a secure adolescent unit because of her violent and antisocial behaviour. She couldn't control her temper and we couldn't control her.'

'By that do you mean you and your husband?' Angel asked.

'I mean her father. We never married, thank God. He was a worthless piece of shit who got drunk one night and tried to rape her. That's when I kicked him out. Three weeks later he topped himself with an overdose. One of the happiest days of my life.'

'How did your daughter react to that?'

She shrugged her bony shoulders. 'Genna couldn't have cared less. She was always a cold-blooded cow. She didn't have feelings for anyone or anything. She once attacked me during a row over the state of her room. Broke my jaw and two of my teeth.'

Temple was surprised by her description. It was at odds with what Damien Roth and Christine Faber had said about Genna.

'How long were you living together?' Temple asked.

She had to think about it. After a few moments, she said, 'She left at eighteen. That's when I started drinking and she started whoring. We stayed in touch, though. She'd call me when she wanted something.'

'So had things got better between the two of you?' Temple asked.

A wry expression touched her mouth. 'For sure, but only because we didn't see much of each other. She'd come over to the flat occasionally, but she was ashamed of me. Can you believe that? A slut who sold her body had the cheek to look down on her own mother.'

She suddenly became pensive and stared off into the distance. Temple gave thought to what she had said. It didn't surprise him that Genna had had a troubled childhood; that was often the case with sex workers. But he hadn't expected to be told that she had a history of violent behaviour. That was an aspect of her character that would have to be explored.

'So when was the last time you saw your daughter?' Temple asked.

A shadow flickered across her eyes. She said, 'That's why I wanted to speak to you. Genna came to see me last Thursday. She was worried about something and that wasn't like her. In fact I'd never seen her so nervous.'

'Did she tell you what she was worried about?'

'No, but she told me she'd got involved in something nasty. That was the word she used. And she wanted to get out of it. She asked me to look after a package for her. Said it was her insurance in case things went wrong.'

Temple's eyebrows shot up inquiringly. 'Where is the package now?'

'Somewhere at home,' she said. 'But for the life of me I can't remember where I put it. I've been trying to think, but my memory is shot to pieces. I usually can't recall what day it is.'

'What does the package look like?' Angel asked.

'It's just a plain brown padded envelope. Normal letter size. Thin, not bulky.'

'Have you any idea what's inside?'

'She didn't tell me and I wasn't interested enough at the time to ask. I'd been on the bottle that afternoon.'

Temple wondered if Genna's flat had been ransacked by someone looking for that very package. If so, then they had been looking in the wrong place.

'The package could be important,' Temple said. 'Would you have any objection if we went to your home and picked it up?'

'If you want. But it could be anywhere.'

'If you let us have the door keys we'll carry out a quick search and bring them back to you.'

'Well don't make a mess,' she said. 'And if you take anything other than the package, I'll know.'

She nodded towards the bedside cabinet. 'Check the drawer. That's where they put the stuff from my coat pocket. The key should be in my purse. If it's not there it'll be in my bag. That's lower down in the cupboard.'

Temple pulled open the drawer. The purse was there, along with her watch and spectacles.

'The nurse said they were going to put those things in their safe, but I think she's forgotten.'

Temple rummaged through the purse until he found a key ring with two keys attached.

'One of them opens the entrance to the block,' Patricia Boyd told him. 'The other opens the door to the flat. It's number seven. I assume you have the address.'

Forty-five minutes later Temple and Angel let themselves into Patricia Boyd's ground floor flat in Portsmouth, a few miles east of Southampton. It had very little going for it except that it was near to the city centre and would have been as cheap as chips.

There was one small bedroom and a lounge that included a compact kitchen area. The furniture was old and faded, the wallpaper bubbled and peeled with damp.

The place looked as though it hadn't been cleaned up in weeks. There were dirty glasses and mugs everywhere. Used plates were piled in the sink.

Temple assumed that since the flat was so small it wouldn't take them long to find the package that Genna had left with her mother. But after searching for an hour they still hadn't found the damned thing.

Temple phoned the hospital and got put through to Patricia Boyd. She was still awake and adamant that the package was somewhere in the flat.

'I would have put it in a safe place,' she said. 'But Lord knows where exactly.'

It was immensely frustrating and after another twenty minutes Temple decided he'd had enough. He told Angel that he was going back to the station. He needed to chase things up and front a press conference. He told her to keep looking and to get help from the uniform division.

'Call me as soon as you find the package,' he said. 'It might well be the key to everything that's happened.'

On the way back to the station Temple stopped at a Tesco Express store and bought a cheese sandwich. He ate it sitting in his car and washed it down with a diet coke. He had a lot to think about and it wasn't easy to make sense of the various threads that were trying to weave together in his head.

He needed to find out why Genna Boyd had tried to stop the Keatons going to King's Manor. Was it conceivable that it had something to do with the strange things that had allegedly happened there? And how did the landlord, Nathan Slade, fit into the equation? Was he the one who had told Genna that the Keatons were renting the house? And if so, why?

Then there was the mystery package that Genna had given to her mother for safe keeping. What had she meant by 'insurance'? And what was the 'something nasty' she had got involved in?

Also, Patricia Boyd's description of her daughter as cold-blooded and violent had added another level of intrigue to the case. Was it possible that Genna had been the victim of a revenge attack? Was the killer someone she had previously harmed in any way?

So far, all they knew for certain was that Genna Boyd had been stabbed twice in the back before being buried on Cranes Moor. And in the days before the killing she had given her mother a package and called the Keaton house in Texas. But beyond that, the dots still hadn't been connected. Was Genna's car dumped before or after she was killed? If it was after then who had parked it in the street near the city centre? If the old guy who called it in was right – and it was a female driver – then was Genna's killer a woman?

31

When Temple got back to the incident room he confirmed that a press conference had been scheduled for that afternoon. But before then, he got the team together for a briefing.

He began with a rundown of his conversation with Jack Keaton and his wife. He told them about the call Keaton had received from Genna and about the weird incidents that had apparently taken place at King's Manor since they arrived.

'It's all very far-fetched so it's difficult to know how much of it is actually true,' he said. 'The couple sound convincing, but maybe there's an element of exaggeration there. As for their daughter, well, from the text messages she's sent it seems clear to me that she's wandered off in a strop over something. Her dad told me she's threatened to leave home in the past. I expect she'll come back with her tail between her legs before the day is out.'

Temple then switched to Nathan Slade. What information had they gleaned? He was told that the team had not been able to track him down. It wasn't known where he'd been living since moving out of King's Manor.

But they had come up with some interesting stuff.

'Let's start with his bank account,' DS Mark Bannerman said. 'We struck lucky because he pays his council tax with a Barclays Bank direct debit. We discovered his account is at a branch in nearby Ringwood. And get this – over the past two months he's been withdrawing cash from ATM machines at a fair rate of knots. Usually in amounts of £200 and £300. Occasionally he's pulled out the maximum sum of £500. So far he's taken out £6,000. There's £2,000 left.'

'When was the last withdrawal?' Temple asked.

Bannerman consulted his notes. 'Five days ago from a branch in Southampton. He took out five hundred then.'

'So why not withdraw it in a lump sum?' Temple asked.

Bannerman shrugged. 'Who knows? But that's not all. We ran a credit check on him and found he has a Mastercard. Two weeks ago he used it to purchase online a one-way ticket to Bangkok. He's due to leave in eight days' time.'

'Sounds to me like he doesn't plan on coming back,' Temple said. 'At least not in the near future.'

'There's more,' Bannerman said. 'Nathan Slade has a criminal record.'

It turned out that Slade was quite an unsavoury character. Four years ago he had been convicted of kerb crawling in an area of Southampton known to be frequented by prostitutes. He was given a fine. A year later he was convicted of indecently assaulting a young woman in a pub in Christchurch. For that offence he was given probation.

'Genna was a glorified prostitute,' Temple said. 'So that could be the connection. He might have been one of her clients. Do we know if his number appeared on her phone records?'

'I was coming to that, Guv,' Bannerman said. 'Slade's home and mobile numbers are on the list. Until recently they were calling each other quite often. Maybe twice a week. It started to tail off three months ago and in the last eight weeks there were no calls between them. So it's possible that Slade told Genna he was renting his house out to the Keaton family. She then decided, for whatever reason, to warn them not to come.'

'So let's consider what we have here,' Temple said. 'There's Slade who is possibly linked to Genna by paying her for sex. He then rents out his house to a family from the States. Before the Keatons arrive here Genna tries to persuade them not to come. We need to find out why.' He paused to look around at the assembled faces. 'We know Genna was a prostitute and porn actress. She's described by her mother as a cold-blooded cow with a history of antisocial behaviour.

'Slade meanwhile has a criminal record and he's disappeared. We know he's been making large withdrawals from his bank account and is planning a one-way trip to the Far East. All very suspicious and it's tempting to draw the conclusion that he's been preparing to flee the country for some time. So was it because he'd been planning to commit a murder?'

Bannerman spoke up. 'Let's say he did kill Genna, for whatever reason. Why would he not leave the country straight away? Why wait another week?'

'Maybe he has left,' Temple said. 'He's pulled out enough cash to buy another ticket to Thailand or anywhere else in the world.'

They discussed this briefly before Bannerman referred back to Slade's phone list.

'We came across another interesting number,' he said. 'It belongs to Damien Roth, the porn producer.'

'This keeps getting better,' Temple said. 'Tell me more.'

Bannerman referred to his notes again. 'Over a period of months Roth called Slade's mobile on five separate occasions. And Slade phoned Roth three times.'

'This needs to be checked out.'

'There's more,' Bannerman said. 'Damien Roth does not have a criminal record, but his name did raise a red flag on the police computer.'

A red flag meant that someone within the police or intelligence services wanted to be informed if an individual became the subject of official inquiries. In this case that individual was Damien Roth.

'Have you found out who put it there?' Temple asked.

Bannerman nodded. 'A DCI Brian Ellroy at SCD9.'

Temple felt a tremor of excitement. SCD9 was short for Scotland Yard's Serious Crime Directorate 9: Human Exploitation and Organized Crime Command. They were primarily tasked with investigating human trafficking, prostitution, obscene publications, money laundering and identity fraud.

'Have you called him yet?' Temple asked.

Bannerman shook his head. 'The info only came through in the last hour.'

'Then leave it with me. I'll ring him myself.'

Temple went on to talk about the chat with Genna's mother and said that Angel was still at Patricia Boyd's flat searching for the package.

'It could be the most promising lead so far – as long as we can find the bloody thing,' he said. 'The trouble is the mother can't remember where she put it and the place is in an awful state.'

Temple was then told that detectives were still working their way through Genna's phone list. Five of the names followed up had turned out to be guys who had used her escort services. Three of them were married and were terrified their sordid secrets would get out. The team had also started checking emails that were sent to Genna via her website. So far they had a list of over a hundred addresses.

Three detectives were out interviewing the other porn artists employed by Filthy Films. The feedback so far was unsurprising. They were shocked and saddened to hear what had happened but had no useful information to offer.

'OK, keep up the good work,' Temple said as he brought the meeting to a close. 'Someone call Damien Roth and set up a meeting for after the presser. And dig deeper on Nathan Slade. I want to talk to him. Trace his friends and relatives. Is he married? Does he have a girl-friend? Children? Try to find out more about his relationship with Genna. And find out if he's left the fucking country.'

Temple got DCI Ellroy's mobile number from Bannerman and then called the detective. But Ellroy didn't answer so he left a message for him to call back.

After that, Temple got on with typing up his report on the case so far while he waited for the call to attend the press conference.

Forty-five minutes later he was fielding questions from reporters who were hungry for the salacious details of the case, like how long the victim had been on the game and how many porn movies she had actually appeared in. Did the police think she was murdered by one of her clients? Was she tortured before her death like the women in her movies? Temple answered every question that was put to him but was more evasive with some than others. When the questions finally dried up, he thanked everyone for coming and returned to his office. Bannerman immediately poked his head in.

'Damien Roth will be here in about fifteen minutes,' he said. 'He was in town when I called and said he'll drop by to save you going to his place.'

'What did you say to him?'

'That we had some follow-up questions about Genna.'

'And how did he react?'

'He said it was no problem and he wanted to do everything he could to help.'

Temple then phoned Angel. She was still at Patricia Boyd's flat and two uniformed officers had joined her in the search for the mystery package.

'God only knows where she put it,' Angel said. 'But this is a thankless task. The place is filthy and full of junk.'

'Well if you don't find it soon go back to the hospital and see if you can prise it out of her.'

Before hanging up he briefed her quickly on what he had learned about Nathan Slade and Damien Roth.

'I'm about to talk to Roth again,' he said. 'I'll let you know what he says.'

Temple closed the door to his office and lit a cigarette. He was desperate for a smoke and reckoned there was just enough time to get one in before the porn peddler arrived.

32

'You need to eat, Jack,' Nicole said.

'I'm not hungry.'

'I don't care. I've made soup. I want you to get it down.'

'I'd rather stay out here,' I said.

She took my arm, steered me towards the front door.

'Come inside,' she said. 'If Tina is watching the house then she's probably reluctant to make an appearance with you standing outside looking as though you're going to give her a major bollocking.'

'I won't be doing that.'

'I know it and you know it. But she doesn't. So come in.'

I'd spent most of the morning outside, wandering around the grounds and praying for my daughter's safe return. Her second text message had completely thrown me. What's more it had convinced the two detectives that she was OK and therefore there was no need to mount a search … and no need to for us to worry. But I still couldn't shake off the feeling that something was very wrong. Call it a father's intuition. Or a refusal to accept that my daughter would take off by herself in the dead of night. Unanswered questions were also still eating away at me. Like how did she get beyond doors and windows that were locked on the inside?

I joined Nicole and Michael at the kitchen table. Michael was spooning piping hot chicken soup into his mouth. He was pale and subdued and had hardly said a word all morning.

My appetite returned with a vengeance with the first mouthful of soup. I hadn't realized how hungry I was.

'This is good,' I said.

Nicole forced a smile and dabbed at her lips with a napkin.

'It's homemade apparently,' she said. 'Mr Slade had frozen it in a carton. There's plenty more.'

Mention of the landlord's name raised my hackles. I'd phoned him twice since the two detectives had left and still got no answer. I just hoped the cops had better luck than me.

For a couple of minutes a heavy silence descended on the kitchen, broken only by the slurping of soup and the chewing of crusty bread. Then Michael sat back, wiped a sleeve across his mouth, and said, 'Is this house haunted?'

We both looked at him. There was no trace of fear in his wide-eyed expression; only curiosity.

'We don't know what's going on,' Nicole said, placing an arm around his shoulders. 'But whatever it is we don't want you to worry. We won't let any harm come to you.'

'But if there are ghosts here then why are they angry with us?' he asked in all innocence.

'Who said they're angry?' Nicole replied.

He scrunched up his shoulders. 'Why else would they try to scare us?'

Nicole looked at me because she didn't know how to respond. I put my spoon down, cleared my throat, said, 'Don't assume that ghosts are responsible for what's happened here, Michael. If they were I'm sure we would have seen one by now.'

Michael tilted his head. 'But I think I have seen one.'

'You've already told us about the figure in your bedroom,' I said. 'But that was a dream. Right?'

'I don't mean that time,' he said. 'I mean last night.'

'So you had another dream?'

'I don't think it was a dream,' he said. 'I think I was awake.'

I felt my spine stiffen.

'So why haven't you mentioned it before now?' There was a sharpness in my tone that made him flinch.

'I forgot about it,' he said.

'Well now you've remembered, tell us what you think you saw.'

He looked at his mother. She ruffled his hair and said, 'I'm not surprised you forgot, sweetheart. We've all been distracted this morning. But we would like to hear about it.'

Michael picked up his spoon and started passing it from one hand to the other. After several long beats, he said, 'Something woke me. I don't know what it was, but when I sat up I heard a noise outside. So I got out of bed and looked through the window.'

Michael's bedroom was at the back of the house. It overlooked the garden and the woods beyond.

'Well go on,' I said. 'What then?'

He swallowed a lump and licked his lips. 'It was dark but the moon was out. I saw someone walking across the grass. At least I think I did.'

'Can't you be more specific? What exactly did you see?'

'That was all,' he said. 'It was just a black shadow that was shaped like a man.'

'You said it was walking across the grass. Was it coming towards the house or moving away from it?'

'Coming towards it,' he said. 'I rubbed my eyes to try to see better but when I opened them again it was gone.'

'So what did you do?'

'I went back to bed. I thought I'd imagined it. But now I'm not so sure.'

A white hot fury swept through me and I jumped to my feet.

'Why the hell didn't you wake us?' I barked at him. 'You should have told us that you saw someone.'

Michael stiffened against the anger in my voice and tears filled his eyes. Nicole leapt to his defence, saying, 'Don't you dare shout at Michael. It wasn't his fault.'

'But Tina's missing, for Christ's sake. Whoever the boy saw might have had something to do with it.'

'That's ridiculous. You said yourself there were no signs of a break-in. And besides, he isn't even certain he saw anything.'

'But what if he did? What if someone came to the house last night? It changes everything.'

'But that still doesn't make it all right for you to turn on Michael,' she said, her lips trembling over the words. 'He's scared enough as it is without you losing your temper with him.'

I felt the blood stir inside me, a hot flush in my veins. I rubbed my hands over my face and blew out a long breath. Michael started to cry then and Nicole pulled his head close to her chest. She fixed me with a brimstone stare that caused the gooseflesh to rise on my skin.

'Are you happy now, Jack? That was totally unnecessary.'

Shame climbed into my cheeks. I opened my mouth to speak, to apologize for my outburst, but the words wouldn't form. Instead, I turned on my heels and hurried out the back door, slamming it behind me. I stood on the patio, my guilt stalking me like a great black shadow. The afternoon light had darkened to a sombre grey, causing my mood to plummet still further.

After about a minute I rubbed my eyes, hard, digging with my thumb and forefinger. At the same time I seized the emotion and shoved it down. I needed a clear head to collect my frayed thoughts.

I looked up at Michael's bedroom window. Below it there was just brickwork. The kitchen door was a few yards to the right and the double doors from the living room were even further over. I checked them again just to confirm what I already knew. There were no scratches on the panels and no broken locks. Even with a key an intruder would not have been able to gain access. I looked around the patio, then wandered onto the small lawn, but saw nothing that could be construed as a clue.

Finally I walked over to the back fence and stared off into the woods. And that's when I glimpsed something. At least, I thought I did, because when I tried to focus it was gone. I screwed up my eyes to sharpen my vision, wondering if I had merely spotted a deer or pony. I scanned that section of wood but there was nothing there. Yet the impression stayed with me of someone standing amongst the trees. It wasn't Tina, though. I was sure of that.

The figure was taller than my daughter and almost certainly a man.

I climbed over the gate and dashed across the narrow stretch of grass to the woods. I stood where I thought I'd seen the figure, but there was nothing on the ground to suggest anyone had been there before me.

I stepped into the woods, my eyes quickly adjusting to the gloom. The canopy of branches and leaves kept much of the daylight at bay. My body was rigid with tension as I trudged across the soft, springy topsoil. Around me shadows blended into deeper shadows.

I took shallow breaths, tried not to make a noise, but the forest was far from still and silent. There were sounds all around me; the crunching of leaves under the feet of tiny animals, the trilling of countless birds, the creaking of tree branches bending in the breeze. I saw a flicker of motion to my left. My eyes lasered in on a woodpecker attacking decayed timber. Then something drew my attention to a dense thicket of hawthorn to my right. This turned out to be only a curious squirrel chewing on an acorn.

I stopped moving and waited for something to happen. Or someone to appear. But nothing happened and no one appeared.

And yet I had the strangest feeling I was not alone. An insistent and growing intuition told me that I was being watched. And it stayed with me as I walked slowly back towards the house.

33

Damien Roth was brought up to Temple's office when he arrived at police headquarters. Roth explained that he'd been shopping in the city centre when he received the call informing him that the police wanted to conduct a second interview.

'The timing couldn't have been better, Inspector,' he said. 'After two hours' traipsing around the shops I'd had just about enough. So I left Belinda in Primark and said I'd pick her up when you've finished with me.'

'Well I appreciate you coming in,' Temple said. 'I'll try not to keep you long.'

Roth sat on the other side of Temple's desk. The chair seemed too small for him – he had the posture and thick cut of an athlete. Temple studied him for a moment and noticed that his dark, sunken eyes were uncomfortably penetrating. It was something he hadn't been aware of during the first interview at his house.

'As I explained to you yesterday, Inspector, I want to be as helpful as I can,' Roth said, his taut, dry voice soft and calm. 'But in all honesty I'm not sure there's anything I can add to what I've already told you.'

'I need to ask you a couple of questions that have cropped up during the course of our inquiries,' Temple said.

'And I'll be happy to answer them. I can't bear the thought that Genna's killer is still at large and free to murder someone else.'

Temple leaned forward on his desk, grimly intent. 'We're determined that won't happen, Mr Roth.'

'So does that mean you're close to making an arrest?'

'Let's just say we're making good progress,' Temple said. Then he flipped over the cover of a leather-bound folder in front of him and glanced at the typewritten note on a sheet of A4 paper. 'Can you start by telling me what your relationship is with Nathan Slade?'

Roth's face turned dark. 'That man is a sick bastard. I don't have a relationship with him.'

'But you know him. In fact, according to his phone records you've called each other on a number of occasions.'

'Unfortunately I do know Slade,' Roth said. 'But I haven't seen him in weeks, thank God. And I hope I never see him again.'

'Care to explain?'

Roth took a big breath, said, 'It was actually Genna who introduced us to Slade. He was one of her regular clients. She would go to his place in the forest at least once a week and he would pay for sex.'

'This would be King's Manor?'

Roth nodded. 'That's right. Weird place. I'm sure it's haunted.'

'So you've been there?'

'Sure, we've shot a couple of movies there. That's how it all started with Slade. When he learned that Genna was doing porn movies he got her to give me a call to see if I was interested in using his house as a location.'

'You mean to film porn there?' Temple said.

'Exactly. I jumped at the chance, of course. The house is big and isolated so it gave us scope to be creative.'

'How often did you go there?'

'Five times in all. The upside was that it was a great location. Plenty of space and light and no problems with the neighbours. And we didn't have to pay for it.'

'And the downside?'

'Well, in return for letting us use the house for free, Slade had to watch all the shoots. He also insisted on taking part in one of the movies. The guy is a pervert and nobody likes him. He creeped us all out.'

'Can you expand on that?'

Roth pondered this a moment and said, 'He was rough with the girls for one thing. I cast him in a bondage scene but he got carried away and we had to stop him from really hurting Genna. He left a bite mark on her left breast.'

'He sounds like a real piece of work.'

'He is. And get this: he has an obsession with snakes. There are a lot of them in the forest. He likes to go out and find the non-poisonous ones to bring back to the house. A couple of times he scared the girls with them and once there was a bit of bother because he answered the front door with a snake wrapped around his neck. It scared the life out of the visitor who happened to be a small boy. The boy's dad came to the house later and threatened to punch Slade's lights out. Me and another guy, who was the talent, had to warn the father off.'

'Do you know where Slade is now?' Temple asked.

Roth shrugged. 'At King's Manor I assume. We haven't spoken since I told him we wouldn't be filming there again.'

'He's renting the house out to a family on holiday,' Temple said. 'So we need to find out where he's staying.'

'I don't know where he is, Inspector, and I really don't care.'

Temple jotted down some notes. 'Tell me about King's Manor, Mr Roth. Why do you think it's haunted?'

'Don't get me wrong,' Roth said. 'I've never believed in all that ghost crap. But things happened there that I can't explain. It got to the point where Belinda wouldn't even go there. It scared her.'

'So what happened?'

'Well just a bunch of strange disturbances such as lights going on and off and doors opening and closing by themselves.'

'I've been to see the family who are staying there now,' Temple said. 'They say they're experiencing strange happenings.'

'Well I pity them,' Roth said. 'That paranormal stuff is OK in the movies and on television. But when it really happens it fucks you up and you don't know what to think.'

'Did Genna warn you about it before you went there?'

Roth nodded. 'She told us she had seen and heard some weird things but it didn't seem to bother her much.'

'Does it bother Slade?'

He smiled without humour. 'The prick seems to think it's funny. He used to joke that he shared the house with a ghost.'

Temple was becoming increasingly interested in Nathan Slade. The guy was now high up on their list of suspects. The sooner they tracked him down the better.

'Have you ever been in trouble with the law?' he asked.

Roth's eyebrows lifted a few centimetres. 'Absolutely not – apart from a few speeding tickets, that is.'

'So were you ever questioned by Scotland Yard's Serious Crime Directorate?'

Roth's mouth tensed. 'Well you obviously know that I was. But that was a year ago.'

'Care to tell me what it was about?'

Roth issued a heavy sigh, said, 'The police were investigating a man who had some snuff movies in his possession. I was in his contacts book because we'd used him in the past as the male lead in a couple of our films. I told them I hardly knew the guy and that was that. No big deal.'

'But it's your understanding that this bloke had bona fide snuff movies?' Temple said, surprised.

'That's what I was told by the officers who questioned me. But my guess is that the films were fakes. Real snuff movies are an urban myth. I'm sure of it. I've never seen one and I don't know anyone who has.'

Temple had never seen one either, but it was his understanding that they were no longer an urban myth. He'd been told on good authority that a number of genuine snuff movies – in which people are murdered on camera for the sake of entertainment – had turned up in recent years. Law enforcement agencies across the world were now taking seriously the notion of an underground film industry that catered for a sick, perverted sub-culture. The internet and mobile technology meant there was less risk attached to making such films. And producing them no longer required expensive equipment and highly trained crews. In addition, the huge increase in the trafficking of helpless young women ensured an endless supply of unwilling victims who would never be missed.

Temple thought it was an avenue of inquiry worth pursuing. Given Genna's dubious professions it wasn't beyond the realms of possibility that she had been murdered to satisfy someone's sadistic sexual fantasy – or that her murder had been captured on tape.

He closed his folder, said, 'Well that was an interesting conversation, Mr Roth. You've given me a lot to think about.'

Roth seemed surprised. 'No more questions?'

'Only one. What was the title of the movie that Slade appeared in?'

Roth told him and Temple recognized the name. It was one of the DVDs they had taken from Genna's flat.

34

I decided not to tell Nicole that I thought I saw a man near the woods. In all probability I'd imagined it. So there was no need to make the situation even more alarming for her.

When I came back into the house she and Michael were in the living room. Nicole was on the sofa reading through the guest folder that Nathan Slade had left for us.

I spent a couple of minutes making grovelling apologies to them for my outburst at the table. They forgave me without hesitation, sympathetic to my excuse that the stress over Tina was getting to me.

I didn't press Michael on what he thought he saw from his bedroom window during the night. How could I? I'd just had a similar experience myself. Plus, I was suddenly too tired to risk upsetting him again. In fact, the tiredness was overwhelming. I found myself wiping my hands across my face to dispel the grogginess. But it didn't really help. My eyelids felt like ton weights and my movements quickly became sluggish.

'I'm guessing I'm not the only one who's feeling drowsy,' Nicole said. 'You look like you're struggling to stay awake too.'

'I am,' I said. 'I don't understand why.'

'Well I feel like I've been injected with a powerful anaesthetic. What the hell is the matter with us?' She turned to her son, adding, 'How do you feel, Michael?'

The boy had parked himself in the folds of the armchair. His face was pasty and drawn and we both watched as he blinked several times and then closed his eyes.

'I'm tired,' he said in a soft, fragile voice.

This can't be right, I told myself. How could we so quickly be consumed by fatigue? And it wasn't the first time it had happened.

Ever since we had arrived I'd felt almost as though I was being sedated. I'd put it down to jet lag and perhaps the country air, but maybe there was more to it. As I looked at Nicole and Michael, both slipping into unconsciousness, a disturbing thought snapped into my mind.

I rushed into the kitchen. Our soup bowls were still on the table. Was it possible the soup had been drugged? At any other time the idea would have seemed preposterous, but in the context of what had been happening here I found it quite conceivable that Nathan Slade's home-made concoction was not all it appeared to be – along with the rest of the food and drink he had left for us. After all, it was usually following a meal that we had drifted into a state of somnolence.

I opened the refrigerator and took out the storage carton containing the rest of the soup. There was a handwritten label on the cover which read 'Chicken Soup'. I opened it and sniffed at the thick, creamy liquid. There was nothing unusual about it. But that meant very little since knock-out drugs were usually odourless and colourless.

Stifling a yawn, I checked through the contents of the refrigerator: bottles of white wine, butter, cheese, cold meats. Then I went through the cupboards. I did not find anything suspicious until I examined an unopened tin of baked beans. My eyes homed in on a tiny hole in the top. It was slightly bigger than a pin-prick. I'd never seen anything like it before and wondered if it was a manufacturing error or the result of a sharp object being inserted into the tin.

I quickly checked all the other tins and food packages and was shocked to find that the same tiny puncture mark appeared in almost every sealed item. I then checked the wine bottles. They were all screw tops and every one had been twisted open, just like the bottle we'd opened earlier.

I went into the living room to tell Nicole, but she was already fast asleep on the sofa, purring like a cat through her open mouth. I sat beside her, my lungs heaving rapidly in my chest. I didn't know what to make of the discovery, but the obvious conclusion to draw was that our groceries had been spiked with some powerful sleep-inducing agent. But why would someone do that? What sinister motive lay behind it?

My mind churned, searching for answers to those questions and a whole bunch of others. I knew I ought to ring the police, but getting up to find my phone seemed like too much of an effort suddenly. I felt vaguely ill as well as exhausted. A dull, leaden weariness pulled at my muscles. I found it impossible to concentrate. My thoughts started spinning without orientation. Finally I couldn't keep my eyes open any longer. Closing them was such a relief. The darkness washed over me and those anxious thoughts gradually shimmered into fragile dreams.

35

Nathan Slade was a striking looking individual – both with and without his clothes on. In the police photograph on Temple's desk – taken after his arrest for indecently assaulting a young woman – he had a cascade of iron-grey hair that spilled over his shirt collar. His jawline was glazed with stubble and as he stared into the camera his dark brown eyes were intense and menacing.

But in the pornographic DVD that was playing on Temple's office TV, Slade looked different as well as older. He wore his long grey hair in dreadlocks and his eyes were hidden behind a pair of dark-framed glasses with yellow-tinted lenses. His body had not worn well since his birth fifty-seven years earlier. His skin was pale and sagging in places and he had a large beer belly that he was clearly trying to suck in.

Temple watched as Slade used a whip on Genna Boyd's bottom, lashing her flesh until red welts appeared. His teeth were bared the whole time in an ugly, lascivious grin. She moaned and cried out but at the same time kept begging him for more and he was only too happy to oblige. After a while he discarded the whip and mounted her from behind as she leaned forward over the kitchen table at King's Manor.

It made for repulsive viewing and Temple could only stick with it for a couple of minutes. Then he switched it off and lit a cigarette. He had never understood those who derived pleasure from receiving and inflicting pain. But there was obviously something in it, since sado-masochism had seen a huge growth in popularity thanks largely to the internet. He had often wondered if all that pain and humiliation was simply an outlet for anger and self-loathing.

He sat back and thought about Nathan Slade. He was obviously a ghastly pervert with an unhealthy sexual appetite, convicted of kerb-crawling and indecent assault. A regular user of prostitutes and a keen voyeur. But was he also a killer? Did he stab Genna Boyd to death as part of some erotic fantasy – like the one he was playing out on the DVD? And was it possible that he had killed her on camera, so he could show it to other sexual deviants?

These questions and more were piling up inside the detective's mind. He needed answers and he needed to start making sense of what had been happening. He still had no idea why Genna had contacted Jack Keaton to warn him off coming to King's Manor. And he did not know if there was a connection between her and the strange goings on in the house, as reported by the family. It was frustrating – and worrying – because the longer the investigation went on, the less chance they had of getting a result.

He stubbed out the cigarette in the waste bin and called Angel, partly to be cheered up by the sound of her voice, but mainly to find out how she was getting on.

She was back at the hospital, waiting for Genna's mother to wake up from a sleep. They had spent several hours searching her flat for the mysterious package that Genna had entrusted to her, but they hadn't found it. So Angel was going to talk to Miss Boyd in the hope that she would eventually remember where she had put it.

Just as he put down the phone, one of the detectives entered his office with some news. Slade's ex-wife, whose name was Audrey Wilkinson, had been traced. She was living in Poole, a coastal town forty-five minutes by car from Southampton.

'At bloody last,' Temple said.

36

The sound of screaming woke me. I sat upright on the sofa. Shook my head to clear it.

It was dark in the living room, but my eyes were drawn at once to a bright, flashing light. It took a moment for my brain to register that it was the TV. On screen a young woman let out another shrill scream as she fled from a man in a black balaclava.

Relieved, I dragged my gaze away from the TV and scanned the shadows that cluttered the room. Everything was as I remembered it before I fell asleep, except that Michael was no longer in the armchair. Nicole was slumped next to me on the sofa, her head resting in my lap, her legs draped over the armrest. My watch said 7 p.m. We had been asleep for several hours. I felt dehydrated, and a dull pain loitered behind my eyes.

I got slowly to my feet, careful not to wake my wife. Three steps took me to the TV. I reached down and switched it off. I could then hear the soft pull of Nicole's breathing and the creaking of floorboards as Michael moved around upstairs.

And then it all came flooding back to me; I was thrust back into the hideous reality that was King's Manor. Tina was still missing, it was likely that we were being systematically drugged, and we were effectively trapped in a house that seemed to have a life of its own.

I felt a sickness in my stomach as I went into the kitchen. The light was on. I filled the kettle and flicked the switch. I was reaching for the coffee jar when it suddenly occurred to me that it might be contaminated. Shit. What in heaven's name were we supposed to do?

The ceiling above me continued to vibrate as Michael stamped across the floor upstairs. I wondered what he was doing and how long he had been awake. I needed to tell him not to eat or drink anything else. We couldn't risk it.

As I moved towards the door, Nicole startled me by appearing in the doorway, bleary-eyed and yawning.

'I feel like shit,' she groaned.

'Join the club,' I said.

She squinted at me, trying to focus. 'Is Tina back?'

I shook my head and moved up to her, put my hands on her shoulders and looked into her face. There was a ravaged expression in her eyes and her cheeks were flushed.

I kept my voice calm as I laid it out for her. Told her what I suspected about the food and drink. The soup. The wine. Everything that had been left for us.

'I'm convinced we've been drugged since we arrived,' I said. 'That's why we've been so tired. Why we keep falling asleep.'

Her tongue moved across her lips, barely moistening them.

'But who would do that?'

'It has to be Slade. Who else could it be? But don't ask me why because I don't know.'

I could feel her shaking, tremors through her entire body.

'I want you and Michael to leave,' I said. 'I'll stay here and wait for Tina to come back. Go to a hotel. I'll call the police. They can take you and help me get the Discovery started.'

A moan of despair issued from her throat. 'But I don't want to leave you, Jack. We should stay together.'

'We can't. You're not safe here. As soon as Tina is back I'll join you.'

She squeezed her eyes shut, held her breath.

'All right,' she said. 'Where is Michael?'

'That's him walking about upstairs,' I said. I paused for a second so she could hear his feet thumbing across the floorboards above us. 'I'll go fetch him and then call the cops. You sit down and get yourself together.'

I legged it upstairs, calling Michael's name as I went. But I got no response. I expected him to be in his bedroom, but he wasn't. I checked the other rooms. All of them. When it got to the point where I was looking in cupboards and under beds the blood in my veins started turning to ice.

I examined every window upstairs – they were all closed. Which begged the question: *Who had been walking around up here?* I hurried downstairs, calling Michael's name and searching every room and cupboard. But he was nowhere.

'What's wrong?' Nicole said, her voice almost a shrill cry. 'Where's Michael?'

'He's not in the house,' I told her.

'But I don't understand. He's upstairs. We just heard him.'

'There's nobody up there. I checked everywhere.'

Shock seized her features. 'Are you telling me he's disappeared like Tina?'

'I'll check outside,' I said. 'He must have gone for a walk.'

'We would have seen him. He would have had to pass us.'

'Not if it wasn't him we heard upstairs,' I said.

She scrunched up her face. 'Then who did we hear?'

I rolled my shoulders.

'We need to call the police,' Nicole said.

I picked up the house phone. No dialling tone as per usual. I felt like smashing the handset against the wall, but I managed to hold back, telling myself I needed to stay in control. We both looked around for my cell. It was Nicole who found it on the table in the kitchen.

'Oh my God there's another message from Tina,' she said.

I took the phone from her, opened the message.

Michael is now on the other side with me. Don't call the cops. You will see us both later tonight.

Nicole looked at me, her eyes bulging fearfully. I wanted to say something, but my face froze over and I couldn't move. Nicole stood there, trying to take in what was happening, her face slowly draining of blood. After an empty, endless moment, she finally broke down, her body shaking with huge, ugly sobs. I took her in my arms and held her tight against me. I shared her despair and her fear. But for me there was also something else – a strong feeling that reality itself was dissolving around us like a slowly fading light.

37

Temple drove to Poole via the A31, which cuts through the New Forest. During the day the views are spectacular, but he had delayed his departure from Southampton so all he could see was an inky black canvas on both sides of the road.

Audrey Wilkinson's son had told him over the phone that his mother would not be home until 7.30 p.m. She'd apparently spent the afternoon visiting a friend in Weymouth. Temple explained that he wanted to talk to her about Nathan Slade. He said he couldn't go into details on the phone but would be there at just before eight.

He had used the time to pore over all the reports from the detectives on the team. There were transcripts of interviews with porn artists who had worked with Genna Boyd, and with some of the men who had paid for her escort services, but nothing leapt off the page at him. Several of the men were now being subjected to further investigation, but Temple still regarded Nathan Slade as their main suspect.

He was surprised it was proving so difficult to run him down. He had not given a forwarding address to the post office and had not set up new accounts with any of the utility companies. So maybe he had gone to ground, or even left the country, following the unexpected discovery of Genna's body. If indeed he was the killer then he would have been expecting her remains to rot in the ground.

Temple felt sorry for Jack Keaton and his family. Of all the hundreds of holiday lets in the area they'd had the misfortune to pick the house owned by Nathan Slade and as a result, they had become somehow embroiled in whatever was going on. He refused to accept that the strange events that had ruined their trip had anything to do with the paranormal, despite what Damien Roth had said about the house. But the family had certainly been spooked by something.

He made a mental note to call Keaton when he got the chance to see if the daughter had turned up safely. If not then perhaps her disappearance was indeed a cause for concern after all.

Audrey Wilkinson was short and plump with silver hair pulled back into submission. Her face looked broken by the years and her eyes were red-rimmed and threaded with veins. She was in her mid to late fifties and wearing a brown cardigan over black, loose-fitting trousers. Her shoulders were bunched, tension apparent in her posture.

Her son, Tom, had answered the door to his first floor flat behind the harbour in Poole. He was about thirty-five with a round face, small eyes and a pinched nose with a strong bridge. He had introduced Temple to his mother after explaining that his father was her first husband. They had divorced ten years ago.

'If they had stayed together she would never have met that scumbag,' he'd said.

Miss Wilkinson made Temple a cup of tea and offered him some biscuits. She was a quietly spoken woman with tiny, irregular teeth. She waited until all three of them were seated in the living room before asking why the police wanted to talk to her about her ex-husband.

'We're trying to trace him and I wondered if you could help us,' Temple said. 'His home in the forest has been let out to a family of holidaymakers and he hasn't given them a forwarding address.'

She looked bemused. 'I haven't seen or spoken to him since our divorce came through a year ago.'

'Does he have another property? Perhaps a house or flat he could be staying in?'

'Not that I know of. We were married for only two years. All of our money went into King's Manor. It's his business as well as his home, although I heard from friends in Burley that he's been struggling to fill the rooms and has kept costs down by closing for weeks at a time.'

'What about relatives or friends? Could he be staying with someone?'

Her lips twisted in a wry smile. 'Nathan has no siblings and no friends, Inspector. He's very much a loner, and with good reason. He doesn't like people and those who meet him tend not to like him.'

'The man's a sleazeball,' Tom said. 'What kind of trouble is he in?'

'None at the moment,' Temple said, 'but his name has come up during the course of an investigation.'

'Well I hope he's done something wrong and you nail him for it. He almost turned my mother into a nervous wreck.'

'Is that so, Miss Wilkinson?' Temple asked.

She chewed the inside of her cheek for what seemed like a long time. Then she said, 'I married in haste, Inspector. I'd been single and lonely for seven years after my first marriage broke down. Luckily I still had a home – I got the house in Ringwood in the divorce settlement. There was no mortgage but I had to carry on working as a cleaner to make ends meet. That's how I met Nathan. He wanted someone to clean his house on a regular basis. It was a full time job. I answered his newspaper ad and he took me on.'

'So you started cleaning King's Manor?'

She nodded. 'I enjoyed it at first. It's a lovely place and at that time business was brisk. Nathan was good to me and generous. He was married before, many years ago, but his wife died. I think he was lonely too. Anyway, we really hit it off.'

'So what started out as a working relationship grew into something more.'

She slowly exhaled. 'He was very attentive. He showered me with compliments and gifts. He's also different to most other men in both his manner and appearance. Some say he's an eccentric. I think that's what I liked most about him. He was fun to be with at the start. Unpredictable.'

'So what happened?'

She smiled again, but this time it was an expression of sadness. 'After we had been together for about four months he asked me to marry him and like a fool I said yes. After the wedding he pressured me into putting my house on the market. When it was eventually sold he used the money to pay off the mortgage on King's Manor without telling me. It was a considerable sum. I should have been more concerned but I was too wrapped up in the joy of a new life with a new man.'

She suddenly turned her gaze away from Temple and directed it out the window. In her face he saw the anguish of resurrected pain.

'It became clear that the bastard just wanted to get his hands on my mother's money,' Tom said. 'What she didn't know at the time was that the bank was threatening to repossess King's Manor. Slade was in the shit financially.'

Miss Wilkinson turned back to Temple and found her voice again. 'He changed almost overnight. He lost interest in me and started treating me badly.'

'In what way?'

She swallowed. 'He was cruel, Inspector. And often violent. He hit me on a number of occasions. During one argument he went out into the garden and picked up a grass snake that was nesting there and brought it back into the house. He then threw it at me, knowing I hated them. I was terrified.'

'I didn't know about any of this until she left him,' her son said. 'I urged her to go to the police but she wouldn't.'

'I didn't see the point,' she said. 'Nothing would have been done.'

'So what, in the end, made you leave him?' Temple asked.

She gnawed on her lip for a moment, then said, 'I discovered some things about him that were distasteful. It made me realize that he has a serious problem.'

'What did you discover?'

'I'm afraid I can't tell you that. It's a private matter and I want it to stay that way.'

'But it might have a bearing on our investigation.'

'I very much doubt that.'

'What if I give you my word that what you tell me will remain confidential?'

She hesitated. 'I don't know you, Inspector. Why should I trust you?'

Temple decided to try another tack. 'Look, would it help if you knew that Nathan Slade is the prime suspect in a murder inquiry?'

Miss Wilkinson's mouth fell open and she glanced nervously at her son.

'You may have heard about the woman who was found dead on Cranes Moor a couple of days ago,' Temple said. 'Well, she was a prostitute and a frequent visitor to King's Manor. That's why we need to find out as much as we can about Nathan Slade.'

Tom Wilkinson took his mother's hand and told her that it was time she opened up and revealed what she knew.

'You've got to stop being scared of him,' he said.

His mother took a long breath and nodded. 'Very well. It started when I found out that he was paying for sex with prostitutes – he made the mistake of leaving a used condom in the back of his car. When I confronted him he admitted it, but promised to stop. Stupidly I gave him the benefit of the doubt. A few weeks later I became suspicious again and when he was out I started looking around the house for evidence. That's when I came across the first hidden camera.'

Temple frowned. 'Camera?'

She nodded. 'In the master bedroom at the Manor there are two wardrobes with mirrors on the doors. I was going through Nathan's wardrobe when I noticed a steel panel attached to the inside of the door. It was about the size of a breakfast cereal box and it was attached with four screws.'

'Had you never seen it before?' Temple asked.

'No I hadn't, but then I'd never had cause to search his wardrobe before. Anyway, out of curiosity I started to examine it and then decided to get a screwdriver and find out what was underneath.'

'And what did you find?'

'I discovered that there was a hole in the wardrobe and through it, a small spy camera fixed to the inside of the box was looking out into the room.'

Temple was puzzled. 'But didn't you say there was a mirror on the door?'

'That's right, but it was a two-way mirror. I was able to look right through it but from the outside it looked normal.'

Temple knew a bit about two-way mirrors, which are also sometimes called one-way mirrors. They have them in police interview rooms and there are plenty for sale on the internet. They work because they're partly reflective and partly transparent. When one side of the mirror is brightly lit and the other is dark, it allows viewing from the darkened side but not vice versa.

'I then started looking around the rest of the house,' Miss Wilkinson went on. 'And to my utter disgust I found cameras in all of the rooms. They were hidden in light fittings, smoke detectors, wall clocks and behind other two-way mirrors.'

'So are you saying that your husband was using them to spy on guests?'

'That's exactly what he was doing. And it had probably been going on for years. He was making recordings and storing them on his computer.'

There had been quite a lot of well-documented cases of landlords and hotel owners rigging up rooms with tiny spy cameras. Temple recalled the case of a peeping Tom hotelier in Manchester who was jailed for six months for spying on guests after installing micro cameras in their rooms. And there was the case of the private landlord who hid cameras in three of his flats – all of them connected to his computer. In fact, this sort of voyeurism had seen spectacular growth thanks to the availability of cheap surveillance equipment on the internet. Plus, there were literally hundreds of websites running hidden camera footage. Some of them even claimed to show 'live feeds' from spy cams in hotels and private dwellings.

'Tell the inspector what you found in the garage, Mum,' Tom said.

Temple waited with bated breath as Miss Wilkinson stared into her lap for about half a minute before speaking. Then she lifted her head and asked, 'Have you been to the property, Inspector?'

Temple said he had.

'Then you would have seen the double garage next to the house. It has a large loft and that's what Nathan uses as his office. You reach it by pulling down a retractable staircase from the ceiling. He always kept the garage locked but I knew where he hid the key. So after finding the cameras I went up there and saw computer monitors that were linked wirelessly to the cameras in the house. From there he could watch and record everything that was going on.'

'The ultimate voyeur,' Temple said.

'Exactly. For me it was the last straw. But when I told him I knew he just said I should keep my nose out of his business. I said I was going to tell the police and he warned me that if I did he would release on the internet dozens of hours of intimate recordings showing me having sex with him. So I said I wouldn't report it and he agreed to a divorce. He insisted on keeping the house but gave me a sum of money and I got away from him as quickly as I could.'

An image from the DVD flashed in Temple's mind: Slade whipping and then mounting Genna Boyd. That sick smile and those absurd grey dreadlocks. It caused bile to rise in his throat.

'So that's why I hate the man,' Tom said. 'He put my mother through hell. I've begged her to let me report him but she fears he'll carry out his threat to release the footage and she can't face that.'

Temple leaned forward, elbows on knees. 'Do you believe that your ex-husband is capable of murder, Miss Wilkinson?'

She didn't even have to think about it. 'He's a brutal man, Inspector. There's no question in my mind that he would kill someone without even flinching.'

38

'If our children don't come back I'll never forgive you, Jack.'

Nicole's words burned into me like hot needles. Her voice rose in a raw, wrenching fury as she glared at me across the kitchen.

'It's your damned fault and you know it,' she yelled. 'We should never have come here. That girl warned you but you chose not to listen and not to tell me.'

I stood with my back against the wall, my heart pounding furiously. Nicole was seated at the table, her face screwed up, her fists bunched in front of her.

Her outburst had been building since we'd woken up ninety minutes earlier to discover that Michael was missing. The text from Tina's cell phone had done nothing to allay our fears. Had my daughter actually sent the message? If not then who had? And what was meant by *'Michael is now on the other side with me?'* The other side of what, for God's sake?

'Right now I hate you for what's happening,' Nicole was saying, her voice quivering with anger and frustration. 'If only you had told me about the call and the warning, I would have been more responsible. I would never have risked our safety.'

I took it on the chin because she was right. And she needed someone to blame. For an hour and a half she had managed to hold her hysteria down while we both frantically searched the house and grounds for Michael and Tina. But now she needed to let it out in a burst of emotion that was, quite rightly, directed at me.

But I didn't want to be distracted by self-recrimination. I needed to focus on getting our kids back. I wasn't prepared to sit around in a state of paralysis waiting for another curious text message or bizarre event.

Nicole ended her tirade and drew in a deep, tremulous breath. Then she made an exasperated noise and dashed into the hall where I heard her break down in tears for the third time.

I thought it best to let her be for a while so I went out through the back door and stood on the patio. I tried for the umpteenth time to get through to Tina's cell phone but it was switched off. I pocketed my own cell and gazed up at the sky, which was dark and foreboding. There were no stars. The mist had cleared and the air felt dead and musty.

What, I wondered, was happening to us? Our children had vanished. Our food had been poisoned. The real world simply did not allow for things like those we had experienced. Did it mean that for us reality had been suspended? How else could you possibly explain it?

I stared out into the blackness of the forest. The last text had said we would see Tina and Michael later. But how much later? And from where would they come? I still found it impossible to believe that Tina had gone off by herself. And it was equally impossible to accept that Michael, at only ten years old, had done the same. Which left me to conclude that they had been taken. But by whom and for what reason?

My brain tried to combat the fear by repeating the mantra: *There has to be a logical explanation.* But if there was then I wasn't seeing it.

The sense of menace in and around the house was tangible. And there would be no escape from it until the kids were back. But the waiting was painful; like nothing I had ever experienced. We were supposed to be on vacation. Enjoying ourselves. Making the most of our beautiful surroundings. Yet it had all gone hideously wrong. Our family had been torn apart – literally. And we had no idea who – or what – was responsible.

A drop of sweat ran down my forehead and into my eye. As I wiped it away I heard Nicole cry out. A new wave of panic coursed through my body as I ran back into the house. I found her in the living room. She was standing in front of the TV, one hand over her mouth, the other pointing at the screen.

'It just came on,' she said. 'What is it?'

The volume was way up and the eerie sound was like wind blowing through a tunnel. There was no picture as such, only pixelated images floating across a snowy background. But the images were slowly taking shape, like figures emerging from a fog.

'Holy Christ,' I said when I suddenly realized what we were staring at.

Their faces appeared first. Then their torsos came into focus. They were lying side by side on a flat surface. They were so close together I couldn't see what it was. Tina was wearing her PJs. Michael was in the T-shirt and jeans he'd had on when we last saw him slumped in the armchair. But their eyes were shut and it looked as though they were asleep – or dead.

It was all too much for Nicole. The shock of seeing our kids on the screen caused her to faint in front of the TV. She went down in a sprawling heap, her fall thankfully cushioned by the thick, grey carpet.

I just stood there – gaping in disbelief at Tina and Michael. Their faces were pale and serene. It was a haunting image.

Through the mind-numbing terror I willed them to move; to show the slightest sign of life. But how could they? It was a still image. A moment frozen in time. Or was it? I couldn't really tell. I tried to move closer to the TV but my body had shut down. What I was seeing was startling, bewildering. It was simply beyond my comprehension.

Then I found myself watching in horrified fascination as the picture began to fade. Light giving way to dark. An insidious shadow crawling over the static forms of our children, until the picture disappeared altogether and the screen reverted to grey reflective glass.

I would probably have continued looking at the blank screen if Nicole hadn't begun to moan. The sound of her voice jolted me out of my trance. I crouched beside her, saw that the trauma had caused her to lose control of her bladder as well as her consciousness. Her face had a greenish pallor and there were heavy shadows under her eyes.

'Are you all right?' I asked. A stupid question.

She looked up at me, struggling to focus. Then she remembered what had happened and gasped as the fear shuddered through her.

She turned to the TV, cried out, 'My baby. Where's my baby?'

I felt a sickening in my stomach, an ache I couldn't fix.

'The picture just faded away,' I said. 'It lasted less than a minute.'

She pulled herself up onto her knees, frowning at the screen.

'But how was it possible? It looked so real.'

'It *was* real,' I said, trying to keep the panic out of my voice. 'That was a picture of our kids.'

She staggered to her feet. I had to hold onto her until she regained her equilibrium.

'Were they alive, Jack? Tell me you saw them move.'

'It was a static image,' I said. 'A photo, I think. So there was no movement.'

She blinked her eyes rapidly several times.

'Then where the hell are they, Jack?'

'I don't know. We'll get them back, though. I swear.'

'But what if they're dead?'

'They're not dead.'

'You don't know that. How can you be so bloody sure?'

'It's what I believe, and you have to believe it too.'

'I don't know what to believe any more. Except that I may have just seen an image of my son from beyond the grave.'

'What you just saw was a picture,' I told her. 'This has nothing to do with ghosts and shit. Some mortal madman is behind this and I reckon its Nathan Slade.'

She looked at me, confusion twisting her features.

'It stands to reason,' I explained. 'I'm sure the groceries he left were injected with a knock-out drug of some kind. He wanted to sedate us. It was when we were out cold that Tina and Michael vanished. That was no coincidence.'

'So you think Slade took our babies?'

'I don't believe they went of their own accord. And I doubt that ghosts are into using tranquilizers. Therefore, it's the only logical explanation.'

'But what about the texts from Tina?'

'They came from her phone,' I said. 'Doesn't mean she sent them.'

A deep furrow entrenched itself in her brow. For a moment she struggled to breathe. I held her arm and squeezed it. Poor Nicole. Her mind was in turmoil. She didn't know what to think and what to believe. For that matter, neither did I. But I knew it was important to stay calm and focus on looking for answers in the real world and not in some imaginary parallel universe. I'd been swept along by the whole paranormal scenario, but it was time to reassert my beliefs and apply more reason and logic to our situation.

I left Nicole standing there in the middle of the room and stepped over to the TV. There was nothing unusual about it. A normal thirty-two inch flat screen on a stand. No video or DVD recorder. I turned it on and the screen came to life. A commercial for toothpaste. I used the remote to flick quickly through the channels. It worked fine. The faces of our children did not reappear.

I pulled the TV away from the wall and checked the back. There were two black cables for the aerial and the power. But there was also a third cable going from a connection on the TV through a hole in the wall. This one was white and I was not sure of its purpose since the property did not have a satellite or cable service.

I felt I was onto something so I started to kneel down behind the TV to inspect it more closely. But I didn't quite get there because the lights were suddenly extinguished. Nicole let out a muted scream and as I jumped up I banged my shoulder against the side of the TV.

The darkness in the room was solid and at first I could not even make out the contours of the furniture.

'Stay where you are,' I said.

I managed to shuffle over to my wife without colliding with the table. She was shaking and sobbing at the same time.

'I have to find the flashlight,' I said, lowering my voice to a whisper.

'Don't leave me, Jack. Please.'

'You'll be OK. I have to—'

I didn't get to finish the sentence because there was an almighty crash in the kitchen. It shook us both to the core and caused the floor to vibrate. We clung to each other instinctively. Nicole's fingers sank deep into the back of my neck.

I could only guess at what had happened: something heavy had smashed onto the kitchen floor. Whatever it was must have been dropped or thrown. But who was out there? What threat did they pose to us?

My thoughts were gnashing in my head when suddenly I was gripped by the sensation that we were being watched – from the doorway. Nicole must have sensed it too because she spun round just as I did.

'Who's there?' I called out.

As I stared across the room to where I knew the doorway to be I saw a movement. A shadow was detaching itself from the darkness and coming towards us. I let go of Nicole and put myself between her and the doorway.

'Who the hell are you?' I yelled. 'What do you want?'

The shadow took shape, an outline against the blackness, a human form with wide shoulders and a featureless head. I took a step forward, anxious to protect Nicole, who was now hysterical behind me.

But when the attack came I wasn't quick enough to stop it. I saw a flash of something just before my head exploded and my knees buckled. I collapsed in a heap on the floor as an excruciating pain detonated behind my eyes and shot down my backbone.

I heard Nicole scream. I felt something brush against my leg.

And then the floor swallowed me up and I dropped into the icy embrace of oblivion.

39

Nathan Slade's ex-wife had given Temple a lot to think about. As he drove away from Poole he mulled over what she'd told him about the hidden cameras at King's Manor. They provided yet more evidence that the man was a deviant pervert. Prostitutes, porno films, secret cameras to spy on people in his house – how sick in the head was he, for fuck's sake?

The circumstantial evidence against him was mounting by the minute. He was one of Genna's sex clients. He had disappeared having pulled thousands of pounds out of his bank account. He'd bought a one-way ticket to Thailand. He had a criminal record and was clearly a dangerous sexual predator.

Temple wondered why it was proving so hard to find him. After all, he had phoned the Keaton family to tell them he would be dropping by the house later in the week. But would he actually turn up? Temple thought it most unlikely.

He lit a cigarette and opened the driver's window. It was half past nine and he felt tired and hungry. He wondered if Angel was still at the hospital with Genna's mother.

He fumbled in his pocket for his mobile and slipped it into the hands-free socket on the dashboard. He was about to press the speed-dial button for Angel's number when the phone buzzed with an incoming call.

It was DCI Brian Ellroy, from Scotland Yard's Human Exploitation and Organized Crime Command. The officer he'd been trying to reach all afternoon.

'I'm afraid I only just picked up your message,' he told Temple. 'I've been flying back from holiday in the Maldives and landed in the UK only a short time ago.'

'No problem,' Temple said. 'I appreciate you calling me.'

'I gather it's about Damien Roth. You responded to the red flag.'

'That's right.'

'So what's going on? Has he been arrested?'

'Hang on a sec,' Temple said. 'I'm driving and can barely hear you. Let me pull over to the side of the road.'

Once the car was stationary and the engine switched off Temple told Ellroy about the murder of Genna Boyd.

'She appeared in a string of porn movies produced by Roth and his partner, Belinda Wallis,' Temple said. 'So we ran a check. I have to say he's been pretty helpful. When I asked him why your lot interviewed him he said it was no big deal – that he knew a bloke you were investigating in connection with snuff movies.'

Ellroy gave a little laugh. 'Well I can tell you it's a bit more serious than that. If you've got a minute I'll give you a rundown.'

'Fire away,' Temple said.

'Just over a year ago a man named Jason Freemont was found dead in a remote farmhouse outside Newbury,' Ellroy said. 'He'd been stabbed repeatedly in the face and body.'

The name rang a bell with Temple. Newbury was in the neighbouring county of Berkshire, about an hour from Southampton.

'The house had been empty for two years and was on the market along with the farmland,' Ellroy said. 'It was in a poor state of repair but still had electricity and some furnishngs.'

'So what was Freemont doing there?' Temple asked.

'He was using it as a location for snuff movies. He had access to the property and others like it in the area through his job as a local estate agent.'

Temple sat back and lit another cigarette from the stub of the first.

'Freemont's body was found in one of the bedrooms,' Ellroy said. 'He was naked. The room was a real mess with blood everywhere. We strongly suspect that something went wrong during the making of a movie. One theory is that the intended victim may have turned the tables on Freemont.'

'I remember the case now,' Temple said. 'But there was no mention of snuff films or anything like that.'

'That's because we got involved and asked for that aspect of the case to be kept from the public. We'd already started an investigation into the snuff business and we didn't want to spook the main players. Besides, it would have served no useful purpose at that time to tell the world what we knew.'

'So what else did you find in the house apart from the body?' Temple asked.

'Not much. Whoever was responsible made a good job of cleaning up the place. No prints were found and there was no camera equipment. They couldn't remove the body, though, because they were disturbed by a young couple who were camping nearby and went to investigate after hearing screams. As the couple approached the house they saw someone watching from a window. So they held back and called the police from a mobile phone.'

'So what happened?'

'The couple watched from nearby woods until the police arrived. During that time they saw three people leave the house in a hurry and make off in a car that had been parked on the driveway. It belonged to Freemont and was later found abandoned in Basingstoke. But they didn't get a description of the suspects.'

'Who got clean away I take it,' Temple said.

'That's right. But when we later searched Freemont's terraced house in nearby Reading we found a box hidden under the floorboards. It contained a selection of extremely violent porn material including three snuff movies on a remote hard drive. They featured the murders of three women who were drugged and tied to beds. In each case the killer, who used a knife, wore a rubber head mask. But we're pretty sure it was Freemont. Same build and same eight-inch cock.'

'Were the movies the real thing or could they have been fakes?' Temple asked.

'These were the genuine article,' Ellroy said. 'No doubt about it. One of the girls had her hands cut off on camera. It was gruesome.'

'I bet.'

'We were able to identify two of the victims. Both were eastern European prostitutes who'd been missing for some months. Their bodies were never recovered.'

Temple clenched his jaw, squeezing the cigarette between his lips. Smoke trailed languidly from his nostrils.

'The detectives were also able to determine that two of the murders took place at the same farmhouse,' Ellroy said.

'So what has this got to do with Damien Roth?'

'Freemont was a part-time porn actor and had been hawking himself around adult film makers for years. He appeared in three legit movies made by Filthy Films. His phone records showed that he and Roth were regularly in touch over the course of a year and a half.'

'And this led you to believe that Roth was involved in the snuff films – and therefore the killings?'

'The pair had spoken on the phone the day before the murder and the detectives who interviewed him were convinced he was lying. But his girlfriend gave him an alibi and they couldn't link him to Freemont's killing or any of the others. He denied he was one of the people who fled the house in Newbury. And he denied any knowledge of snuff movies. We kept him under surveillance for a few months but he stayed clean so we had to give up. That's when I red-flagged him.'

'This is crazy stuff,' Temple said. 'How long had Freemont been doing it?'

'We don't know for sure. Possibly years. He was a loner. Single. No friends. Spent all his time downloading extreme porn, including bondage, fetish and bestiality. Turned out he was abused as a child and his mum was a prossy. Classic psychopath material.'

'So what more do you know about Damien Roth?' Temple asked.

'We looked into his background. He started making porn movies at university. One teacher there described him as an oddball. That's where he first met Belinda Wallis, who had a reputation for being aggressive and antisocial. She started appearing in his films but then later they formed a company together. I interviewed both of them several times and each time I came away thinking I'd been manipulated. They're among the new breed of porn peddlers – savvy, erudite, inconspicuous and computer literate.'

'I'll haul them in again,' Temple said. 'Maybe get a warrant to search their place.'

'Bear in mind that if Roth is involved he'll be covering his tracks well. That's why it's so hard to catch these bastards. Snuff movies have gone from being an urban myth to a multi-million pound international business. We believe there's now a large creation and underground distribution network in operation. Paedophiles have shown all the other scumbags how easy it is to make movies and get them circulated to a depraved audience that's willing to pay top dollar. Not only that, but the films are becoming increasingly elaborate.'

'What do you mean?'

Ellroy cleared his throat. 'In the past, snuff movies were made on the cheap in abandoned buildings and grim cellars. The victims were usually drugged, tied to a bed or chained to a wall. But that's all changed. Now the movies are proper production numbers with build-up scenes and even storylines.'

'You've got to be kidding me.'

'I wish I was. The producers are even trying to better each other by making their movies stand out, with high production values and unusual settings.'

'Is this just based on anecdotal evidence?' Temple asked.

'Not at all, and I can give you a recent example. A year ago two teenage girls disappeared while walking home from a college in Hamburg, Germany. It was assumed they'd been abducted but nobody knew for sure what happened to them – that was until six months ago when a snuff film surfaced on the internet. The two missing girls were in the movie. They were shown being chased through woods by three men wearing masks. When they were caught they were stripped, tied to trees and brutally cut up. I could give you more examples but I don't want you to have a sleepless night.'

'That's bad shit,' Temple said.

'You bet it is. The internet has unleashed an enormous audience for porn and tough competition and consumer desensitization have pushed the industry towards hardcore extremes. Every bizarre taste is catered for. In fact, according to the latest data, simulated rape movies are among the most popular downloads. But when it comes to snuff, well, that's Holy Grail for a lot of jaded people. The ultimate turn-on. And the internet gives them access to it.'

'It's a shocking thought,' Temple said.

Ellroy agreed. 'Shocking, but not surprising. I'm afraid we live in a world where life is cheap. Thousands of people disappear off the streets every year and nobody gives a shit. Gone are the days when snuff was just industry folklore.'

The two detectives talked for another ten minutes, by which time Temple felt thoroughly depressed. The beginnings of a headache were growing at the base of his skull.

He ended the conversation by asking Ellroy if he had heard of Nathan Slade. The name meant nothing to him. However, he said he would run it through his division's database. Temple then thanked him for the information and promised to keep him updated on their dealings with Roth.

When he came off the phone Temple struck up another cigarette. He sat smoking for a while, letting the shock of what he had heard work its way through him. He was still sitting there five minutes later when his phone buzzed. It was Angel. She said she had been trying to contact him.

'Sorry. I've been talking to someone.'

'I gathered that,' she said. 'I wanted to let you know that I've got the package Genna Boyd gave to her mum.'

Temple sat up straight, threw his half-smoked cigarette out the window.

'Where was it?'

'In her bag would you believe? All along it was in the cupboard next to her hospital bed. She'd completely forgotten that she'd put it in the bag. I found it when she asked me to get something out for her.'

'So what's in it?' Temple asked.

'Two unmarked DVDs.'

'Have you checked them?'

'Not yet. I've only just left the hospital. Heading back to the station. Where are you?'

'Coming back from Poole. I've spoken to Slade's ex-wife.'

'Did she have much to say?'

'Plenty. I'll brief you when I get in.'

'Are you coming straight back?'

'No. I need to make a little detour first. But I won't be long.'

Temple hung up and switched on the ignition. He intended to drop in on King's Manor. He wanted to have another chat with Jack Keaton – and warn him about Nathan Slade's hidden cameras.

40

I was slow in coming round. It was like crawling out of a dense, cloying fog.

The pain hit me the moment my senses started to kick in. My head throbbed with an intensity I had never experienced.

I was lying on my side, my left cheek pressed into the floor. I saw the blood as soon as my eyes flickered open; the stain on the carpet was so red it was almost black. I could even taste it, like molten metal on my tongue.

I rolled onto my back. The ceiling light stabbed at my eyes, forcing me to shut them again. I groaned loudly and reached up with both hands to cover my face. My fingers made contact with a lump the size of a golf ball. This time I shrieked in agony. I felt myself being yanked back into the blackness. It was hard to resist. I took a couple of deep, ragged breaths and somehow found the strength to haul myself into a sitting position.

The living room spun. A wave of nausea swept through me. But after a few seconds the spinning stopped and the room came into focus. That's when I realized I was alone. Nicole was no longer in the room.

Suddenly oblivious to the pain, I tried to think back to what had happened. For a second or two my mind was a blank. But then it came to me, an abrupt recognition of events and circumstances. The vision of Tina and Michael on the TV raged in my head. I remembered the lights going out, the dark figure emerging from the shadows. Nicole screaming just as I took a blow to the head.

So how long had I been unconscious? Where was my wife? Who had attacked me? As I struggled to my feet, the silence of the house closed in on me. I called out for Nicole. She didn't respond. A ball of nerves bounced in my gut as I stumbled across the living room and into the hallway.

Empty.

Then into the dining room.

Empty.

The kitchen.

Empty.

My eyes were drawn to the microwave, which was lying upside down on the floor. Its door was hanging off and the glass window cracked. Hadn't we heard a loud smash in the kitchen seconds before the figure appeared? Someone must have hurled it onto the floor. Probably in order to scare us. I was in no condition to wonder who or why.

As I pulled myself up the stairs the pain returned with a vengeance. It made me feel sick and dizzy and confused. I was glad all the lights were on because I would have struggled to find the switches. I reached the landing. It appeared to stretch forever. Lots of doors, all of them closed. Christ knows how long it took me to look into every room. But when I finally found myself in the master bedroom I knew the house was empty. Nicole was gone, along with Tina and Michael.

A sense of unreality consumed me. Surely this wasn't happening. How could it be?

I was standing next to the bed I'd shared with my wife. In front of me was one of the wardrobes with the mirrored doors. The shock of seeing my own reflection struck me like a jolt of electricity. Blood covered my face. It soaked the front of my shirt and streaked down over my jeans. It had congealed around the huge swelling on my forehead where the skin had been torn apart by whatever weapon had been used on me. I looked like a fucking zombie. And the longer I stared at myself the harder it became to stay awake. I could feel myself letting go, my mind retreating in desperation from the onslaught of pain and terror.

My vision went first. Then my legs. Finally, I blacked out just before I hit the floor.

41

Temple cursed out loud when he realized he was on the wrong road. This one did not lead to King's Manor, he was sure of it. He must have missed a turn as he came out of Burley.

But it was no great surprise. Driving at night in the New Forest is notoriously difficult, sometimes even dangerous. There are no lights and very few signs. The roads twist and turn capriciously. It's hard to concentrate on where you're going because you're constantly worried about running down a pony or deer.

But Temple knew the house was around here somewhere. There were woods on his right and he had an idea he should have been on the other side of them.

His headlights picked out a Forestry Commission car park up ahead. Rather than drive around aimlessly he decided to pull over and check the Ordnance Survey map in the glove compartment. It was 10 p.m. when he turned into the gravel parking area, one of many dotted about the forest. The Forestry Commission sign identified the location as Conifer Wood.

Temple stopped the car, turned on the overhead light, opened the glove compartment. From a selection of maps, he took out the one he wanted. He unfolded it across the steering wheel and located Burley with his finger, then the track leading from the road to King's Manor. Conifer Wood was directly behind where the house would have been if it had been shown on the map. He spotted the car park and worked out that all he had to do was drive on for another half a mile, take a right turn and follow a winding lane into the valley beyond the woods. Piece of cake.

He put the map back in the glove compartment, switched off the overhead light and started to execute a three-point turn. The headlights swept over the wall of trees and, to Temple's surprise, revealed a vehicle on the other side of the car park.

He hadn't noticed it before because it was shielded from the road by a grassy bank. It was a white Citroën. He couldn't see anyone inside and there was nobody wandering around. He grabbed the torch he kept in the door pocket, switched off the engine and got out. The night closed in around him, dark and foreboding.

He switched on the torch, which cast a pale yellow light on the ground. He took out his phone. He was relieved to find that he had a signal, albeit a weak one. He noted the vehicle registration and called it in. He said he wanted to know who it belonged to and asked for a call back asap. Then he walked across the car park. He shone the torch inside the Citroen. It was empty; no personal items lying on the seats. He tried the front door. Locked.

Temple was puzzled and a little curious. This was unusual. People rarely left cars unattended in the forest at night. He looked around and spotted a well-trodden path going from the car park into the woods.

Just then his phone buzzed. He flipped the cover and answered it.

The result of the vehicle check sent his pulse racing. The owner of the Citroën was none other than Nathan Slade.

Temple speed-dialled Angel. The call went to her voicemail. He left a message asking her to ring him back as a matter of urgency.

He thought about the Citroën. Slade must have left it here for a reason. So where was he? What was he doing here this late at night?

Temple experienced a flutter of excitement. This was an unexpected turn of events. A lucky coincidence that might well lead to something significant. But why should he be surprised? Serendipity had always played a part in his investigations.

He looked again at the path and realized that it probably cut through the woods to King's Manor. He walked over to it and shone his torch into the trees. Then he came to a decision and started following the path. Without the torch it would have been virtually impossible.

Trees crowded in on either side of him. During the day it would have been a picturesque trail through lush vegetation, but right now it was eerie and claustrophobic. Temple tried to ignore the chatter of forest creatures and focus on what might lie ahead.

If Nathan Slade had dropped in on the Keatons then why hadn't he driven up the track and parked on the driveway? Was it because he didn't want them to know he was here? Was that why he had left the Citroën in the car park beyond the woods?

Temple decided to call for some backup now, rather than wait for Angel to ring him back. She was probably tied up viewing Genna Boyd's DVDs.

He fished out his mobile, only to find that he no longer had a signal. But he'd come too far into the woods to turn back. So he continued onwards, and kept checking his phone.

A light breeze wrestled in the branches above him. The chilly air was thick with the scent of pine needles. He walked doggedly along the path, which in places narrowed to the point where branches whipped at his hands and face and snagged at his suit jacket.

He thought it would be a long haul so he was surprised when the trees petered out and the path came to an abrupt end. Ahead of him stretched a black mass of heathland. Above it a silver moon peered through a crack in the clouds. King's Manor was over to the left about fifty yards away. There were lights on inside.

Temple checked his phone. Still no signal. Before returning it to his pocket he switched it to vibrate. He thought briefly about playing safe and retreating to the car park, but decided it was out of the question: he wanted to find out what was going on and he needed to make sure that the Keaton family were not at risk from the man who might have murdered Genna Boyd.

He stomped across a stretch of grass towards the house. He knew the layout from his previous visit. As he approached, he thought he saw something behind the garage. A spark of light – like the glowing tip of a cigarette. He switched off the torch and stopped walking, but it didn't happen again and nothing was moving ahead of him so he carried on. In less than a minute he reached the rear of the garage where he saw that the back door was open. Then he noticed that the lock was broken and the wood splintered. Had someone forced it open?

What Miss Wilkinson told him about the garage leapt into his mind. The roof space was where her sick-in-the-head husband had his office.

And from there he used to monitor the hidden cameras he'd installed in the house.

Temple could feel the adrenaline gushing through him. He could also smell smoke. Someone had been here seconds ago enjoying a cigarette. So he hadn't imagined it.

He peered inside the garage. A dull light was coming from somewhere. It enabled him to make out piles of storage boxes and crates. Holding his breath, he ventured inside, trying not to make a sound.

He noticed that the light was coming from an opening in the ceiling over by the wall to his right. It illuminated the retractable staircase that Miss Wilkinson had told him about. Someone had obviously pulled it down.

There was no time to wait around for backup. If Nathan Slade was up in his office spying on the Keaton family, then Temple could think of nothing better than to catch the perverted voyeur in the act.

He trod carefully across the garage, weaving between the storage boxes and other junk. Faint sounds drifted down from the loft but he wasn't able to identify them.

An image of Nathan Slade having rough sex with Genna Boyd on the DVD flashed in his mind. The lecherous grin, those absurd grey dreadlocks, the pale, flabby body that reminded him of a gargoyle.

There was every reason to suspect that the bastard was now satisfying some warped sexual appetite by violating the privacy of the Keaton family. He had probably been doing it since they arrived at King's Manor. Temple wondered if that was why Genna had phoned Jack Keaton to warn him not to come to the house. She'd found out about the cameras and felt compelled to do something about it.

He reached the staircase. Through the open loft hatch the light flickered and, looking up, Temple could see the sloping underside of the garage roof. But that was all.

He stood stock still and listened. All was quiet now, except for the beating of his own heart.

He took a deep breath and started up the stairs, pausing after each step to listen out and look around. He was half way up when his phone started to vibrate. He ignored it. He had no choice if he wanted to surprise Slade.

Five more steps to go. His nerves jangled and his chest heaved. At the top of the stairs he slowly raised his head through the hatch, not knowing what to expect. It was reckless, even downright dangerous, but he was fully committed by now to getting to the bottom of what was going on.

The first thing he saw was the sauce of the light. It was coming from two large monitors on a desk against the far wall. There were two chairs in front of the desk but no one in them. Temple was close enough to make out the images on the screens. What he saw caused his jaw to drop. This was far worse than he could ever have imagined. He wasn't prepared for it and the shock almost made him lose his balance. He had to grip the sides of the hatch to steady himself.

Then he started to turn around to take in the rest of the loft and to assess the level of threat. That's when he felt cold metal press against the side of his face and a voice say, 'If you move I'll blow your fucking head off.'

42

When I came awake my head was smouldering with a deep, hot pain.

I remembered fainting in front of the mirror, overcome by the sight of my own blood-drenched reflection, but I had no idea how long I'd been out.

Once again, getting up was an ordeal. And once again the terrifying reality of what confronted me was almost paralyzing. That image of Tina and Michael on the TV seared at my retinas.

As I stood up my chest tightened with panic. I forced myself to look in the wardrobe mirror, and this time I managed to hold it together. I looked like a dead man walking. But I wasn't dead. I was alive. And despite the pain and the blood I was still able to function, which meant that all was not lost.

I refused to believe that my family were dead. They were close by. I could sense their presence, feel them watching me. It gave me strength, made me determined to hold back the emotion and focus on finding them, wherever they were.

Whoever had attacked me had taken Nicole. That much was obvious now. And the same person must have abducted our children. The text messages had almost certainly been a cruel ruse to stop the police from getting involved. As long as the cops thought Tina was planning to come back there was no need to take her disappearance seriously, or mount a search. But why were they taken and where were they now? These questions shuddered through me.

I stomped into the bathroom and doused cold water on my face. It revived me somewhat but did nothing to alleviate the crippling pain in my head. I was aware that I might have been concussed and if so my condition might quickly deteriorate.

As I walked out of the bedroom onto the landing I clenched my teeth and tried desperately to think what to do next. The answer didn't come until I was back downstairs. In the living room I went straight over to the TV. Earlier I'd discovered a cable going from the back of the set into the wall. What purpose it served was not evident. I knelt down and examined it, but still I couldn't work out why it was there.

It was a partition wall and beyond it was the dining room. I hurried in there and saw that the cable did not come out the other side. So it must have been routed elsewhere within the cavity. To me it was an important discovery – and a relief – because it explained how the image of Tina and Michael could have been relayed to the TV from a remote location. Rather than being some paranormal phenomenon the image was almost certainly transmitted through a basic cable or wireless connection.

But the intention had been to put the fear of God in us; to make us think it was coming from beyond the grave. And Nicole, bless her, had fallen for it. But then I couldn't blame her for that. After all, I'd been sucked into the whole supernatural thing since we arrived. But not any more. Whatever sick game Nathan Slade was playing it was coming to an end.

I went into the hall, intent on going outside to search the grounds. But as I approached the front door, a high-pitched scream came from upstairs. Every muscle in my body froze. It was Nicole. She must have found her way upstairs when I was unconscious.

The shock hit me like a falling wall and for several seconds I couldn't move. But then something snapped into place inside my head and I whirled around and bounded up the stairs.

43

'When we've put it together it'll be a masterpiece. The ultimate fucking horror movie. The fear and the dying will be genuine. No actors, no make-up, no artificial gore. Just honest to goodness terror.'

The voice came from behind Temple, along with the foul stench of tobacco breath. The words were as chilling as the images being displayed on the monitors. He had no choice but to watch and listen because they'd tied him to one of the chairs in front of Nathan Slade's desk above the garage.

'So that's what this is all about,' Temple said, astounded. 'A big budget snuff movie.'

The man behind him exhaled a loud, exasperated breath.

'It's more than just a snuff movie, Inspector. We're creating a new genre – authentic horror. We're breaking new ground with this. It's the realization of a dream, the high point of our careers. People will be talking about it for years to come.'

As the insane rant continued, Temple switched his horrified gaze between the two monitors. One showed an overhead live feed of three people lying side by side on a king-size bed. The mattress beneath them was bare and they were secured to the bed with black duct tape that had been wrapped around their legs and chests. Strips of tape covered their mouths.

Temple recognized two of them – Nicole Keaton and her son, Michael. He assumed that the third person, the girl, was their daughter, Tina. They were fully clothed and their eyes were open. Even from a distance he could see the fear reflected in them.

The other monitor displayed a split screen. It was divided into four squares. Each square showed the feed from a different camera hidden in the house. There was a wide-angle shot of the hallway, a shot looking down the stairs, another showing the kitchen. And the shots were constantly changing. It seemed the house had almost total surveillance.

Temple was therefore able to watch as Jack Keaton stumbled around the house frantically searching for his wife. His every move was captured and recorded.

'There are twenty cameras altogether,' the voice behind him said. 'All with night vision capability. They're hidden in smoke detectors, clocks, light fittings, wall sockets, pictures and mirrors. Four cover the outside. That's how we saw you coming. We don't like surprises.'

Temple knew he was in deep shit; he should have waited for backup. In spite of all his experience as a copper he had allowed himself to be drawn into a situation that was both bizarre and dangerous. He had no idea what was going to happen.

His heart was still thudding madly against his ribs; it hadn't stopped since he was yanked by the hair through the loft hatch half an hour ago. The double barrels of a shotgun had been used to prod him towards the desk. The muzzle had been placed against his head as they'd secured him to the chair with duct tape.

Questions had been fired at him. Why had he come to King's Manor? Why had he left his car beyond the woods? Who else knew he was here? He said he'd been told about the cameras by Nathan Slade's ex-wife and had dropped by to inform the Keatons. But he'd lost his way and had, by chance, come across the car park. His suspicion had been aroused because Slade's car had been parked there, so he followed the path and when he got to the property he'd seen the garage door open.

He told them that his colleagues knew he was here and that backup was on the way. But when they searched him they took his phone and listened to a voicemail from Angel which had only just been left. She was returning his call, she said. She asked him where he was and when he would arrive back at the station. She said she wanted to talk to him urgently. His captors had quickly responded to the voicemail with a text message telling her that he, Temple, was following up a lead and wouldn't be back for several hours.

Clearly relieved, they'd decided there was no need to panic. So they'd told him to sit tight and enjoy the entertainment. And that was when Temple truly realized he was at the mercy of a pair of psychopaths.

On the desk was a computer keyboard with a games-type console attached. Belinda Wallis, one of the two directors of Filthy Films, sat in front of it operating the cameras with a joystick. She was able to zoom in, pull out and pan left and right. She was also able to operate the software that produced what she had just described as their 'special effects'. Temple had so far witnessed only one example – the scream that had just lured Keaton back upstairs. It was indeed his wife he'd heard, but the scream had apparently been recorded earlier. The audio was simply fed through to one of the hidden speakers concealed in the rooms.

But Keaton didn't know that and Temple's stomach churned as the poor man went from room to room calling her name. Temple had never seen anything so cruel.

The other director of Filthy Films, Damien Roth, was the person standing directly behind Temple giving a running commentary. He clearly expected the detective to be impressed.

'You're privileged,' Roth was saying. 'You're getting a preview of what will become the most sensational underground movie ever.'

'You're fucking mad,' Temple sneered.

'And you're a narrow-minded plod. I wouldn't expect you to understand. Your creative juices have probably remained dormant since the day you came into this world.'

Temple was about to respond when his attention was drawn back to the screen. Jack Keaton was standing in the master bedroom, his fists bunched at his sides, his face screwed up. He continued to shout his wife's name, his voice quivering with anger and frustration.

Temple had never seen someone in such a state. Keaton looked like road kill. He was bruised, battered and bloodied. It was almost too painful to watch. He knew the image was locked forever inside his mind.

'You have to stop this,' he said. 'It's fucking cruel.'

Roth showed no trace of emotion. 'His suffering is almost over. Just a few more pages of the script to go.'

Temple was gobsmacked. His eyes narrowed to slits he could barely see out of. 'You're working to a fucking script?'

Roth let out a single bark of laughter. 'All good horror movies have a developing plot, Inspector. You build the tension gradually, scene by scene. That's what we've been doing over the past couple of days. Scaring them, confusing them, making them think the house is haunted.'

Roth stepped forward and leaned his large frame across the desk. He stared intently at the screen as Jack Keaton collapsed in a tearful heap on the bedroom floor. The spectacle pleased him. A grin crawled across his mouth, sleazy and unpleasant.

'Think about it,' Roth said. 'A real family, terrorized, tortured and eventually murdered. Every reaction is recorded. Every scream and drop of blood is genuine. There's intrigue, tension, shocks, outrage, panic. This will raise the bar and set a new standard. It'll put to shame every other horror movie that's ever been made.'

44

Temple knew now that they were going to kill him. Not just because they enjoyed murdering people, but because they would need to cover their tracks. If they let him go their insane movie would never be made.

Roth and Wallis continued to stare at the split-screen monitor, as though willing Jack Keaton to get up from the floor and do something. But the American looked like a broken man. He was still sitting on the floor of the master bedroom, his face in his hands, his shoulders heaving as he sobbed. He was totally wrapped up in his own despair.

'You must know you can't possibly get away with this,' Temple said.

Roth let out a sneering laugh. 'Is that right? Well it might interest you to know that we've been making snuff movies for three years and we've killed twelve people. I don't see anything stopping us from carrying on for years to come. Do you?'

There was shameless pride in Roth's voice. He was boasting. He wanted Temple to know that they were special, and gifted, and not subject to any law or moral code. In that respect they were like those serial killers who yearn for recognition. They want others to look up to them as they look up to themselves. That was why they were forcing him to watch them do their thing now. They were showing off; trying to prove they were brilliant and untouchable.

There had been others before them who had recorded on video the death throes of their victims. And there'd been plenty of serial killers who had worked in pairs – from Myra Hindley and Ian Brady to Fred and Rosemary West. But Temple thought this duo were in a class of their own when it came to sheer ambition and creativity. They were committing recreational homicide on a spectacular scale.

'Keaton has had about all he can take,' Roth said. 'Maybe it's time we moved towards the final scene.'

'Not just yet,' Wallis said. 'This is emotive stuff. We should make the most of it.'

She was grinning as she spoke, and her features were taut with anticipation. Temple could see that she was in her element, enjoying every second of Keaton's agony. In fact he was amazed how absurdly relaxed they both seemed, as though they had all the time in the world to carry out their plan.

'Try flushing the chain again,' Roth said, with a malicious sparkle in his eyes. 'See how he reacts this time.'

Temple watched, spellbound, as Wallis tapped the keyboard in front of her. A second later he heard a toilet flush.

'It's in the en-suite bathroom,' Roth explained. 'Nice touch, eh? A device in the cistern lets us trigger it from here.'

On the screen Keaton leapt to his feet and dashed across the room, pulling open the door to the en-suite. Wallis tapped the keyboard again and there was a shot change. Another camera and another viewpoint – this one looking outwards at Keaton as he peered into the empty en-suite.

Wallis cackled loudly, like a witch. 'This is so fucking easy,' she said. 'He still can't be sure that he's not witnessing paranormal activity.'

'Let's try the voices again,' Roth said, and Wallis tapped again at the keyboard.

This time Temple heard what sounded like a muted conversation coming from the monitor. Keaton must have heard it as well because he pricked up his ears and rushed out of the bedroom. His progress down the stairs was captured on various cameras.

He came to a halt in the living room, at which point Wallis tapped the keyboard again and the voices stopped, leaving Keaton looking angry and confused. He collapsed on the sofa, closed his eyes and started mumbling to himself.

'We've rigged up the house so that we can override the electrics and the phone,' Roth said. 'We can turn the lights and the TV on and off, bypassing the switches. As you can see we can also introduce sounds. Footfalls on the floorboards are so creepy.'

'Plus, we can squirt foul odours into any room through the air conditioning vents,' Wallis said. 'I wish we'd done that more than once. The reaction we got provided some cracking footage.'

'It's all quite simple,' Roth explained. 'A few cables and gadgets strategically placed under floorboards and inside wall cavities. It took a bit of time and money but it was a worthwhile investment.'

'So you've been here since the family arrived and they haven't spotted you,' Temple said.

'The cameras have been rolling all the time but we've come and gone,' Roth said. 'Keaton saw me earlier at the edge of the woods when I was leaving here to come into town to meet you. I was careless, but I quickly lost him. Another time he and his wife broke into the garage looking for their daughter, but they didn't notice there was a room up here.'

Temple clenched his jaw. 'They told me they found a snake in one of the beds.'

Roth nodded. 'We thought it would be a great way to set the scene. An attention grabber. It just so happened that there was an adder nesting in the back garden. All we had to do was give it some poison and lay it to rest.'

'So the daughter's disappearance was part of this ... script.' He spoke the last word as though it had a foul taste.

'Indeed it was – designed to put them through hell and to stop them leaving the house. We sent the text message from her phone to keep you lot from getting too involved.'

'But how did you do it – take her, I mean?'

'We injected a sleeping drug into the groceries we bought them. We avoided what they would most likely eat and drink for breakfast. Didn't want them going to sleep before we were ready to snatch the kids.'

Temple lifted his chin towards the monitor showing Keaton's family. 'So where are they?'

'In the basement,' Roth said. 'The American doesn't know that the house has one. We concealed the entrance. It's how we've been able to get in' and out with all the doors and windows locked.'

Temple was appalled and yet fascinated. The amount of planning and effort that had gone into this whole depraved set-up was just stag-gering. Despite himself he found it hard not to feel a grudging admiration for what they had done.

'So where does Nathan Slade fit into all this?' he asked.

Roth pursed his lips and said, 'Slade gave us the idea. One evening when he'd had too much to drink he told us about his hidden cameras. He'd installed no less than ten to spy on guests. It started us thinking about how great it would be to use the whole house as a film set. So Belinda and I worked up a script. Since the house is supposed to be haunted we used that as the theme and it grew from there. It quickly became an obsession with us. We added our own cameras and made some changes to the King's Manor website then waited for the bookings to come in. Unfortunately for the Keatons they were the first to get in touch by email. After their booking was confirmed we stopped checking the emails so I have no idea how many other families were interested.'

'So Slade gave his blessing for all this?' Temple asked.

Roth shook his head. 'Nathan Slade has been dead and buried for almost two months. The creep knew nothing about our plans and we didn't want him to get in the way. So we snuffed him out.'

'But Jack Keaton said he received a call from Slade.'

'That was me. Keaton was getting over anxious. I wanted them all relaxed enough to have dinner and an early night, so I could get the daughter out.'

Temple arched his brow. 'So now you're setting Slade up? It's you who's been withdrawing money from his bank. You also bought the airline ticket. You want to make it look like he's been planning to flee the country.'

Roth smiled. 'And why not? That way nobody will suspect us. Sadly we won't be able to bask in the glory, but we will be free to make more and even better movies.'

45

Temple sensed that things were coming to a head. On the monitors nothing much was happening. Keaton remained seated on the sofa, exhausted and dispirited. The camera had been placed high up, shooting downward on the room. Wallis was having fun with the controls, zooming in slowly for close-ups of Keaton's gaunt, terrified features.

His wife and kids continued to stare skywards, unaware of what fate had in store for them. Their ordeal was nothing short of barbaric.

Temple's whole body was charged with fear and emotion. He didn't want to die, especially not now that Angel had brought new meaning to his life. But even so he found it difficult to focus on the hopelessness of his own situation. His concern was for Jack Keaton and his family. He wanted to help them. He couldn't bear to watch them suffering like this.

But there was nothing he could do except perhaps keep Roth and Wallis talking and hope for a miracle.

'Did you kill Genna Boyd?' he asked. 'We had Nathan Slade in the frame, but he obviously didn't do it.'

Roth stood up straight and folded his arms across his chest. As he looked down at Temple his furtive eyes became intense and menacing.

'She got cold feet,' he said. 'We suspected she might. She called Keaton from the house to warn him. She'd arrived to meet us and because my car wasn't here she thought the place was empty. But Belinda had dropped me off earlier and I was checking the cameras. I got to Genna before she could ring him back.'

'And then you buried her on the moor.'

He nodded. 'While Belinda abandoned Genna's car in the city centre I took the body to Cranes Moor in Slade's Citroën. But I fucked up. I rushed it. The grave should have been deeper and better hidden.'

'But surely you'd had enough practice at digging graves,' Temple said.

'Those other times it was planned. The holes in the ground were dug in advance. With Genna it was different. A lot of other stuff was going on. We were working to a timetable and having to deal with her was a distraction.'

Temple shook his head. Talk about cold-blooded, he thought. This guy was a fucking monster.

He inhaled deeply and said, 'So to begin with Genna was an accomplice in all of this?'

'Of course she was. She's been part of the team since the night she killed Jason Freemont. But when it came down to it she couldn't bring herself to kill children. All our previous victims were either worthless tarts or pervy scumbags.'

Temple felt the skin on his face tighten. He said, 'Tell me about Freemont.'

Roth took a breath and turned to check the screens. A soft smile brushed across his lips. He was clearly pleased with the way things were panning out.

'Jason was the original member of the team,' Roth said. 'He started appearing in our bondage films and got a huge kick out of inflicting pain. It didn't take me long to realize that he was just like us, so we started to use him on the snuffs. Sometimes he'd work alone, other times with me or Belinda.'

The cold, callous way that Roth referred to what he did sent a shiver up Temple's spine.

'So how did he come to be murdered by Genna?' Temple asked.

Roth gave him a grim smile. '*She* was meant to be the victim. After picking her up off the street in Southampton he drove her to the farmhouse where we'd already set up the cameras. Genna was game for some S&M and was happy for Freemont to wear a mask. But after they got started she refused to be restrained because she didn't know him. So he tried to put a sedative in her drink. She cottoned on and went ballistic. He then produced a knife and threatened her. Big mistake. She managed to grab it and use it on him. She was like a wild animal. I rushed into the bedroom to try to stop her but it was too late. She cut him up bad.'

'What happened then?'

'I managed to restrain her. After she'd calmed down I told her we needed to get away before the alarm was raised. Belinda had spotted someone on the driveway who must have heard all the screaming.'

'Did Genna know what you had been up to?' Temple asked.

Roth shook his head. 'Not right away. But she was in shock so she let us get her dressed and out of the house. We considered killing her but I figured that would be a waste of her obvious talent. So we took her to her flat and gave her a choice – work with us or we'd send the tape of her killing Freemont to the police.'

'And she agreed?'

'She jumped at the chance. She said she'd been looking to get into porn for some time. And she admitted that slicing up Freemont had been a big turn-on. Make no mistake, Genna Boyd was a real head case. That's the reason we didn't get rid of her then. We saw that she had enormous potential. And we were right. It was a shame that she suddenly developed a conscience.'

'How many people did she kill on camera?'

'She didn't actually kill anyone apart from Freemont,' Roth said. 'That's my job. Genna would help us lure the punters in and drug them. Then I'd appear and do the business. But she would watch. She enjoyed that.'

'After she was killed did you ransack her flat?' Temple asked.

Roth nodded. 'We wanted to find out if she had anything there that might incriminate us. We had a good look round and took her laptop, but we didn't find anything.'

'But you left her DVDs.'

'We took the view that it didn't matter because we knew you'd find out she was working for us anyway.'

Temple's whole body felt numb and hollowed out. He now knew who had killed Genna Boyd. All the questions relating to her death had been answered. Crime solved. And yet it looked as though he'd be taking that knowledge to his grave. Nathan Slade would then be held responsible for the murders of Genna Boyd and the Keaton family. And when the movie featuring the Keatons eventually surfaced he'd be blamed for that too.

'Let's record the grand finale,' Wallis said, breaking into Temple's thoughts. 'I'll put the wife and kids back on the TV.'

Roth nodded. 'And I'll go to the basement. Make sure you get good close-ups of Keaton's face from the start.'

Temple cleared his throat and spoke with a nervous wheeze. 'What are you going to do?'

Roth walked over to a low metal filing cabinet pushed up against the wall and Temple craned his neck to watch him. Roth then took off his shirt. Beneath it he was a muscular brute with a six-pack and solid pecs. He dropped the shirt onto the filing cabinet, then reached down to a rucksack on the floor. From this he took out a kitchen knife and a black rubber head mask with slits for the eyes and mouth.

Then his lips curled into a slow, cruel smile.

'All great horror movies end with a bloodbath, Inspector,' he said. 'The youngsters will be shot and the mother will have her throat cut – as per the script. And to add to the drama we'll record Jack Keaton watching it live on TV. It'll be the most unforgettable scene ever shot.'

'You sick bastards,' Temple shouted. 'This is insane. You'll be arrested within days. There's a ton of forensic evidence here.'

'There soon won't be,' Roth said. 'When we leave here tonight we're going to set fire to the house. That's how the movie will end – with Keaton burning alive. Then we'll leave Slade's car in town – complete with the murder weapons and traces of Genna's blood. Oh, yeah, and we'll have to get rid of you.'

Roth gave Wallis a kiss on the mouth before slipping the mask over his head. Temple winced. The crazy monster looked like a figure from a nightmare. As Roth moved towards the hatch Temple started yelling and begging for them to spare the family. But his entreaties fell on deaf ears.

'If you don't shut the fuck up you'll get this in your eye,' Wallis shouted.

She produced a hypodermic syringe from the breast pocket of her shirt and brandished it like a dagger.

Temple felt all vestige of hope desert him.

He clenched his eyes shut and started to pray.

46

I sat on the sofa for several minutes, trying to silence the screaming in my head and the relentless thudding in my chest. I needed to pull myself together and focus. I had to find a way through the abject terror that was consuming me.

But when I opened my eyes a new wave of panic surged through my body. I took a deep breath, held it for a few moments, then let it out in a slow stream.

That's when I noticed Nathan Slade's guest folder, the one containing the information on the house and the forest. It was lying open on the coffee table, right in front of me.

It seized my attention because I recalled that Nicole had been reading it when I came back into the house after losing my temper with Michael. As I stared at it now I felt my forehead crease into a frown. What did it contain that had puzzled me when I first glanced through it? And why did I have the strangest feeling that whatever it was it might somehow be significant?

I reached over and picked it up. It was open somewhere in the middle. On the left side was the leaflet on the house.

I suddenly remembered what had struck me as odd about it. On the cover it described King's Manor as a 'stunning six-bedroom guest house'. Yet there were only five bedrooms. On the other side of the folder was a laminated A4 sheet containing typewritten information about the house, along with two small photos dated 1910.

One of the photos showed a man wearing a cloth cap who was pouring coal into a chute set into the ground at the rear of the house. The other photo was of Elizabeth Maddox, the widow of the original owner who was said to haunt the property.

Despite all that was happening I found myself intrigued by the leaflet and the photos. It was as if a voice inside my head was telling me I should be seeing something here that wasn't immediately obvious.

I opened the leaflet. It was well produced and in glossy colour. Inside was a montage of photos showing interior and exterior shots of King's Manor. My eyes were drawn to one particular photo. I stared at it for a long time before what I was seeing fully registered.

It showed an exterior door at the bottom of a short concrete stairwell. The wording beneath it read: *One of our bedrooms is in the basement and has its own entrance at the rear of the house. What was once a large cellar for storing coal has been converted into beautifully appointed accommodation.*

Instinctively, I looked again at the photo of the cloth-capped man pouring coal into the chute. Had the chute been turned into the basement entrance? But if so why hadn't I seen it? And why hadn't Slade told us about the extra room?

I turned again to the leaflet and studied the other photos. There was one of the living room, and others showing the bedrooms and kitchen. The rooms did not look much different to how they looked now, though some of the wall colours had changed. But there was one exception – the hallway.

If I hadn't been studying the photos so closely I probably would have missed it. But now I could see it clearly. In the alcove under the stairs there was a door and it was slightly open.

I dropped the folder on the table and hurried into the hallway. The muscles in my stomach clenched as I stared into the spacious alcove. Where the door should have been there was a wall with patterned wallpaper and several framed pictures. It was immediately obvious what had happened. Both entrances to the basement bedroom had been blocked off and concealed.

But why?

I was about to move closer to see if the old door was still there when I heard a noise in the living room.

It sounded like an explosion of static and I realized that the TV had 'magically' come back on.

I rushed back into the living room. Shock and outrage forced a shrill moan out of my mouth when I saw what was on the screen. I fell to my knees in front of the TV, then reached out and ran the tips of my fingers across the glass.

Nicole, Tina, Michael.

It was a scene straight out of hell. I had to will myself not to buckle under the crushing weight of despair. But at least they were together – and alive.

They were secured to a bed with black tape. Their eyes were open, thank goodness. Tina and Michael were moving their heads and looking around fearfully. But Nicole's head remained still and she stared straight at me.

Or rather straight at the friggin' camera.

The picture changed suddenly and I saw the bed from a different angle. It was a wide shot this time, revealing more of the room they were in. I saw bedside tables, a brown carpet, a wall with a door set in it.

Something in my brain sizzled and I began to feel dizzy. I tried to concentrate, to focus, to think.

A bedroom. It had to be close by. The cameras must have been linked to the television. And then it clicked: the basement. My family were in the fucking basement. Right below where I was standing. It explained a lot, and at the same time raised a whole set of new questions.

Go get them, screamed a voice in my head. *You know the way. Go now.*

But just then the door on the far side of the basement room was thrown open. I watched, mesmerized, as a bare-chested figure wearing a black mask stepped into the room. In one hand he carried a shotgun, in the other a large knife.

Fear clutched at my stomach as I watched the hulking figure tower over my family. He was no ghostly apparition; he was real and he was terrifying.

I could see the blood rush into my wife's face as she fought desperately to wriggle free.

The man stepped up to them. His movements were slow, deliberate, and it was clear he wanted to prolong the terror. He shoved the knife into his belt and reached over to rip the strip of tape from Michael's mouth. The boy immediately let out a pitiful scream before he started coughing and choking on his own phlegm.

The man then leaned over Michael and tore the strip from Tina's mouth. She started gulping in air like someone who'd been saved from drowning. What was happening was truly grotesque and inhuman. I could barely believe it wasn't part of some horrific nightmare.

Don't just stand there. Do something. Find the door. There's still time.

The voice in my head jarred me into action. I forced my eyes away from the screen and dashed across the room. In the hallway I made straight for the alcove below the stairs and began searching frantically for its guilty secret. It did not take me long to find it. There was no handle, but up close I could see the outline of the door, which, from a distance, was camouflaged by the patterned wallpaper. The frame had been removed so the door was flush against the wall.

I tried pushing at it but it wouldn't give and there was no way I could get my fingers in the gap to try to prise it open. So I used brute force. One, two, three heavy kicks and the door crashed inwards, taking a large chunk of plasterboard with it. Ahead of me was a short wooden staircase. At the bottom was another door and it stood open. Through it I could see the brown carpet I'd just seen on the TV.

As I started down the stairs, I prayed that I wasn't too late to save my family.

47

Belinda Wallis started yelling at Roth through the microphone. 'The door's open. He's coming down.'

Temple's eyes were darting between the two monitors. He saw Roth step away from the bed to wait for Keaton to appear in the basement. He was holding the shotgun against his waist and his sweat-soaked body was rigid with tension.

'I'm coming over,' Wallis announced, jumping to her feet. 'Be careful.'

She was in a panic and looked scarily unpredictable. Temple's heart started to gallop.

'Let them go,' he pleaded. 'Stop this now. Please!'

'Like fuck,' she growled.

Then she turned to him and he saw the syringe in her right hand. Before he could react she plunged the needle into the side of his neck. He pitched sideways with a loud shriek. A searing pain erupted in his neck and for a moment everything went out of focus.

'That'll keep you quiet for a while,' Wallis said, as she withdrew the needle and dropped it on the desk.

She then moved swiftly towards the hatch, leaving Temple feeling weak and light-headed. But he wasn't going to let that stop him from trying his best to avert a bloodbath.

His wrists were bound together behind his back and the duct tape was also attached to the chair. So when he hunched forward and put his weight on his feet, he took the chair with him. Even so, he managed to scuttle across the floor with his knees bent.

Wallis had one leg through the hatch when she turned towards him. But it was too late to stop Temple from slamming into her. She cried out, lost her footing and tumbled through the hatch.

The momentum carried Temple head first through the hatch after her. He went with such force that two of the wooden chair legs snapped off because the opening wasn't wide enough to take them. As he crashed down the stairs the remaining two legs also broke off. One of them bounced up and struck him in the face.

But that was nothing compared to the battering the rest of his body took en route to the garage floor. He ended up in an untidy heap next to Wallis. She was lying on her back, unconscious. There was a nasty gash on her forehead and blood was seeping from it.

Temple could taste his own blood from a cut lip. When he moved, a wave of dizziness engulfed him. He closed his eyes for a second, took a deep breath.

Then he tried again and this time it wasn't so bad. He quickly took stock of his situation and realized that the tape attached to the chair had snapped. So although his wrists were still bound, he was able to lift his arms free of what remained of the chair.

He struggled to his feet and hurried towards the garage door. But before he got there he heard an explosion and knew instinctively that the shotgun had been fired in the house.

48

The masked man shot me as soon as I burst into the basement bedroom. In desperation I'd entered without fear of the consequences.

The blast was deafening and the pain was excruciating as the slug slammed into me. I was hit in the shoulder and the impact threw me against the wall. I slid to the floor, clutching at the wound as blood poured out through my fingers.

At once, shadows began forming at the edges of my vision. I could feel myself slipping towards unconsciousness.

'Don't die, Pops,' I heard Tina cry out. 'Please don't leave us.'

My daughter's voice pulled me back from the edge. I clenched my jaw against the pain, opened my eyes, lifted my head.

The madman was standing over me, smoke issuing from one barrel of the shotgun. Through the slits in the mask I could see his cold, dark eyes. The expression in them was one of sheer exhilaration.

'Why?' I managed to say. 'Why have you done this to us?'

He raised the shotgun, aimed it at my face. That's when I saw that he also had a knife tucked into his belt.

'Because you were the ones who came here,' he said. 'If it hadn't been you then it would have been another lucky family.'

What kind of stupid answer was that?

I was about to ask him when someone else came tearing into the room. As the gunman spun round I saw that it was the cop who had come to see us, DCI Temple. His hands were behind his back and he had blood on his face and suit.

He barely had time to take in the scene before the shotgun exploded again. But this time the guy's aim was off and the slug smashed into the wall a few inches from the cop's head. The cop lost his balance and keeled over. The gunman was on him in an instant and threw a kick at his face, but the cop turned and the boot struck him on the back of the head. He howled in pain and brought his knees up against his chest.

I saw an opportunity then. I just hoped I had the strength to seize it. My head was full of fog from the pain and loss of blood, but I managed to get myself up and hold my balance. I wasted not a second thinking about what I had to do. I scrambled across the floor and flung myself at the gunman. I took him unawares and the impact winded him. We both went over, hitting the floor with a sickening thump.

He was dazed by the fall so I pressed my advantage and drove a powerful punch into his throat. He groaned out loud and rolled on his back. The guy was big and strong and I knew that if he could get into a position where he could deliver a blow to me it would be over in an instant. The loss of blood was making me weaker by the second. Plus, I was on my own; the cop was barely conscious.

The knife in the guy's belt was my only hope. And it was there for the taking, if only I could get to it. But he read my thoughts and we both tried to grab the weapon at the same time. He got there first and clamped his fingers around the handle. I seized his wrist, but he whipped his arm back and crawled away from me on all fours.

As he started clambering to his feet, I felt all hope slip away. My mind conjured up an image of the brutalized bodies of my family. The bed soaked in blood. The fear frozen on their faces. Their unanswered cries for help.

And then I heard the voice in my head again.

Stay with it. Stay alive. There's still hope. Just one more big effort.

The guy was on his feet now, trying to get his balance. I saw my chance. My last chance. I stretched out my good arm and managed to get a firm purchase on his left ankle. Then I yanked it towards me with all the strength I could muster.

The brute fell on his back right in front of me and I saw the knife drop from his hand onto the carpet. I grabbed hold of it before he even realized what had happened.

He cottoned on fast, though. He heaved himself into a sitting position and tried to snatch it back. But as he lunged at me he left his torso exposed and I shoved the knife into his stomach with thunderous force. His blood sprayed my face and air gushed out of his mouth like a punctured balloon.

The shock in his eyes was a pleasure to behold. I just wasn't in any condition to fully appreciate it.

Suddenly he fell backwards onto the floor. The room went quiet. But after a couple of seconds the silence was shattered by an ear-splitting scream.

I whirled around and stared in disbelief as a woman I had never seen before came bearing down on me. She had blood on her forehead and was holding the shotgun by the barrels. As I opened my mouth to speak she rammed the stock into my face with a savagery born of incandescent fury.

49

Temple was still clinging to consciousness so he had seen the entire bloody sequence. He hadn't expected Wallis to appear and blamed himself for not making sure she was out of action.

The drug she'd shot into him was swamping his senses and he was losing the battle to stay awake. His limbs were heavy and unresponsive. The kick to the back of the head hadn't helped so he was having to contend with a throbbing pain on top of everything else.

He was lying only feet away from Keaton and Roth. He didn't know if the American was alive or dead – he couldn't see his face. That last blow to his face had been ferocious and Temple had heard the crack of bone. But Damien Roth, damn him, still hadn't taken his last breath. A tearful Wallis was on her knees cradling his head in her lap. She had removed his mask and he was trying to speak to her.

It was all so surreal. There was so much blood that the room resembled a slaughterhouse. The Keaton kids were crying and Temple pitied them and their mother because all hope of saving them was now gone.

Suddenly Wallis started to sob more loudly. Temple lifted his head and saw that she was stroking Roth's cheek.

'I'll see it through, my love,' she was telling him. 'Just as we planned it. It'll be my tribute to you.'

Roth had a coughing fit, during which he brought up blood. It went on for several seconds. Then he arched his back and abruptly became still. His last breath sounded like a huge sigh.

Wallis looked up at the ceiling and let out an agonized wail. She then wept for about a minute before carefully laying her lover's head on the carpet.

As she stood up she caught sight of Temple. 'It wasn't meant to be like this,' she said. 'He was my life.'

'You have to stop this now,' Temple told her.

She glared at him through a veil of tears.

'I'll stop when I'm finished. And I won't be finished until all your bodies are burning.'

She reached down and gently pulled the knife out of Roth's stomach, then wiped his blood on her jeans. She glanced at the bed and Temple saw that her eyes held not a trace of compassion for Keaton's family.

She crossed the room to the door, the knife still firmly grasped in her hand.

'Where are you going?' Temple said in a croaky voice that was only just above a whisper.

She looked back at him briefly. Her jaw was set tight and her eyes burned holes in the air. 'To check the cameras,' she said. 'But don't worry. I'll be back in a couple of minutes to finish off the final scene. As they say, the show must go on.'

She disappeared through the door and he heard her climbing the stairs.

He lost all track of time then as he floated in and out of delirium.

Fight the drug, he told himself over and over. Fight the drug. Push it aside and find the strength to save Keaton's wife and kids. But in his heart he knew that he couldn't. He was struggling just to stay awake, let alone drag himself across the floor with his hands bound behind his back. The space between where he lay and the bed seemed to stretch for miles.

He could hear Tina and Michael sobbing, but their throats were drying up and their hope was fading.

The end would not be quick. He knew that. The psycho bitch was going to vent her anger and grief on all of them. She would take her time for sure, and wallow in the bloodlust as a bizarre tribute to her depraved boyfriend.

Temple didn't want to die in this house of horrors, but knew he was going to. He was resigned to it. But acceptance did not distil the terror that gripped him. When he heard the footfalls on the stairs a black wave passed through his mind. He yearned finally to give in and succumb to the bliss of unconsciousness.

But it wasn't to be. He heard Wallis enter the room. She made a strange sound deep in her throat, as though the air was being sucked out of her lungs. Then she approached him. He could almost feel her body ruffle the stillness in the room. He took a deep, rasping breath and braced himself for what was to come. Would she cut his throat or stab him in the chest? Would it depend on what would look best on the screen?

He forced his eyes open and looked up just as she came into view. He gritted his teeth and pulled back his lips. He wanted his last facial expression to be a defiant one.

Wallis stood over him. She was now wearing her late boyfriend's mask, no doubt because she didn't want to be identified committing five murders on camera. Her chest was heaving and her eyes were wide and hostile.

Then, through the slit in the mask, Temple saw her smile, her small, sharp teeth white like shards of bone.

'Time for a barbecue,' she said.

She lifted an arm and Temple saw that she was carrying a red petrol can. The smell hit him the moment she started pouring the contents over his legs.

'You're going to burn alive,' she told him. 'A just reward for fucking everything up.'

Temple lay helpless on his back as the madwoman poured petrol over his shirt and jacket. Then she turned and proceeded to spread it around the room. The cloying stench filled his nostrils and made him cough.

He managed with great effort to pull himself up onto one elbow. Through the fog of his vision he saw her empty the last dregs over the three figures on the bed. Mrs Keaton and the two youngsters were crying and struggling against the duct tape that restrained them.

Wallis had her back to Temple and he watched her toss the empty can across the room. Then she extracted the knife from her belt and stood over Michael Keaton who was on the side of the bed nearest to her.

'Please don't,' Temple managed to utter. 'Let them go.'

Wallis swivelled round and looked at him. Her eyes were now flat, like old coins.

'Do you really think I would do that after everything that's happened?' she said, her voice full of contempt. 'I owe it to Damien to see this thing through.'

'But they don't deserve to die.'

Wallis shook her head. 'You just don't get it, do you? The movie is all I have left. It means everything to me now. These pathetic creatures mean nothing.'

Temple made an effort to speak again, but this time he no longer had the strength to push the words out.

Wallis turned back to the bed and Temple felt his nerves shriek. He tried to move but the drug had finally seized his muscles and his senses. He prayed he would slip into unconsciousness before the fire reached him.

His breath caught as Wallis raised the knife above her head and held it there as she stared down at the boy she was about to murder.

But then he witnessed something totally unexpected.

Jack Keaton, his face smothered in blood, stumbled into Temple's line of sight.

Wallis became aware of him only when it was too late. She spun round, the knife still in the air, and was caught completely by surprise.

She cried out as Keaton rammed his shoulder into her. The force of it caused her to lose her balance and tumble sideways, dropping the knife in the process.

Keaton went over with her and together they hit the floor with a loud thud.

Temple watched, awestruck, as the American grappled with her, even in his weakened state. Spurred on by the fear of losing his entire family, he had somehow managed to summon the strength to get to his feet, despite his appalling injuries.

He attacked her with ferocious intent, grabbing her hair and slamming her face against the floor until she stopped moving. Then he rolled onto his back, his face scrunched up in pain, his chest rising dramatically with every wheezy breath.

After maybe ten seconds Keaton closed his eyes and slipped into unconsciousness, almost certainly unaware that his wife was calling his name and his daughter was pleading with him to stay awake.

And then it was Temple's turn to drift into the darkness.

The last thing he heard before passing out was the faint sound of distant sirens.

50

Three days later

They said I was lucky to be alive. The ambulance got me to the hospital just in time.

My blood pressure was so low it was almost off the charts. I was given an immediate transfusion. Then they'd set about fixing my nose, which had been badly broken when Belinda Wallis smashed me in the face with the shotgun.

The slug wound was pretty serious, but it was all tissue damage. No vital organs were harmed. My shoulder would heal soon enough, but I'd be left with a scar.

So it could have been a whole lot worse, and it surely would have if the police hadn't arrived when they did. We had DC Metcalfe – or Angel – to thank for that.

Her suspicion had been aroused when she received the text from Temple telling her he wouldn't be back at the station for several hours. It just didn't ring true, she said, for two reasons. Firstly, Temple – who I now knew was her lover – did not put a kiss at the end of the message like he always did. And secondly, he had been desperate to talk to her just a few minutes earlier.

Angel had therefore hurriedly checked the GPS signal on his phone. When she discovered where he was she became concerned because of what she'd seen on Genna Boyd's DVDs. So she'd got the cavalry together and they arrived before I bled to death and Wallis regained consciousness.

According to Temple, the two DVDs had been shocking and illuminating. One was footage of Nathan Slade being bludgeoned to death by crazy man Damien Roth. Apparently Genna had managed to get a copy of the 'snuff' movie without the others knowing.

The second DVD lasted ten minutes and featured Genna's confession to a web camera in which she told the complete story about what they had been up to. She described it as her insurance policy in the event that things went wrong and she was threatened in any way. If she'd been able to tell Roth about it before he decided to kill her she might still be alive.

I still couldn't take it all in; how we'd been unwitting participants in a grotesque 'real life' horror movie. The hidden cameras. The drugged food. The fake paranormal happenings. The concealed basement doors. According to Temple, we hadn't spotted the exterior entrance to the basement because the cover was flush with the ground and hidden beneath a section of removable turf. The trouble they'd gone to defied the imagination.

The story was big news and reporters had been laying siege to the hospital and to the hotel where Nicole and the kids were staying. My family were physically OK but they were all in an emotional state, especially Tina, who couldn't stop crying. Family therapists were already involved in helping them through it.

There was still a lot that I didn't know about what had happened, like how I'd found the strength to stop Wallis from slaughtering my family.

But thank God I had. They were still alive and we were still together. That was the important thing.

The blows I'd inflicted on Wallis had not caused too much damage. She'd suffered a fractured cheekbone and mild concussion. She was already well enough to be questioned about where the bodies of their victims – including Nathan Slade – were buried. So far she had refused to provide the information, but DCI Temple reckoned it was only a matter of time before she did.

The detective had already charged her with attempted murder and with being an accomplice in the murders of Genna Boyd and Nathan Slade. She was facing a lifetime behind bars.

Temple himself was almost fully recovered from his ordeal, the drug having worn off. He had cuts and bruises, but they didn't amount to much.

Of course, I'd thanked him for saving our lives. If he hadn't come bursting into the basement when he did we would all have been killed.

Temple had assured me that none of the video footage from the hidden cameras would ever be made public. After Wallis's trial in the New Year it would all be destroyed. His assurance had come as a great relief. The last thing I wanted was for any of it to turn up on the internet.

We had agreed to return to England for the trial. But it was something we wouldn't have to think about for a while.

In the meantime, I intended to organize another birthday surprise for Nicole. I felt I owed her that much.

But this time it would be in a five-star resort in Florida or the Bahamas. Far away from any haunted houses and desolate moors.